HEN
ALOHA CHICKEN MYSTERIES: BOOK 4

ALOHA CHICKEN MYSTERIES 4

Josi Avari

• • • •

Quill Canyon Press

www.josiavari.com

Cover art and illustrations by Richard Lance Russell

• • • •

Also by Josi Avari

The Aloha Chicken Mysteries Series

Nest Egg (Book 1)
Hen Party (Book 2)
Hard Boiled (Book 3)
Hen Pecked (Book 4)
Home to Roost (Book 5)

HEN PECKED

First edition. April 26, 2019.
Written by Josi Avari.

CHAPTER 1

S affron Skye tried to memorize the sound of the tires. She'd seen on movies that it was possible for a kidnappee to know where they were by listening to the music of the road beneath them.

She'd never been kidnapped before now, so she'd never had a chance to try it out.

The tires of the old car made a jumble of sounds. First humming, then a steady thumping, then a soft shushing sound. None of them seemed particularly useful for navigation purposes.

"You'd better let me go," she said, but the man driving the car didn't acknowledge that she had spoken. He was a small man, wearing a dark satin jacket with a ribbed collar. He had a bathtub ring of colorless hair arching from his neck to his ears. His hands on the wheel were small and pale, but Saffron's acute color recognition picked up something odd about the fingertips: they were stained a watery moss color. Maybe he smoked? But Saffron didn't smell smoke. She smelled garlic and sweat.

She thought about opening the door and jumping, but the headlights of a car close behind them were making fireworks in the rearview mirror. If she jumped, there would be no way that car could avoid running right over her. Saffron ran a finger across the useless phone in her pocket. Its battery had died just after she'd run out of gas heading home from a quick trip into the little Hawaiian town of Maika'i. She'd thought she would just walk back to the Oceanside Cafe, where she'd met an old friend, Nik Samson, recently returned to their little town from a long surfing trip around the islands.

Nik's olive eyes and sandy hair flashed through Saffron's mind. If only she could tell him what was happening. She had no doubt that he'd be at her side immediately.

She wanted to call Keahi, her more-official boyfriend, but he was in Boston, half a world away. She tugged on the gold bracelet he'd given her before he left. It was a 24-carat circle of plumeria flowers, each delicately made, that she never took off. She'd developed a habit of tugging on it when she was anxious.

She never should have accepted a ride from this stranger. Growing up in Washington, DC, she had known that safety principle since she was a kid. But living in the friendly little island town of Maika'i had changed her, had restored her trust in people. The man had offered her a ride home, and she had hopped right in the car.

The storm was so fierce that she couldn't tell exactly where they were. It was a road she'd never been on before, thick with vegetation on either side. The trees were dense, and in the dark night, they blended into one blurred shadow streaking by the window.

If her phone was working, she could call Bradley, the town's one police officer. If the phone was working, she wouldn't be in this mess at all.

She had thought to grab the charging cord and adapter from her car before she got out. It was coiled in her pocket around the smooth weight of her dead phone. She ran her eyes along the door panels, hoping to see a power point. The only power point she could see was up near the driver. The car was an old beige sedan that smelled of fish and smoke. Saffron had a special ability to see color. She could see more shades than other people, and it was usually a benefit. Here, though, everything seemed drained of color—the man, his car, the bleak stormscape outside. It made Saffron feel off-balance.

"Just stop, and I'll get out," she said. "You can drive off. You're going to be in a lot of trouble if you don't."

The man's voice was too small for his size, "I'll be in more trouble if I do."

Saffron asked what that meant, but she was met with stony silence. There was only one thing to do—wait until the car stopped, then run.

So when the car squealed into an otherwise empty two-car garage and slammed to a halt, Saffron threw the door wide and jumped out.

As she did, she ran smack into a tiny woman in a fuzzy scarlet bathrobe. The woman had short hair the color of onyx, and her hands were raw and as red as her bathrobe. In one of them was a short-nosed handgun. Saffron froze and watched the garage door creak closed behind her.

She glanced around. There were no windows and only one door. Based on its orientation, it led into the little beach house she'd glimpsed through a tangle of bushes as they arrived. There were no doors that led directly to the outside.

From somewhere behind her, Saffron's kidnapper spoke. His voice was small and sounded grainy, like an old cassette tape recording. "I'm sorry," he said. It was unclear whether he was speaking to Saffron or to the woman.

When the little woman spoke, Saffron was surprised at the forcefulness of her voice. It wasn't loud, but it filled the whole garage. The fluorescent lights seemed to flicker at the sound of it. "Shut up, Milo." She waved a hand, "lock the car up."

He shuffled around the car, slamming Saffron's door before retreating back to the driver's side and using a key to lock it.

Saffron had been in difficult situations before. Gun or no gun, a show of confidence was essential. "You'd better let me out of here," she said, more loudly than she'd intended.

The woman's face was unreadable. "You're not going anywhere, Miss Party Planner."

Saffron's stomach twisted. She was at a disadvantage. She ran an event planning business: Brightblossom Events. The woman obviously knew more about her than she did about the woman.

"We're just all going to stand in this garage for the rest of our lives?" Saffron asked, trying to keep the shiver out of her voice.

"You are," the woman said. The implication made Saffron feel dizzy. How long would the rest of her life be? She tried a different tactic. "What do you want?" Honestly, Saffron was afraid to hear the answer, but she asked the question without blinking.

The woman's sable eyes were steady, as was her hand on the gun. "Not much. You're just going to tell me all about the Kimball wedding you've been working so hard on."

Saffron's heart sank. The wedding was tomorrow. It was the union of a mature couple, who'd come to her begging for a beautiful beach ceremony—and complete secrecy. Only seven people even knew the wedding was happening: the bride and groom, the bride's adult son, the Kahu who would perform the ceremony, Bernadette from the Oceanside Cafe, who was providing light refreshments that Saffron was supposed to pick up in the morning, a lawyer from Mai'kai, and Saffron, who'd planned the whole thing, from the attire to the jeep the couple would drive off in after the ceremony. And of those seven people, Saffron was the only one who knew all the details, including where the wedding would take place. The bride had whispered to Saffron that she wanted to get married next to the enormous, deafening waves on Uwē Beach. Even the groom, whom Saffron hadn't met yet, didn't know he was getting married at the little beach with the big shorebreak that caused towering waves. The beach was so dangerous that Saffron had spent an entire day scouting out the only location where the wedding could take place and the wedding photos wouldn't include a "Proceed at Your Own Peril" sign. It seemed a bad addition to a wedding montage, if an accurate one. Saffron was supposed to pick up the three guests in a minivan tomorrow and meet the couple at the beach.

"You're surprised I know about it? Well, I do. You're not the only little detective in this town." The woman stated.

Saffron didn't know what to say. This woman knew who she was, what she did, and the secret that she'd done her best to keep.

She even knew that Saffron dabbled in solving mysteries. Saffron felt exposed.

"Dorah," the man spoke up, moving around the nose of the car, "this isn't the way."

Without altering her stance, the woman turned her seething anger on him. "I told you to shut up, Milo. I don't want to hear your nasal whining." Saffron saw the words hit the man like blows. He flinched as they fell on him and he froze in front of the door that Saffron guessed led into the house. She suddenly became very afraid that he would go through it and leave her alone with the woman.

"That's pretty harsh," Saffron said.

"Well you have to be harsh if you're married to an idiot," the woman said. "His stupid hobbies, his slow wits. I've put up with it for years. And I slave around here, working my fingers to the bone cleaning up his messes, but he keeps dragging things in and making more work for me," She sighed, and it was a heavy sound, "you have no idea what it's like being married to someone like him. May you never find out."

"There's not much danger of that if you don't let me out of here," Saffron said, glancing around for anything she could use as a weapon.

The garage was conspicuously bare. The far wall, behind Dorah, was lined with shelves that were mostly empty except for some old beach gear, odds and ends, and a few shells and chunks of coral. The only other thing in the garage was a big black cylinder near the front of the car, on the wall where the door was. It made a humming, swooshing sound, and pipes running from it through the wall made Saffron guess it was some kind of water heater. There was nothing she could see that would stop a bullet.

"I told you, you're not going anywhere until you tell me about my sister's wedding."

Her sister? Doe-eyed Rachel Kimball was this cruel woman's sibling?

"What do you want to know?" Saffron was stalling, "the gown is ivory lace, the bouquet is tiger lilies."

But the woman cut straight to the one thing Saffron couldn't say. "What time and where is it?"

Saffron deflected. "You're going to jail, you know."

Dorah didn't react, but Milo did.

"Dorah, listen to her. We have to let her go. We have to. The police will come."

"Not if they don't know she's here," Dorah said.

"We'll go to jail."

"*You'll* go to jail. You kidnapped her." This made Milo duck his head.

"We have to let her go some time. You said we would." He said in a small voice.

There was an emptiness in Dorah's eyes that scared Saffron. The woman's next words didn't surprise her. "I said we'd *probably* just let her go."

Milo took a step forward. "No, Dorah. No. We can't do anything awful. It's not her fault that your sister's getting married, or that she didn't invite you. It's not her fault about the will. You have to see that this girl's innocent in all this."

Saffron saw where this was going. The woman hadn't planned to let her go, even if she told her about the wedding. Saffron had to get out of here.

Milo made a small, pleading sound. Dorah glanced at him, and in that moment, Saffron bolted for the door.

Saffron was ready to plow into him, ready to scratch and bite and kick through him to the door, but as she reached him, Milo stepped aside. Instead of reaching for Saffron he moved toward his wife, putting himself between them.

Saffron snatched at the door handle, twisting and throwing her shoulder against the surface. But the door didn't budge. It was locked tight.

Saffron threw herself against it again, but it didn't give. She turned, scrambling, searching the wall for a button that would open the garage door. There was none. It must be inside the door.

If she hadn't glanced over to see where the gun was, she wouldn't have seen Milo put his big hands on his wife's small shoulders. And if she hadn't been watching, she wouldn't have believed what happened next.

Dorah struck out, landing a vicious blow to Milo's throat that made his arms fall to his sides and his knees go slack. He crumpled to the cement floor, gasping in a ragged way that made Saffron feel sick. The woman's eyes were empty and cold, without pity or regret, and Saffron suddenly felt a depth of fear she'd never experienced before.

Dorah didn't look at him, there on the floor. She looked directly at Saffron. Raising the gun, she ticked the barrel of it sideways. "Get away from the door."

Saffron stumbled to her right, putting the car between herself and Dorah.

"Come on," Dorah said to Milo, who trembled on his hands and knees in front of her.

She walked to the door. "Maybe a little time in here will get you ready to talk," she said, tossing the words over her shoulder at Saffron.

Milo crawled, then struggled to his feet. His ragged breathing sounding like the far-off cry of a wounded bird. Tears were streaming down his face. He didn't look at Saffron again as his wife procured a key from the pocket of her robe and snapped the door lock open. She ushered him through, then closed the door behind them.

The click of the lock sounded through the empty garage just as the lights turned off, plunging Saffron into complete darkness.

She leaned against the car. It was still slick with rain, and the damp soaked through her jeans, but she didn't care. A tremor shook her. She had never seen anyone with such a complete lack of human compassion.

She had to get help. There was no light, not even a thread of illumination around the place she thought the door should be.

Saffron felt for the phone in her pocket, praying there would be just enough charge to make a phone call. But pressing the power button did nothing. The screen didn't glow to life like she had hoped. She pulled the cord from her pocket and reached for the wall. She felt along it for an outlet, but the smooth wall only led her to the chill metal of the garage door.

She worked her way to the middle of the big door, then slid the phone back in her pocket as she pushed her fingers under the spongy seal at the bottom of the door and heaved. The garage door sat like stone.

Saffron felt her way to the wall full of shelves that was opposite the car. She pulled her finger back from the sharp point of what might have been a broken shell or a dried anemone. It stung, and she wiped it on her jeans as she proceeded to explore the shelves with more care.

There were more shells, a boogie board, a fishing net. She found what felt like a bucket with holes drilled all over it and tried not to imagine what it was used for. She felt a little bottle that rattled when she shook it—pills of some kind, maybe. She found swim fins and a snorkel mask, and the coral she had seen earlier was rough under her fingers as she brushed across it.

Under the fishing net, she found a little pile of sundry tools: a hammer, two screwdrivers, and a roll of what felt like duct tape.

Touching the tape brought her abduction back to the front of her mind. They hadn't duct taped her mouth and wrists yet, but it wasn't out of the realm of possibility. She threw the roll and sent it shushing off into some unknown corner of the garage. She stuck the screwdrivers in her back pocket and gripped the hammer—at least she'd have something to defend herself with when that door opened again.

But there was no outlet and no light switch that she could find. She suppressed the thought that the room had been built for the purpose of keeping someone captive. More likely, she supposed, the garage had been built on after the house, and it had been easier to run the electrical wiring off already-existing switches inside the house. Either way, it made for a very effective cell.

Saffron felt vulnerable, exposed. She couldn't see what was around her. Even though she knew that the only other thing in this big empty space was the car, she had to keep telling herself that nothing and no one was behind her.

Without light, she was robbed of her color sense, which usually helped her orient herself in her surroundings better than most people. Without light, her advantage was gone. She felt dizzy, as if the whole world was spinning. Reaching out, she shuffled toward the car, craving some kind of solid object in the void.

She was turned around, and she found herself touching the garage door even though she thought she had been heading toward the car. It was simple, though, to follow the door to the opposite wall, then follow that wall to the car.

She felt the bumper against her knee, then slid a hand across the trunk until she felt the slick plastic of the taillight.

The image of a bright red taillight exploded in Saffron's mind. Even without switches or outlets, she had all the light and power she needed. She just had to get into the car.

And she had a hammer now.

Working her way to the back door on the driver's side, she raised the hammer and swung it with all her strength into the window. She expected to feel it shatter, to hear falling glass. But instead, the hammer popped off the window at an angle, its head narrowly missing Saffron's cheek. She pulled her jacket sleeve over her hand and felt the window. There was no chip, no fracture that she could feel. She raised the tool and aimed directly at the window again. Again, the hammer bounced off.

Saffron felt another wave of panic. If she couldn't get into the car, if she couldn't get help, she would have to face Dorah and her handgun again alone.

She swung harder, stepping aside to get a better angle. She swung again and again until her shoulder and wrist ached from the impacts, but the window held firm. Saffron supposed it was safety glass, but she'd had no idea it was so durable.

When her arm gave out, she dropped the hammer at her feet. Hot tears made her eyes sting as she pulled the screwdriver from her pocket and jammed it into the door lock. She had no idea how to pick a lock, but desperation had set in. She wrenched the screwdriver from side to side, and at one point she thought she felt a little give inside the lock, but the door handle didn't move when she tried to open it, and she felt the crushing disappointment of yet another failed attempt.

Frustration rose in her chest like a hot tide. She stabbed at the car with the screwdriver, feeling the paint scratch away and hearing the screech of metal on metal. It got her no closer to opening the door, but it felt good. She did it again and again, popping the screwdriver's sharp point against the car door.

In the dark, she couldn't tell where she was aiming. At one point she lodged the screwdriver in the crack of the door, and at another point she hit the rubber window trim. When, with one particularly violent stab, she felt the tip of the screwdriver slip against glass, she knew she had hit the edge of the window.

As she did so, the window shattered with breathtaking suddenness, the falling glass pinging like windchimes against the cement floor.

Saffron stood with the screwdriver in her hand for a long heartbeat, unbelieving. The pounding blood in her ears whooshed like the big cylinder on the wall. When the reality hit her, she reached through the broken back window and unlocked the driver's door.

Her legs trembled with relief and fear as she slid into the seat. The window had broken almost silently, but she was still afraid they had heard her. She felt for the headlight switch and flooded the garage with light.

CHAPTER 2

The return of color was a triumph, a celebration for Saffron's eyes. Even the dull khaki interior of the car was welcome after the space of time in the dark. She jerked the charging cord out of her pocket and fitted it with the car adapter, then plugged in the phone. The screen didn't spring immediately to life. Instead, a battery icon with a lightning bolt inside it lit up on the screen. She clenched her fists, willing herself to be patient.

Saffron got out and paced around the room, looking again for any visible means of escape. She searched behind the shelves for any light switch she may have missed in her first blind inspection.

There were the bucket and the net. There was the little bottle. She picked it up and flinched as she read its label: sodium cyanide.

Saffron stared at the bottle. Was this actually possible? Were these people so blatantly evil that they had *cyanide* in their garage?

She thought about the woman's threats, about the coldness in her eyes. Poisoning didn't seem impossible, somehow.

Saffron dropped the cyanide tablets and kicked them back under the shelf. At least they'd have to look for them if they wanted to use them on her.

The room was full of the sound of the cylinder in the front corner. The car lights shone on it, and Saffron crossed the room to inspect it. She needed to keep her mind busy while the phone charged. The cylinder was black, almost as tall as she was, and alive with that steady whooshing. The pipes around it were sealed with crumbling spray foam insulation, and Saffron picked at it absentmindedly while she planned her next steps. To her surprise, a piece of the insulation pulled free, leaving a little gap around the pipe. She pulled at another chunk, and it came loose, too.

Saffron used the screwdriver to remove even more, and through the gap around the pipe came voices. She leaned down and peered through the wall directly into Milo and Dorah's living room.

It was a small room, and unusual. It took Saffron a moment to understand what she was seeing. The wall was moving. Like living wallpaper, brilliant tropical fish glided through an enormous tank on the far wall.

The cylinder wasn't a water heater at all. It was a colossal aquarium filter.

The fish were mesmerizing—their brilliant colors were like candy to Saffron after her time in the dark. A school of lemon-yellow ones sailed by behind Milo, who seemed to be packing something in a box.

Dorah was sitting on a worn couch in front of the tank. She had a bucket on the floor in front of her and a scrub brush, and she was talking fast.

"If you're not going to keep these things clean, I'll have to do it."

Milo responded in a slow, measured way, "I would appreciate it if you'd just leave them in the tank. They're new. They have to get accustomed."

I won't have filthiness in this house!" She barked. Saffron could see the woman's crimson hands from here. She was obviously obsessed with cleaning. The house was old, but scrubbed.

The tanks were immaculate. Saffron wondered if Dorah got anything else done in a day besides cleaning.

"The fish will clean them," Milo said, "and the filtration system."

"Not if you keep shipping the fish out all over the world," Dorah said. "You remember to leave my fish alone."

"I will. I won't bother him." Saffron thought she heard a slight distaste in Milo's voice.

Saffron tilted her head and pressed her forehead against the wall to align her eyes with the crack so that she could see Milo better. He was seated at a small desk, wrapping a bag of water in newspaper. He must be a tropical fish breeder. Saffron assumed there were fish in the bag. He must be getting them ready to ship.

"I do have to ship some of them out. We have to make a living, Dorah," he said patiently. "And at least this way, they get to go out and see the world, even if we can't."

Dorah's hands stilled. She looked up toward Saffron. Saffron froze. Could the woman see her? What would she do if she knew Saffron was spying?

But Dorah didn't focus on the spot Saffron was peering out of. She didn't focus at all, actually. Instead, she stared blankly, as if she were day-dreaming. "Not for long," she said.

"Dor, not that again. We've got to let that go, live our lives. And we've got to let that girl in the garage go, too."

"That girl has to tell me what she knows. We can live our lives as soon as I talk to my sister."

"That's what I mean. Don't try to stop the wedding. Let it go. Let Rachel get married and be happy for once in her life."

"She's always been happy!" Dorah howled. Her tone was pained, as if the words were being wrenched from her. "Unlike me. She married well the first time, had that son of hers—"

"We could have had children if you hadn't been obsessed with your father's money." Milo's voice was so bland that Saffron couldn't tell if he knew what rage those words would evoke or not.

Without warning, Dorah threw the scrub brush she was using. Her aim was good—the brush clunked into the back of Milo's head, and he yelped in surprise and pain.

Dorah's voice trembled, "That money is rightfully mine. And I wasn't about to lose it by breaking the stipulations of the will just so I could change diapers. Anyway," she sneered, "the world doesn't need any more of you, Milo Harrison."

Saffron wondered briefly what it would be like to be so mean, to say things just because you knew they'd hurt someone. The thought made her shiver. Dorah reminded her of Bossy, the meanest old hen back at Hau'oli ka Moa Egg Farm, where Saffron lived and worked.

Bossy was a Golden Comet hen, a cross between a Rhode Island Red and a white Plymouth Rock chicken. She was the color of blood oranges splashed with cream, and Saffron steered clear of her. She was in a pen by herself right now, because she'd relentlessly taken feathers from any hen who was unlucky enough to be her roommate. It was a horrifying habit, one that left the victim pale and hunched around a bare patch of exposed skin where Bossy had plucked the feathers away.

The feathers grew back as soon as Bossy was out of the coop, but the chickens who'd roomed with her remained flighty and fearful. Saffron saw that same look in Milo's drawn shoulders, in the way he pressed his feet against the floor and his elbows against the table, as if bracing.

Milo didn't speak, and Dorah didn't stop. "My father said in his will that he didn't want me to have children, and I respected his wishes."

Milo's voice was smaller than before, but he spoke up anyway, "He also said that he wanted her married by her fifty-fifth birthday. If you really wanted to honor his wishes, you'd let her have her wedding."

Saffron was impressed. If there was a will, and if it had those two stipulations, Milo was clever to see how Dorah's actions were contradictory.

Dorah didn't acknowledge the contrast. Instead, she cried out, "Don't you want me to get that money? Aren't you the one that wants to travel the world?" She didn't give him time to answer, "I deserve that money! I was a better child to him than she was! If there's no wedding tomorrow, then she's broken the stipulation of the will that she must be married when noon of her fifty-fifth birthday rolls around, and all the money is released to me." Dorah leaned forward, and Saffron saw a strange change in her. The woman's voice was softer now, and she used it to lure Milo into looking up at her. "To *us*," she said.

It was almost more painful to see him respond to her gentle words than it had been to see him react to her cruel ones. At the new tone in her voice, he looked up.

"I want this for us," she said, "for our future together. We can be happy when this whole inheritance business is behind us."

Milo's voice was achingly hopeful, "Do you promise, Dor? Do you promise no more terrible things once you've got that money?" Saffron wondered what other terrible things could be laid at Dorah's feet.

"Of course I do," her voice was smooth, "I promise only wonderful things."

It was at that moment when the two kidnappers were gazing across their living room at each other, and their voices were stilled, that Saffron's phone rang.

The lilting tune of the Chicken Dance seemed to explode in the quiet garage. Saffron scrambled away from the hole in the wall and vaulted into the front seat of the sedan. Snatching the phone, she hit the green button to stop the ringing before she even read who was calling.

"Hello?" her voice was hushed.

"Saffron?" Nik sounded worried and very loud in her ear. "Where are you? You left your purse in the cafe, and I brought it to your house, but you weren't here, so I waited, but it's been hours."

She chose her words carefully, hunching down into the car and easing the door closed to muffle her voice. "Nik, I've been kidnapped. I need you to call the police."

"Kidnapped?" His voice raised in alarm. "Where are you? I'm coming to get you."

"I don't know," she felt tears stinging her eyes. "I don't know where I am."

"How do I find you?"

"Call Officer Bradley. The people who kidnapped me are named Milo and Dorah Harrison. I'm locked in their garage. My phone was dead. Now it's charging, but I'm afraid to talk very much in case they hear me."

"I'll call him," Nik said. "But I'm coming, too. Bradley takes forever to do anything. You have to tell me what you know. Did you see any landmarks?"

"No. It was too dark and rainy, and there were too many bushes. I think we turned onto a bumpy dirt road about five minutes before we got here, though."

"Saffron, tell me, can you hear the ocean?"

Saffron opened the door of the car as softly as she could. She sat listening, but all she could hear was the whoosh of the big filter. She slipped out of the car and walked to the garage door, where she pressed her ear to one of the joints.

There it was, the constant, calming rhythm she'd grown accustomed to in her little bungalow by the beach. She climbed back into the car and eased the door closed again before she spoke. "Yes. I can hear it."

"Okay. And was there a lot of vegetation along the side of the road?"

Saffron didn't see how that would be helpful. There was vegetation everywhere on the island, but it felt good to be talking to someone outside this nightmarish situation. "Yes. That was all I could see."

"Could you see any lights? Houses? Boats?"

"No. Everything was dark outside."

"Okay. I think I might know where you are. I'm going to call Bradley."

Part of Saffron wanted to beg him to stay on the line, but logically, she knew they had to call the police. "Okay," she echoed.

"Saffron, I'm coming," Nik said, and the words that came into the bleak garage were as bright as the headlights of the car.

When they hung up, Saffron set her phone to vibrate and left it charging on the seat. She crept back over to the hole in the wall. Her abductors must not have heard the phone. She was grateful for the noisy filter and the thick walls. The kidnappers were in precisely the same places, and Dorah was pecking at Milo with more sharp words.

"If you hadn't gone to jail, we could have taken care of this a long time ago."

Saffron wondered why Milo had been in jail.

"I don't like to talk about that," Milo said, "I told the parole board, and I told you—I don't ever want to think about that awful night again."

"You did what you had to do," Dorah said, "for me."

At this, Milo perked up again. He straightened and glanced at his wife, "I did do it for you." Saffron hated that Milo still held affection for someone who treated him this way.

Dorah didn't respond. "My head aches," she said, stifling a raspy cough. "I'm going to bed. Deal with the problem in the garage. Make her talk, Milo. I need to know where that wedding is taking place. I have to talk to my sister and stop this thing."

She stood and left the room. Saffron watched Milo's shoulders raise and lower with a heavy sigh.

• • • •

THE PHONE WAS FULLY charged when Saffron pulled it out of the car and stuffed it and the charger into her pocket. She sat behind the steering wheel, thinking about popping the car into neutral and pushing it back through the garage door. At least she should be able to knock the door off its tracks, which might leave a big enough opening for her to escape through. She got out to examine it.

The opening of the door to the house made Saffron jump. Instinct made her dive back into the sedan, then reach up and snap the doors locked, even though she realized the back window was broken out and the car offered little protection now.

Milo looked mildly surprised to see the window, but as he shuffled forward, Saffron didn't detect any anger in his expression. He leaned down and spoke through the passenger's side window. She could hear him easily because of the broken window behind her.

"I'm not going to hurt you," he said. "Come on, I'll get you out of here."

Saffron was surprised. She didn't move. "What?"

"I'm sorry I brought you here. I know it has been scary. Come through the house with me, and I'll take you out the front door."

"Why don't you just open the garage door?" Saffron asked.

"Too loud. Dorah is sleeping, and we can hear that door all over the house. If she wakes up, it's going to be bad. I need to get you out of here before that happens." He paused, his limpid eyes the color of boiled basil. "I'm sorry you're scared. Just trust me, and I'll let you go."

Saffron didn't have much choice. Feeling for her phone in her pocket and gripping the screwdriver in her right hand, she climbed out of the car. Milo shuffled back to the door and opened it carefully. He stood inside and listened, then waved her after him. His eyes swiped across the screwdriver, but he made no attempt to take it from her. Instead, he gave a little nod, as if it were probably a good idea.

Saffron stepped into a little utility room. She saw the light switch and the garage door control as she had suspected. She also saw a plethora of nets, cleaning supplies, and tanks with dozens of different kinds of fish swimming lazily through them, oblivious that this was one of the most terrifying nights of her life.

Milo followed her gaze. "Teardrop Butterflyfish," he whispered, gesturing at a tank full of striking yellow and white fish with black markings. Saffron nodded. Milo stopped near another tank and whispered, "Moorish Idol."

Saffron tried to quell her annoyance. She wasn't on a tour here. She was fleeing for her life. Her head ached, and she was working furiously to suppress a cough that tickled in the back of her throat.

The little house was a maze of hallways and tank-filled rooms. The air hung heavy and damp.

Fish of all sizes glided through their tanks in an unending dance of flashing colors. The tanks were brightly lit, their sides reflective. It made Saffron feel as if she were sneaking through a kaleidoscope.

Twice they had to freeze as Dorah's snoring was interrupted by breathless moments of a wheezing cough. The woman was obviously having trouble breathing, and Saffron understood why. The air in the house was heavy with humidity and probably chemicals from the tanks. When they made it to the front room, Saffron's heart was pounding so loudly in her ears that she was afraid the sleeping woman would hear it and wake up.

Saffron glanced down into the bucket that Dorah had been scrubbing in and saw big chunks of slimy rock and coral. She looked at the desk where Milo had been sitting and saw several bagged fish waiting to be packed in shipping boxes. They must breed all these fish to sell through the mail. Maybe they sold coral, too. It seemed an unusually bright hobby for such bleak people.

They had reached the door. Milo unlocked it and pulled it open.

Like a wild animal, Saffron saw the opening and bolted through it, running blindly down the steps, across the lawn, and out onto the wide sand of the beach.

She felt hunted. All she wanted was a screened place to hide and call Nik. But what would she tell him? Where was she? How could he find her? She stood on the sand and looked around. In the pale moonlight, she saw them—the colossal waves of Uwē Beach.

CHAPTER 3

The sun had filled the front room of Saffron's little bunga-low. She sat with a cup of hot herbal tea cooling on the cof-fee table in front of her, huddled into the protective arch of Nik's arm.

He was on the phone with Officer Bradley.

"I understand. Okay. I will." Nik hung up. There was a tight-ness in his voice that Saffron recognized as worry. "Bradley has been out to Milo and Dorah's house. They weren't there. He searched it and found their car still there—with the window bro-ken, just like you said, so he's finding them, and he'll arrest them for kidnapping."

Saffron hated the word, hated the shaky feeling she had about the whole thing. She was glad to have Nik close by. She was even glad to have the guests staying in the three little cot-tages behind the bungalow. She was glad they were all full—an old couple, a widow, and a family. Even if the widow—Mrs. Jones—was continually showing up and snapping photos with-out asking, and then rapping on Saffron's door to complain about tiny things, and even if the kids from the family spent all afternoon yesterday chasing her rooster, Curry, around the yard, she was glad to have people around after the very long night she'd spent in the aquarium of terror.

She glanced at the clock above the door. It was decorated with chickens, and it read 8:47.

Saffron gasped. After she'd called Nik last night to tell him where she was, he'd come and picked her up, and they'd gone to tell Bradley her story. Nik had brought her home and stayed with her. But she had wasted hours waiting for the couple to be arrested. Now she had just a few minutes to get ready and pull off the wedding.

"I have to get showered," she said, pulling away from him.

"Saffron, you're not still going to do that wedding, are you?" Nik's brows were drawn together over his bright green eyes.

"Yes." She had thought this through last night. "I don't know what all has happened with Rachel and her crazy sister, but I do know that if this wedding doesn't happen, Dorah wins. She gets the inheritance, and Rachel gets nothing. I don't want her to win."

Nik shook his head and got to his feet beside her. "I just think it's dangerous. You said the wedding is right outside their house. What if they show up with their gun to try and stop it?"

"Then we have Bradley there to arrest them," she tried to sound braver than she felt, and surer.

"I'm coming, too," Nik said. Saffron nodded her agreement. There was no room for argument in his tone, and Saffron didn't want to go alone anyway.

She left him there and stepped into the bathroom. She peeked out its window to breathe the fresh island air for a moment, then ducked immediately back behind the curtain. Mrs. Jones, her nosy and cantankerous guest in the Coral Cottage, was standing outside with a camera, snapping pictures of the house and, probably, the impressive mountain behind it.

Saffron was used to people with cameras. It was a fact of living in Hawaii. Just as people in Los Angeles had to deal with traffic, people in New York had to deal with tiny apartments, and people in Minnesota had to deal with grueling winters, people in Hawaii had to deal with malihinis—tourists.

Saffron sighed. Mrs. Jones was challenging to deal with, but she was a guest. Saffron hoped that she was having a good time. Saffron turned on the shower. As the water heated up, she pulled out her phone and dialed Keahi. She wished he were here instead of thousands of miles away in Boston. He was the strongest, most dependable and reassuring person she knew, and Saffron would give anything to step out on her lanai and see him standing under the big monkeypod tree out front.

As the phone rang, she tried to think of what she would tell him. He was bound to panic when he heard she'd been abducted. Maybe he'd even insist on coming home for a short visit. But she had to let him know that she was really okay, that it had turned out for the best. She squirmed at telling him Nik had charged out in the night to rescue her, but Keahi knew he had her heart still, so he should be objective about Nik. She ran a finger down her arm to tug on her bracelet, but it was gone.

She glanced around the little bathroom, on the floor, and on the countertop, as she answered the phone.

All her planned phrases fled when she heard the voice on the other end of the line.

"Hello?" It wasn't Keahi's deep bass, his rumbling tones, that filled her ear. It was the lilting, musical voice of Evelyn Fairbanks, Keahi's old flame.

"Keahi?" Through the fog of her terrifying night and the shock of the voice, it was all Saffron could think to say.

"Oh, hi, Saffron!" Evelyn's voice dripped with forced chumminess, "Doc can't talk right now. He just ran out to catch us a cab."

"Cab?" Saffron willed herself to make complete sentences, but none would come.

"Yeah, we're just heading to lunch. We've had such a long morning at work," Saffron calculated—it was almost two o'clock there in Boston, "Keahi is the lead on this incredibly complicated pediatric surgery case, and he requested that I be the lead nurse. He's such a big shot around here that they immediately changed my shift so I could assist him. It's really complex, and it's just totally consuming him. We haven't had a break all morning, and we're starved. Do you want me to give him a message?"

Saffron shook the image of them sitting down to a cozy lunch together from her mind. "Ask him to call me, please."

Saffron thought she heard a hint of genuine concern in Evelyn's voice as the girl asked, "I will. Are you alright, Saffron? You sound upset."

Saffron felt tears spring to her eyes. She tried to keep the tremor out of her voice as she said, "I'm fine. Just have Keahi call me, please." She hung up without saying goodbye.

Why was Evelyn answering his phone? Why were they going to lunch? Why was he thousands of miles away when Saffron really needed him?

Her bracelet wasn't in the bathroom. It wasn't in the pocket of her jeans or in her jacket. It was, she assumed, lost somewhere on Uwē Beach in the bushes.

• • • •

SAFFRON WAS SURPRISED to see the groom, Blake, waiting patiently at the curb with the lawyer when she went to pick up the guests. He was wearing a straw boater hat and a white suit. Saffron nodded approvingly as she introduced herself. It would go well with Rachel's dress. The groom didn't take off his sunglasses as they rode, so she could only guess how he felt about being driven to his own wedding in a crowded minivan.

"I thought you were riding out with Rachel?" she asked as he climbed into the minivan behind her. She was sitting in the passenger's seat, letting Nik drive. It seemed like a good idea after her long night.

"Rach said she didn't want me to see her in her gown. She said she'd had enough bad luck. She wanted me to meet her there."

Saffron shrugged. It was a minor change in the plan. She could adjust to that. The two keys to being a successful event planner were adaptation and innovation.

Nik kept up friendly chatter with the three wedding guests as he drove the minivan out to Uwē Beach.

Blake, the groom, was in advertising. He bragged that his most significant account had been for a line of dinnerware. Nik asked follow-up questions, and Saffron was glad. Without him, the drive would probably have been long and awkward.

"How did you land that account?" from Nik's rapt attention, an onlooker might have thought he was in advertising himself.

Saffron only half listened as Blake talked about how he was known in the industry for anagrams. He was the king of anagrams, he said.

"I use them in all my concepts," Blake said. Saffron could tell he was passionate about advertising. "In the Clarion Dinnerware ads, I used an anagram for plates: petals." Saffron tried to sort that in her mind. Yes, she realized, the word 'petals' was made of the same letters as the word 'plates.' "We worked with our art department to create billboards, commercials, and print ads showing a set of dishes arranged like the petals of flowers—it was a huge hit."

"I remember those ads!" Nik said excitedly. Saffron was grateful for his effervescence. His bright conversation, paired with the cloudless day outside, brought back some of Saffron's enthusiasm for the ceremony she'd worked so hard to plan.

The lawyer, Mr. Cutler, cleared his throat. "Is this going to be a long drive?" he cut in.

"No, no, we're almost there," Nik said. Saffron looked up and saw that he was right. The drive had gone so quickly. She thought through her checklist as he pulled off the road into the little parking area.

There was one car parked at the beach, and Saffron saw a figure walking toward them far down the sand. She recognized the breezy ivory wedding dress she'd picked out for Rachel.

Saffron took twenty minutes to set up the little refreshment table and the arch under which the couple would wed, then the ceremony began.

Bradley had pulled up sometime during the setup, and he stood leaning against his car, watching the proceedings.

A few other tourists were visiting the beach, but they stayed back and let the couple have their space. Saffron noticed with annoyance that Mrs. Jones's island exploration had brought her here, too, and she was snapping photos of the wedding, the beach, the ocean, and the other tourists. The woman's steel-wool hair and domineering attitude radiated from her, even at a distance. Saffron hoped Mrs. Jones wouldn't see her and want to air some complaints while they were here.

Saffron refocused on the ceremony. Tourists were a part of Hawaii, and you couldn't let them bother you. And it was understandable why they came, and why they wanted photos to hold onto their moments here. The golden beach, the azure sky. Saffron soaked in the colors. The jades and emeralds and olive greens of the foliage, dotted with bright blossoms in every hue were as important as food and water to her. Her unique color sense made all of it more vibrant, more complex.

She breathed in. The sweet Hawaiian breeze blew all the tension away. Saffron loved planning weddings for this reason—no matter what went wrong before, no matter what hiccups obstructed the way or what annoyances cropped up, once the couple was at the altar nothing else mattered.

Weddings were new beginnings.

Saffron stood back from the ceremony, snapping photos discreetly with a telephoto lens. She didn't like to interrupt, but this moment was significant, and she wanted to capture it. Usually, she would have hired a photographer from Maika'i, but this wedding wasn't usual. She had agreed to act as a photographer to limit the number of people who knew about the wedding.

Taking the will into account, there was even more reason to have photo documentation of the event.

Saffron captured the anxious look on the groom's face, the triumphant look on the bride's. She captured the smiling Kahu as he pronounced the words of the ceremony and the gleam of the ring as the groom slipped it onto Rachel's finger.

It was when Saffron pulled the telephoto back to capture an overall shot that she saw a smudge on the sparkling blue water behind the couple.

She glanced at her lens, but there was nothing on it. Saffron raised the camera and peered through the viewfinder, then, slowly, focused in on the swaying dark spot in the water.

The party on the beach must have seen it, too, and they must have had a better view than Saffron, because before she could zoom in fully, Saffron heard a scream.

Through the lens, Saffron saw why.

The dark spot in the water was a body. As the waves carried it to the beach and laid it down lightly as seafoam, Saffron recognized the blazing red bathrobe and sodden black hair. It was Dorah.

Bradley must have seen it, too, because as Saffron and Nik made their way across the sand, he loped ahead of them. He was turning her over as they reached him.

She was dead. Saffron saw that immediately. She was not the same color as she had been the night before. Bruises covered her face and one arm that was exposed where the bathrobe sleeve had been torn. They were the color of old vegetation, brown and black and dull.

Saffron's keen sense of color picked out the ragged edges of several small cracks on the woman's fingers, where her skin had been cracked by her obsessive cleaning. They were bleached whiter than the rest of her hands, and a matted spot on her hair looked deep red.

"Dorah?" Rachel's hands were over her mouth, but they didn't muffle the wails that began to fill the beach.

"You folks better take a step or two back," Bradley said, closing Dorah's staring eyes and standing. He stepped with authority between the onlookers and the woman's body, "We've got ourselves a crime scene here."

• • • •

NIK WAS VEHEMENT IN his dislike of Dorah. As Saffron sat in the sand with him waiting to talk to Bradley, she couldn't argue with Nik's criticisms. The woman had held her captive, and in the short time she'd known her, had made a terrible impression overall.

She and Bradley talked for a long while in the police cruiser about Saffron's adventure in the victim's house last night. She told him everything, especially about Dorah and Milo, how she treated him, what they'd said about stopping the wedding.

"Sounds like he was sympathetic to Rachel. Maybe he killed Dorah so she couldn't mess up the wedding like she wanted?" Bradley was in a brainstorming mood.

"Possible," Saffron said. "There was certainly tension about the subject."

Bradley seemed particularly interested in the information Saffron could provide about the will, and in the contents of the garage, particularly the cyanide tablets, which he hadn't seen in his cursory inspection of the place.

"That could be a means," he said, "I mean, she obviously has a head wound, too, but I wonder if she was poisoned first, maybe figured out that she was, and started fighting back, which could have lead to more physical violence."

Saffron ran a hand across her forehead. The car was hot with the morning sun, and she was trying to sort through her memories of terror to find any other evidence for Bradley.

"You know," she said, "Dorah was coughing."

"Oh?" Bradley noted it down on his clipboard. "When you were there?"

"Yes. She had a really ragged cough, and she said she had a headache and was dizzy, so she was going to bed."

"Mmm-hmmm," Bradley nodded sagely. "That sounds like cyanide. We'll have to find that bottle. Good work, Gumshoe. Even when you were in danger, you were still picking up clues."

She and the officer had been through a few strange situations together, and lately, he had taken her into his confidence concerning various local cases. He'd also given her the nickname Gumshoe. It made her feel welcome and as if they had a rapport. Even though Bradley was overworked and often underconcerned, he was a good officer who had the citizens' best interests at heart.

Even after they were done talking, Bradley didn't dismiss Saffron. In fact, he waved her over as he questioned the others, and Saffron hung out in the back seat of his cruiser, listening to the information they offered and trying to piece together the puzzle of Dorah's death. What had happened after Saffron had fled into the night?

They learned more about the will from the lawyer at the wedding than they did from Rachel or her new husband.

The lawyer was, at the moment Bradley called him over for questioning, getting Rachel and her new husband's signatures on various legal documents that would release the remainder of her father's estate to her.

He was very forthcoming.

"The father did not think much of his daughters," the lawyer said, pushing his wire-rimmed glasses up on his nose. He wore a slate blue button-up shirt and a tie, along with slacks and black wingtips. He carried a briefcase, which he set down in the sand. Saffron wondered briefly if grains sifted in among his papers. The lawyer went on, "the will stated that the money was to be divided between them if two conditions were met."

"And those conditions were?" Bradley asked.

"Rachel must be married by her 55th birthday, and Dorah must have had no children—natural or adopted—by that date."

Saffron couldn't keep quiet. She spoke up from the back seat, "But why? Why would someone make such stipulations?"

Cutler glanced over his shoulder, the razor-sharp edges of his glasses glinting, "Because he was controlling. He had to have everything his way, and he thought that Dorah was too cruel for children and Rachel was too incompetent to be alone."

Cutler had that lawyerly way of speaking that laid things bare. It was almost too blunt. The stark assessment stunned Saffron into silence.

Bradley picked up the line of questioning again. "You said she had to be married by her 55th birthday. When is that, Mr. Cutler?"

"Tomorrow."

"And she's married now." Bradley glanced back at Saffron, "the Kahu finished the ceremony, right?"

"Right. He pronounced them man and wife."

"So Rachel's met the stipulations. What would have happened if one of the sisters didn't meet the conditions?"

"The compliant party would receive the whole amount."

"What if neither of them had done what he said?"

"If the children were found incompetent or ineligible, the money was to be donated to a non-profit called the Fantail Foundation."

"And now?"

"With Dorah's death, Rachel will receive the whole amount at noon tomorrow—on her 55th birthday. Provided," he cleared his throat, "she is still married."

And still alive, Saffron thought.

Bradley shook his head. "Well, I guess she's our prime suspect then, huh, Gumshoe?"

"I guess," Saffron shrugged. Rachel didn't seem the type to kill for money, but Saffron's life had taught her that it was hard to really know people.

"Me?" Rachel chimed in from several yards away. "I wouldn't do that—" she gestured at the body, which the coroner was zipping inside a black bag. Rachel's hand fluttered in that direction, but she didn't turn her eyes toward it.

"You have a better suspect?" Bradley asked, his slow drawl lending an air of calm to the horrific situation.

"What about Uncle Milo?" These words came from the bride's son. His name was Dylan, and he was a lanky young man with a skiff of dark, straight hair falling into his eyes. "He's already done it once."

"Hmmm?" Bradley urged the kid for more information.

"My dad," Dylan said. "Milo went to prison for killing him."

The words hit Saffron like the waves that pounded the shorebreak. So that's what Milo had been in jail for. That was the terrible thing he'd regretted. She shivered when she thought of how close she'd come to being his next victim.

Rachel jumped in, a little too quickly, Saffron thought, "And Dorah was horrible to him," Rachel said, "He'd have a better motive than I do. Years of cruelty."

Saffron shivered again when she thought of Milo out there on the loose somewhere. Bradley still hadn't found him.

Bradley turned to Saffron, "You saw any evidence of cruelty last night."

Saffron was about to answer when Rachel spoke up. "Last night? What happened last night?"

Bradley, never one to keep juicy details to himself, said, "Your sister kidnapped your wedding planner here."

"What?" Rachel's hand flew to her mouth. "Why?"

The lawyer spoke up, though he was crouched down running a pocket handkerchief over the sandy tops of his leather wingtips.

"That's very in-character," he said, "she would have wanted to stop the wedding."

"How would she have even known about the wedding?" the groom snapped. "I thought this was all hush-hush."

Rachel looked down.

"Something to say, Ma'am?" Bradley asked.

"I know how she knew. She saw me on the beach. I was here yesterday—I just came for a second, and I didn't get out of the car. I just wanted to see Uwē Beach. I just wanted to dream about our wedding here. I shouldn't have come."

Something occurred to Saffron. "Why get married here? Why right in front of her house?"

Rachel's eyes snapped, and her mouth drew into a flat line. For the first time, Saffron saw a family resemblance between the sisters. "Because it's not her house. It's our house. It's where we grew up! She just weaseled her way into it when Dad died. I have as much right to be here as she does!" She choked a little on the word, and her voice was more subdued as she amended, "as she did." Rachel looked with pleading eyes at Saffron, then at Bradley, "you don't know how our father was, or how Dorah was. They had to control everything. I had my first wedding far away so she couldn't interfere, but I have always wanted to get married here. On my beach. And I'm not sorry I did, even if she wouldn't have liked it."

Mr. Cutler, the lawyer, straightened. "Forgive me," he said, "but that all seems a little irrelevant when you realize that there is a much more likely suspect here."

Bradley tipped his hat back and raised a skeptical eyebrow at the lawyer, "the son?" he said, jerking a thumb toward Dylan.

"No," Cutler's voice was cold, and he blinked his round eyes slowly behind his glasses, "The wedding planner."

CHAPTER 4

Saffron had to admit that after Cutler laid out the case against her: motive, opportunity, the fact that she was the last one to see Dorah alive, it was pretty convincing.

And he didn't even know the details, like the screwdriver she had taken with her or the cyanide tablets she had found. Bradley did, and he put those pieces into the puzzle, too.

"You know I'm going to have to ask you a few more questions," he said, his earlier camaraderie waning. He didn't even call her Gumshoe.

"I know," she said.

"That's totally ridiculous," Nik growled. "I can't believe you would single out the victim in all of this as the suspect. If anyone's to blame in this, it's that crazy dead woman herself."

Cutler turned a cool gaze on Nik. "What about you, then?" he asked. "You seem sufficiently emotionally compromised. What would you be willing to do to protect this young lady?"

Saffron was stunned into silence by the accusation, but Nik didn't even blink. He stepped forward, peering down at the thin little man. When he spoke, his voice was as menacing as the sound of the breakers behind them, "You don't want to know."

Bradley, blinking at all these new revelations, stepped up and put a hand on Nik's arm. "Okay, now, easy. We're going to question everybody thoroughly. Right now, I have a mountain of paperwork to do with the coroner, but stay in town, all of you, and I'll be around to talk to each of you. The likelihood is that the husband did it, but we're going to investigate every possibility."

Nik stepped back, and his arm slid around Saffron as they walked to the car.

• • • •

AS THE NEWS SPREAD, it became apparent that they were not the only two who might have wanted Dorah dead. At the Oceanside Cafe, over a burger she didn't feel like eating, Saffron heard three different conversations about how Dorah had treated people around Maika'i with contempt and derision for decades.

No one seemed to like her in the least. The general consensus was that the world was probably better off without her in it. That struck Saffron as very sad.

She was in a melancholy mood when, back at the egg farm, she wandered down to gather the eggs. Nik had dropped her off and headed to his job at the surf shop, and she knew that getting back into her routine would help ease the turmoil of the last two days. She checked her phone to see if Keahi had called her back. He hadn't. She tried not to be hurt by that. It sounded like he'd had a hectic day. But she had so much to say about the situation with Rachel and Dorah, and she had spilled all her thoughts to Nik. It felt so good to talk about it, and she felt guilty that Keahi didn't know anything about her ordeal yet. Shouldn't she be sharing everything with him instead? Not for the first time, she wished Boston was much closer than it was.

When she entered the egg house, Saffron was surprised to see chickens milling about outside their pen. The door to one of the pens had come open, and about twenty hens were wandering around.

Bossy, Saffron's mean old hen, was protesting loudly from her pen because she wasn't allowed out like the others.

Saffron spent a few minutes rounding them up. A handful of grain tossed into their pen sent them all bouncing back where they were supposed to be. The fact that they got a treat, in addition to a vacation outside their enclosure, was more than Bossy could bear. She set up a racket, scolding Saffron with loud cackles.

The indoor pens all had little doors that opened out onto outdoor enclosures, and from outside, above the noise of Bossy's displeasure, Saffron heard a strange sound.

It was a chicken sound, but not one Saffron was used to. Bossy ran outside, and Saffron walked into her pen to peer through the wire-covered window and see what was happening.

Outside, just on the other side of Bossy's enclosure, was a rooster. This was not Saffron's usual resident rooster, Curry, who lived on the porch of Saffron's bungalow and warned her of approaching visitors. This was a tall, gangly, red rooster with an enormous comb. He was making the funny sound: a tapping squeak that was accompanied by a head-bobbing dance. He pranced in a circle, raising his wings lightly and looking up at Bossy through the wire every few seconds.

It was a strange dance, and Saffron watched until the rooster caught sight of her. She shifted, and his gaze fixed on her. They regarded each other for a long moment, then the rooster fled into the underbrush, leaving Bossy clucking with annoyance.

Saffron left the pen and latched the door before Bossy got back inside from her outside enclosure.

The egg house was equipped with two long conveyor belts, one on each side of the aisle, which ran behind the nest boxes down the length of the egg house. The eggs rolled out of the nests and Saffron cranked the conveyor to carry the swaying ovals toward the work areas at the front of the long building.

There was a good crop today. She'd just switched to adding a higher-protein feed supplement, which was made by her fisherman friend Akoni out of the leftovers of the fish he caught and sold. He must have been here today because two new bags of it sat solidly in the work area. She hefted one onto the lift and cranked, raising it to the feed bin, where it tipped and poured in, sifting down among the feed that was already in the hopper. She wound another crank and sent the mixture rattling down several pipes into the feeders in each pen. She repeated the process on the other side of the egg house.

She was glad for the new supplement. Feeding it to the chickens had markedly increased their egg output. The conveyor belt that ran under the egg boxes was laden with eggs today.

Saffron plucked each egg from the conveyor and moved it to the bristly egg washer. From there, the eggs moved through a big contraption that scrubbed them in a stream of clean water, then rolled them along through a series of chamois cloth drying channels until they swayed gently into a padded holding tray at the end. From there, Saffron put them in the cartons, selecting either all brown or a rainbow assortment, depending on what her customers had requested.

The Hau'oli ka Moa emblem was emblazoned on each carton: a chicken made of a pineapple. The whole process was familiar, repetitive, and calming. Saffron eased into a meditative state as she placed the eggs in the cartons. She had learned a lot since taking the farm over. For example, the eggs needed to be stored pointy-end down. In the opposite, more blunt end of each egg was an air sac that a developing chick would use to breathe while it was hatching. Though most of Saffron's eggs weren't fertilized, so there was no chance of a chick hatching, they still contained the air sac, and if it were stored at the bottom of the egg, it would eventually begin to rise, pushing the yolk away from the center of the egg and shortening the time the egg could be stored before it spoiled.

So, row after row, she put the pointy ends down.

Each carton was like a palette. Sometimes Saffron sprinkled the blue, green, pink, white, and brown eggs randomly throughout the container, sometimes she aligned the different colors into bands that made a rainbow effect when the customer opened it. Sometimes she did all one color and arranged the eggs from lightest to darkest.

Saffron was aware that most people would open the carton and see far fewer distinctions between the colors than she did, but even people without her color perception could appreciate the basic variations in the hues of Hau'oli ka Moa eggs.

At first, she forced herself to concentrate on packaging the eggs, but the repetitiveness of the task lent itself to mental processing. While she worked, her thoughts tugged toward the strange happenings of the last few days.

Dorah was mean, but she hadn't deserved to die. Milo was mistreated, but that didn't excuse murder. Rachel carried more baggage from her strange family situation than Saffron had realized when she'd first met the bride.

It struck Saffron as sad that none of them seemed happy. Of course not now, after the unexpected discovery of Dorah's body, but even before. The sisters seemed to have a strange competitiveness that had eaten at them their whole lives.

It seemed to come from their father. He must have been a strange character to assert such control over their lives. Dorah had forgone children just to comply with his stipulations. And imagine someone not trusting their own child to have children. And why force your other daughter to be married? That seemed a recipe for disaster. It was hard to believe that anyone would be so arrogant as to think he could control his daughters' lives, even from the grave.

Of course, Saffron knew little about fathers who were even marginally involved in their children's lives. Her own father had left when she was very young, and she hadn't even known he was alive until a few months ago.

She thought of him now, the man who had abandoned her and her mother to come back here to Hawaii and look after his brother. That part wasn't so bad, but the fact that he never came home still stung.

She wondered where he was now. She wondered how much he knew about her. She wondered why she was wasting time wondering about him.

Parents, she decided, had so little awareness of how their actions rippled through the lives of their children. Rachel and Dorah had spent their whole lives navigating the crashing waves left behind by their father.

Saffron was so deep in thought that her phone had rung four times before she surfaced enough to snatch it from the counter in the work area and tap it to life.

"Saffron?" Across the miles, Keahi's voice was a ribbon tied around Saffron's heart. She felt its tug, and she could barely speak.

"Keahi."

He knew immediately. "What's wrong? Are you okay?"

She took a deep breath. Hearing his concern, she felt both reassured and guilty for making him worry. Of course, she was okay. There was no need to scare him. She suddenly thought of the case he was dealing with at work, of how hard it was for him to operate on pediatric patients after he'd lost one several years ago, and her little overnight adventure didn't seem quite so urgent. She steadied her voice.

"I'm fine. Just a little excitement around here. But I'm just fine. I'm—I'm washing eggs."

There was a pause. Saffron could tell that Keahi knew she was lying. They had come to know each other's speech patterns so well over the last few months since he'd been gone and all their contact had been on the phone. Though she missed his strong arms and his steady smile, she had come to love his breaths and his inflections just as much.

"Keahi? Are you still there?" She missed having her bracelet to tug on. She opened and closed the egg carton in front of her to make up for its absence.

"Yeah. I'm here. I just—I saw that you called earlier. I was afraid something was wrong."

"You *saw* that I called?"

"Yeah, on my phone."

"Didn't Evelyn tell you that I called?"

"Evelyn?" He said the name like he'd never heard it before, with a forced lightness in his voice that made Saffron immediately suspicious.

"She answered when I called. I asked her to have you call me. Must have slipped her mind. Or else she didn't want you to know." Saffron wasn't proud of the bitterness in her voice, but she didn't try to hide it, either.

"Hey, now," he said, half reproving, half consoling, "I'm sure she just forgot. It's been a busy day up here."

"I'm sure it has," Saffron said.

He paused, assessing her tone, Saffron assumed.

"You're not—" he started, then softened his voice before he continued, "you're not *worried* about Evelyn, are you, Ipo?" His voice was low and gentle on the word *ipo*, which was his term of endearment for her—like *sweetheart*.

Saffron wanted to be magnanimous and mature, but after the long night, after the long months, she couldn't manage it. "Why should I worry about Evelyn?" She snapped back, "She's doing fine. She's getting everything she wants."

"Saffron, what—"

She cut in, "She's got you, Keahi. She's going to be fine."

"She doesn't have me," there was a defensive edge in his voice.

"Doesn't she? You work together, you eat together, you probably even—" Saffron stopped herself before she went too far.

"There's nothing between us," Keahi said. Saffron could picture the lines on his face, his forehead puckered above drawn eyebrows.

"Then why are you spending so much time with her?" It was a question she'd wanted to ask for a long time. She went on, "I don't want you to work with her anymore, Keahi. I can't stand thinking about you being together all the time."

"Honey, I don't have a lot of say about—"

"She told me, Keahi. She told me that you requested her."

He was quiet. "You guys had quite a conversation."

"If it's that easy to ask that she work with you, it should be just as easy to request a different nurse."

There was a long pause. When he spoke again, Keahi sounded apologetic, but also a little angry. "I can't do that, Ipo."

Now the word was like a slap. How could he call her that while he was insisting on seeing Evelyn?

He went on, "I don't know how to help you see, Evie's a *good nurse*." He emphasized the words. "She's better than that. She's great in the operating theater. She's really good at what she does. I've got this major surgery coming up, and, Saffron," his tone was pleading, "*I need her*."

The words stung. It was like swallowing hot saltwater, and Saffron, without thinking, pressed the button on the phone and hung up on him.

She tossed the phone onto the counter and paced away from it. Her heart was pounding. She had never wanted to hear him say that. Today he needed Evelyn's help in the operating room. Tomorrow, maybe he would need her companionship.

It was a risk she had taken by supporting his return to Boston, his return to medicine. She had known when he went that Evelyn would be there. But Saffron had believed in the way they'd felt when they were together. She'd believed they could stay close even with five thousand miles—half an ocean and a continent—between them.

Now, she wasn't so sure.

She didn't pick up the phone when it rang again. She was embarrassed that she'd hung up, and she was afraid of where their conversation had to go from there.

Saffron finished putting the day's eggs in the cartons. She put the packages on the wheeled cart that she used to get them to the house. She picked up her now-silent phone as carefully as if it were an egg and slipped it into the pocket of her apron.

Back at the house, Saffron filled the avocado-colored egg fridge with the fresh crop of eggs. Tomorrow, early, people would drive out and make a long line from the highway to the house to pick them up.

The phone felt heavy in Saffron's pocket. She walked to her other fridge and opened it. She was hungry. It had been a long time since she and Nik had eaten at the Oceanside Cafe.

A fresh bowl of lomilomi salmon greeted her. Akoni must have left it when he dropped off the new feed. It was now all she wanted to eat.

Lomilomi salmon was a delicious cold concoction that started with Akoni's salmon, cured in a bath of sea-salt and pineapple sugar. He cured it for days, then broke it into small pieces by hand. That was why it was called lomilomi. The word meant massage, and the whole dish was broken and mixed by hand. Akoni then added chopped tomatoes, chopped onions, rice vinegar, ginger, and garlic. It was a savory-sweet concoction that Saffron could never get enough of.

She pulled one of the bowls from the cabinet. In the bottom, a painted rooster stared back at her. She scooped in several spoonfuls of the salmon and made her way into the living room.

It was a beautiful room. Especially now, as the sun was setting. The light was warm and yellow, and the ocean outside caught it and tossed it back to Saffron in sparkling bits.

The salmon was firm and flavorful, the tomatoes perfectly ripe. Saffron hadn't known that there was such a difference in onions until she came to the islands and tasted a true kula onion. Also called Maui onions, they were grown in the rich volcanic soil of Maui's Mount Haleakala, and they were sweet and mild. Akoni used the traditional raw chopped onions in his Lomilomi salmon, but he also was the only person she knew of that took about half of them and sauteed them until they were lightly caramelized. It gave the dish an extra depth of flavor, a richness that set off the salty salmon perfectly.

Curry, Saffron's porch rooster, was clucking contentedly outside. She could see him through the window, silhouetted against the sea, framed by two palm trees as he perched on the railing of the lanai.

Saffron wondered if he knew about the other rooster, the one she'd seen by Bossy's pen. If so, the knowledge didn't seem to be bothering him. Her memory flitted to Keahi. She should call him back, though it would be late there by now. She still didn't know what she would say, or how she would explain hanging up on him, and she still didn't like the thought of him spending so much time with Evelyn, but Saffron and Keahi had been able to talk about hard things since the day they'd met, and she was sure they could do it now.

She pulled her phone from her apron pocket. Just as she tapped it awake, though, it started to ring. Nik's face popped up on the screen. She checked the time. He must have just gotten off work.

"Hello?" she answered.

"Hey! How are you tonight?"

That was hard to define. Saffron was noncommittal, "I'm okay." She changed the subject, "how was work?"

"Great! I've got a surprise. Are you busy tomorrow?"

"I just have the egg line in the morning, and I have to gather tomorrow night. Somewhere between there, I have to plan the

Letoa's anniversary party. They're having it out at that old lodge—the Piscine Lodge?—and I need to make sure I've got enough centerpieces. Other than that, I'm open."

"Awesome! I think we need a little outing—just something fun—Can I pick you up at noon?"

"Where are we going?"

"It's a surprise."

Nik's voice was light. It glowed through the phone and lit up Saffron's living room. The sun outside had sunk into the gentle waves. "I love surprises," she said.

CHAPTER 5

"Okay! Open it!" Nik wore a Christmas morning expression as he gestured at the back door of his station wagon. Through the rear window, Saffron could see a beach blanket spread across something lumpy. She raised an eyebrow. This date—not a date, she reminded herself—was full of mysteries. First, he'd insisted that a bathing suit was the best choice of apparel for this outing, then he'd taken her to lunch but driven her around the island for an hour afterward.

Now they were standing at the edge of a crowded beach, one Saffron hadn't visited before. Families dotted the sand and bobbed in the water, retirees lay stretched out on rows of beach chairs, and boogie boarders rode the ridges of the gentle waves. Out in the ocean, she could see flat, circular coral outcrops.

Saffron raised the back window and lowered the tailgate below it. This space was usually filled with Nik's surfing equipment—a couple of boards, tins of wax, and a tangle of towels and wetsuits, but the boards were gone. From the corner of her eye, she could see Nik bouncing on his toes with excitement. She grasped the blanket and pulled it off with a flourish. She stood looking at a pile of flippers and snorkeling masks.

Nik didn't wait for her questions. He leaned close and started pulling things out, loading her arms with gear. "See? My work was getting rid of this stuff! They gave it to me for free! I got it for us to go snorkeling!"

Nik's enthusiasm infused the air like plumeria perfume. Saffron almost forgot to be nervous as they maneuvered around the beachgoers and waded into the water.

Nik pointed with a free hand toward the coral disks in the surf. "We're going to head over there. It's easy swimming for your first time snorkeling."

He had his gear on before Saffron could even figure out which side of her mask was up.

These were different than the snorkels she'd played with in the pool as a kid. Those had a hooked snorkel pipe, goggles, and an awkward mouthpiece that always made her jaw hurt. These were sleek domes of clear plastic, with a seal around the back and a stubby air pipe at the top, near the forehead.

"How can these possibly work?" Saffron asked.

"They're full-face masks," Nik called. "They cover your whole face. You don't have to put anything in your mouth. They have a little float in the snorkel that stops water from coming in. You're going to love them. It's like looking through a window right into the reef."

She nodded, wrestling with the thick rubber strap on the back.

"I'll help." Nik splashed close to her, and the two of them swayed with the incoming waves as he reached for the mask. Taking her face in his hands, he carefully swept the hair back from her forehead.

Saffron's skin tingled where he touched her. He smelled like salt and sunshine. His hands were gentle as he fitted the mask over her face and eased its rubber strap past her ears.

A big wave surprised her by washing in past her hips and lifting her feet from the sandy ocean floor. Saffron scrambled and grasped at Nik, catching his shoulder in one hand and his opposite bicep in the other. Instinctively, she pulled closer to him as he slid his hands around her waist to steady her. The wave retreated and set them down. It felt like dancing.

Saffron blinked and breathed, testing the mask and trying to hide her suddenly racing heart. When she looked at Nik, his eyes were on hers. There was a gentle amusement there, evidenced by the light creases reaching from the corners of his eyes. But there was something else there. A focus that told Saffron his heart was racing, too.

She stepped backward, floundering, as the next wave found them. He steadied her again, this time with a single hand on the small of her back, and pulled his mask down with his free hand.

"Here you go," Nik said, his voice muffled by the full-face mask. He seemed to sense that she wasn't ready for that kind of closeness, and she liked that he pulled back, despite the intensity she'd seen in his eyes, "this way."

Saffron watched as he pushed off into the next wave, letting his body go horizontal on top of the water. He reached back for her hand, and she did her best to follow his example. Nik's strong hand closed around hers, and together they half-swam, half-floated into deeper water.

The feeling of swimming through the water with the help of the fins was incredible. Every kick rocketed Saffron through the warm gentle waves.

The sounds of the beachgoers cut off abruptly as Saffron lowered her face into the water. It took a bit of deliberate effort to overcome her initial resistance to the motion, but once her face was submerged, she was riveted on a little meandering blue fish. She pointed excitedly and turned to see Nik's million-dollar smile flashing back at her.

He mouthed the words, "just wait." Saffron found that strange.

They followed the little fish, who swam in a more or less straight line along the golden sand. Below him, the ocean floor became rougher, more rocky. A few more fish darted in and out of sight.

Nik's admonition suddenly made sense as the little fish led them to their destination.

It was a new world—one she'd never even thought of from the shore. Below them was a cityscape of coral populated by the most beautiful creatures she'd ever seen.

It was a delight for her eyes—colors even she'd never seen before. She tried to tell Nik, but there was no hearing each other through the masks and the water, so she just pointed urgently at a school of brilliant yellow fish—like gold coins swaying and turning in the little currents below them.

It was like flying, gazing down on the inhabitants of a miniature world who were, for the most part, utterly oblivious to them.

Saffron cataloged every color: the narrow scarlet and white fish, the sunset-orange one. She let go of Nik's hand and carefully followed a brilliant azure fish as he skimmed along a small canyon in the coral.

He led her over a coral hill right into the reef, where she was delighted to find lemon-yellow fish, pink fish, and a school of bright white and black striped fish grazing delicately. Around them, on the rough coral, were basketball-sized spiny sea urchins with foot-long spikes the color of eggplants. She wondered if they were as sharp as they looked.

This world, this whole world, had been here all these months that she'd been in Hawaii. She had never thought about what was beyond the surface of the sea that she gazed at every day.

The fish came and went like the people in Maika'i. Little ones made way for big ones, big ones skimmed along on their own urgent business.

A school of bright orange and blue fish arched and swayed in a choreographed performance that seemed to catch the attention of several other fish, which held steady in the current and watched them as if they were on stage.

Saffron imagined that the spectator fish had shown up just to see the dance. She imagined little flyers in little fish cafes: "Don't miss it! Tangerine Dream School Recital!"

Two ice-blue fish swam side by side past the show, and Saffron followed them. A couple? On a first date maybe? They darted into a coral arch and were hidden from view, apparently away from prying eyes, or perhaps away from a bizarre fish that was approaching. About the size of Saffron's hand, the fish was all made of spikes and fans. It was striped from front to back with thin radiating white stripes and thicker cinnamon ones. Along its back were thirteen spines, each as long as Saffron's fingers. Its lower fins were as long as its body, and so wide they looked like palm fronds attached to the fish. It swam forward, toward Saffron, unafraid. She reached toward it, and Nik scrambled through the water to catch her hand and pull it back before she could touch it. His sudden motion scared the fish, and it darted in the opposite direction.

Nik pointed up, the signal for Saffron to meet him topside. As they popped out of the water, the water drained from her ears and the sounds of the world returned, including Nik's voice.

"Don't touch those," he said.

"I'm sorry. Does it hurt them?"

"It'll hurt *you*. That's a lionfish, and those spines are venomous."

Saffron curled her fingers into her palms involuntarily. "Venomous?"

"Very. All those spines along their backs have poison in them. I had a buddy get spiked by one in the foot when we were surfing, and he passed out, it was so painful." She could see lines of solemnity in his face. It was an unusual look for Nik. The memory must have been particularly unpleasant.

Saffron's stomach knotted. "Wow. It was weird how he came right up to me, though."

"They're predators, so they're a lot less easy to frighten than most of the fish down there."

"I won't touch them," she reassured him. "In fact, I won't touch anything."

Nik smiled, the severity fading from his features. "Okay. There's more to see, though, so we have to go back down."

Saffron stuck a little closer to Nik when they went back under, and she kept an eye out for anything spiky, prickly, or jagged. Though there were urchins with long spines and several rough-looking coral outcroppings, most of the sea life was bright, slick, and shining.

Saffron felt a hand on her back and turned her head to see Nik, his face framed by his mask, smiling at her. She smiled back. He gestured toward a spot directly below them.

Saffron looked. Vibrant fish—cobalt and pineapple colored—darted between them and the jagged coral floor. She nodded. They were thin and delicate, and she saw their beauty, but they weren't the flashiest she'd seen. She turned her head away.

Nik tapped her again, and she turned back, glancing at him. She read in his expression an urgency, an excitement, and she looked at the spot again. Knobby coral. Little fish. Spiky urchins.

Until he reached his hand down slowly toward the ocean floor.

Saffron gasped as a knobby protrusion of olive-colored coral abruptly transformed to a desert-red octopus as smooth as a ripe mango. It had been perfectly camouflaged. It gathered its spread tentacles around it and rocketed away from them, navigating the narrow channels of coral with precision.

How could she have not seen it? Could its disguise have been that flawless? She kicked, following it, and felt Nik beside her.

The octopus settled on an ebony and slate patch at the edge of the coral, tucking its long legs into the crevices. Saffron felt her breath quicken as the creature instantly changed to fit the surroundings.

Its skin puckered to the exact texture of the reef. The brick-red color shifted to patches of gray and charcoal. As Saffron watched, it disappeared.

She blinked, looking for its edges and not finding them. She turned her wide eyes to Nik, who was grinning broadly.

She looked again. The octopus was gone. Only she knew it wasn't. She knew that directly where she was looking was something she couldn't see.

· · · ·

SAFFRON WOULD HAVE stayed in the water the rest of her life, watching the underwater soap opera that was the reef. But as the afternoon had gone on, an umbrella of clouds had moved in, and the air above the water had cooled. Also, more and more people had shown up, and it became a little tricky to avoid crashing into other snorkelers.

Nik had apologized several times. "I didn't expect it to be that busy. I haven't been to that beach in forever."

"Don't worry. I didn't mind the tourists. It was completely magical anyway."

"Magical." Nik grinned. "That's such a Saffron word."

"Magical?" She asked. "No, it's not. People say magical. Everyone says magical."

He fixed her with his green eyes. "No, they don't."

"What do they say?"

"Awesome. Radical. Sweet. Amazing."

"Okay, okay. It was those, too." She thought about it. "But none of those capture the real feeling."

"Which was?"

"Magical."

He laughed, and the sound was light and comfortable. It was the perfect sound to accompany the swaying palm trees that lined the Kamehameha Highway. His voice was smooth, "So many people there, though. That's why I like surfing the big waves. That weeds out most of the malihinis."

Saffron felt the stars in her eyes. She was still dazzled by what they'd seen. She had barely noticed the tourists. "But you can't see the reef when you're surfing."

"That's true."

Saffron closed her eyes and pictured it again. "I had no idea that was out there."

Nik chuckled. "That's just the beginning. There are reefs all around the island, and beyond that, a whole ocean full of even more *magical* things."

Saffron had, at some level, known this. But she had never actually seen it before, had never felt it like she did now.

"Do you ever think about how much you don't know?" she asked.

Nik shrugged. "Not really. There's too much." He tossed a smile across the bench seat of the station wagon. When he saw her, though, his brows drew together. "Are you chilly?"

Saffron was shivering a little, but she wasn't sure whether it was from excitement, hunger, or her wet hair and suit. "A little," she admitted.

Nik patted the seat next to him and invited her over with a little jerk of his head.

Saffron knew she was crossing a threshold. She knew that accepting his invitation meant more than just warming up from a swim. But she was glowing with the excitement of snorkeling, and she felt close to him already from the events of the last few days. It was easy and natural to slide across the seat and into the crook of Nik's arm.

The drive was different from over there. The turquoise hood of the old station wagon stretched away in front of them, and his arm was warm around her shoulders.

Nik was so natural, so relaxed. It was something she loved about him. He embodied the Hawaiian surfer spirit, the sense that there was nothing you couldn't conquer if you just read the waves right and positioned yourself to ride them. He didn't seem to worry.

It hadn't been that way when she first met him, when he was worried about his great-grandfather's death and his twin sister, Naia. But now she was safe and happy and thriving at the University of Hawaii, and Nik didn't seem to carry a single anxiety about anything.

The road was surprisingly open. "Most of the malihinis must be at the cove we just left," she teased. Then she mused, "Can I say malihini? How long do you have to live here to start calling other people tourists?"

"Oh, I think you've earned your local status. You're a farmer!"

This jolted Saffron. "I'm not a farmer."

"You're not?"

"No. Farmers wear overalls and drive tractors."

"Okay."

"No, really. I'm not."

"How many chickens do you own?" Nik slowed the station wagon as they drove through Maika'i.

"A lot," Saffron admitted.

"More than fifty?"

"Is that the official cutoff for farmer status?" She asked. She had way more than fifty. Over twice that many, and she didn't want to tell him.

He switched his approach. "Why don't you want to be a farmer? I think it's great."

"I think farmers are great, too. I guess I just am not sure how attractive it is to be a single thirty-something female farmer."

Nik squeezed her shoulder, pulling her closer to him. "I'll put those fears to rest. It's very attractive."

Saffron's cheeks heated up. She didn't pull away. Some part of her brain sent off an alarm, but she silenced it. She couldn't stop the next words from tumbling out. "Do you really think that?"

He glanced over, his eyebrows raised. "Why wouldn't I?"

Saffron knew she was different from other women he spent time with. She was tall and strong and had always been curvier than her peers. She could probably starve her way to a leaner figure, but she believed that good food was part of a happy life. Also, her genes seemed to resist that, and she had long ago come to love her body. Nik, though, spent his days surfing with girls with string bikinis and angles instead of curves. She'd assumed that was his type. Nik nosed the car off the road and down her long driveway as all these thoughts streaked through her head. She tried to articulate them. "I just—I'm not—exactly a supermodel."

Stopping the car in front of the spacious lanai, Nik put it in park and reached for her face with his left hand. His green eyes fixed on hers, he spoke clearly, emphasizing every word. "Saffron, I think you are absolutely beautiful." He leaned in and kissed her softly, and she didn't pull away. From the other side of the car,

Nik had seemed so carefree, so reckless. But at that moment he was remarkably focused.

Saffron was smiling when they parted.

A slight movement directly in front of the car caught her eye, and she glanced at the lanai. There, in one of the comfy deck chairs, was Keahi's grandpa Mano.

Saffron didn't mean to wince. She didn't mean to pull back from Nik so abruptly, but Mano's gaze told her that he'd seen the kiss, and she scrambled back across the seat and popped the big door open with a half-formed explanation on her lips.

Holding her wet towel, she climbed the stairs to the lanai and called him by the Hawaiian word for grandfather as she approached.

"Tutu!" It had been a long time since she had met him without a smile. "I—I'm sorry. I can explain."

The weight of his years was evident as Mano stood. His slippahs—what Saffron might have called flip-flops before she came to Hawaii—were beside him on the lanai. Saffron wondered how long he'd been waiting.

"I just—" she began.

But Mano said nothing. Instead, he reached for Saffron's shoulders, and without a word, laid his nose and forehead against hers. The flow of her words ebbed as they both inhaled. This was the honi, a traditional island greeting that symbolized acceptance, love, and respect through sharing space and the breath of life. Saffron's heart pounded. She wished he had just yelled at her, rather than showing such tenderness in this moment when she was so ashamed of herself.

As they parted, her words tumbled out. "Tutu, I can explain. See, we went snorkeling, and—"

He held up a hand, worn and finely creased like palm bark, calloused from his woodcarving. "Moʻopuna," she felt even worse as he called her *grandchild*, "I understand. I miss him, too."

Saffron felt a longing to be like Mano—calm and accepting, understanding, loving. She wondered how he had become that way.

Mano changed the subject. "I brought some scraps out to the chickens. I was over at the luau this afternoon, and they sent them for you. I tossed them in the pens."

"Thank you," she said, still wincing when she met his eyes.

"You have a visitor at the egg house," he said.

"Another one?"

"A bird one."

She gave him her best quizzical look.

"There's a rooster working hard to get Bossy's attention."

"Oh, him!" she remembered the rooster she'd seen yesterday.

"You should probably call Birdy and have her come over and take him to the sanctuary," Mano said. Birdy was Saffron's friend who ran the Friends of Hens organization, dedicated to helping deal with the feral chicken problem in Hawaii. They had a beautiful temporary sanctuary here on the island and a huge one on the mainland.

"I will."

Mano scooped on his slippahs with his feet. He reached for Saffron's hand and squeezed it lightly. "I have to get back to town. I'll see you soon, eh?"

She watched him walk off the lanai and pat the hood of Nik's car as he passed it. He stooped and smiled through the window at Nik and Saffron tried not to remember the sadness in Mano's eyes.

Nik smiled back and climbed out of the station wagon as Mano passed. The old man tossed him a shaka, the Hawaiian hand sign of greeting and friendship, and Nik threw one back. Saffron couldn't understand how they could be so relaxed in such a tense situation.

Nik came up onto the lanai with a sheepish smile. "I'm sorry, I didn't know he was here."

"Neither did I, obviously," Saffron sighed.

"I'm not sorry about the kiss, though. That was *magical*." Nik's grin was genuine and warm. Saffron felt her embarrassment slipping away, but she grasped onto it and held it close.

"Nik, what was that? What is this? You've only been back a couple of days, and here we are together. Are you really interested in me? In—" she waved a hand between them, "in this?"

Nik's smile burst into a laugh. "I would have thought that would be pretty obvious. Yes. I'm interested."

Saffron didn't return his smile. "But Nik, since when? You weren't interested when you left—"

"That's not true. I was interested. I just had a lot of other stuff on my mind—my sister, my grandpa's death—it was a crazy time. But Saffron," He stepped closer to her, "I thought about you every day while I was on that trip. And you know what? Every day I regretted not doing something about the way I felt. I told myself that if you were still here when I got home, I would." Nik held out his hand toward her.

His eyes were shining with sincerity. The air on the lanai was heavy and warm around them. He was handsome and kind and fun and close. Saffron reached out and took his hand.

CHAPTER 6

"You don't really think I could have killed her, do you, Bradley?" Saffron had answered all of the officer's questions, and she was ready to ask a few of her own.

"No. I don't. There are a lot more likely people than you, Gumshoe."

She was relieved to hear him use her nickname.

"Like who?"

"Like everyone in town and everyone she ever knew." Bradley swept his hat off and wiped a hand across his forehead. It was incredibly humid lately, due to the morning storms and afternoon sunshine Maika'i was experiencing.

"Any leads on Milo?" Saffron asked.

"Nope. I've got the neighbors keeping an eye out, but they haven't seen anything, and his fish keep getting fed, so either he's got a helper, or he's getting in and out of the house somehow."

"Why don't you stake out the place?"

"Can't. Not enough manpower. There are other things I have to do, you know."

Saffron did know. As Maika'i's only police officer, Bradley was called on for everything from escorting funeral processions to getting cats out of trees to hanging Christmas lights on the main street.

Saffron considered offering her help, but if she was honest, she didn't ever want to go back to that house again.

"So who's on your list?" she asked.

"Honestly, the kid. Dorah's nephew."

Saffron nodded.

"And the sister," Bradley looked out past the monkeypod tree and shaded his eyes.

"Rachel?"

"Yeah. You can't deny the motive, and she was out on that beach all alone just before the body was found."

"How about Milo?"

"Absolutely. He's the top. Because he's disappeared, and he had a motive, the means, and an opportunity."

That reminded Saffron. "Means? Do we know what killed her yet?"

"No coroner's report yet, but it seems obvious that the trauma to her skull had something to do with it, and the ocean didn't help the situation."

"Someone hit her and threw her in the water?"

"Where she drowned."

"Oh," Saffron breathed, overcome with pity for the woman.

"And then there's the cyanide you found. We got the tablets, and we're looking into that, too."

"Anything I can do to help?"

"Actually," Bradley seemed to consider for a moment, then reconsider, "No, no," he shook his head, "nothing you need to worry about. Unless you remember anything else."

"What were you going to say?" Saffron asked, leaning forward.

Bradley shifted, his eyes narrowing in thought. "Well, I am having a little trouble with one detail. Maybe you could find out something I can't seem to. There's something we found on the victim that seems . . . odd."

Saffron tried not to let the tantalizing sense of curiosity arise in her mind, but there was no stopping it. As soon as she heard that something was out of place, she always had the urge to put it right.

"What was it?" She looked out the front window nonchalantly, trying to conceal her interest.

He pulled from his pocket a small plastic bag. In it was a necklace, carved from what looked like pitted stone, in the shape of a fish. Bradley handed it to Saffron. Looking closely, she could see bright red tufts clinging to its points. She recognized them as the fibers of the bathrobe Dorah had been wearing. She asked Bradley about them.

"Found this tangled in the bathrobe," he said. "No prints on it. I was going to do some asking around town about it, but sometimes people seem to clam up when they see the badge. You seem to have more luck getting people to open up." He laughed. "Of course, you're used to cracking tough eggs."

· · · ·

THE LETOA ANNIVERSARY party was growing by the second. Saffron had three RSVP calls just during the drive to town. She stopped in the little grocery store: the Paradise Market, to drop off their weekly egg order. The new owners were a dynamic couple from Botswana, and they always greeted her warmly.

"Dumela mma!" The wife, Tale, gave a quick hug. Saffron inhaled the scent of strawberries and mango that the grocer always seemed to carry with her. Tale ran a hand down her cheek. "Glad you came today—we're low on eggs." Tale's skin was the rich umber of a leopard's spots, and her eyes were a dance of deep brown. She seemed always to be smiling.

Her husband, Baruti, was tall and angular. His hair was styled in a tight jet flat top, adding to his height, and his voice was a deep baritone. He reached for Saffron's hand. It had only taken a few awkward encounters for Saffron to get the hang of the Botswanan handshake. It started with a quick Western clasp like Saffron might give anyone, but then Baruti swung his hand back and bent his wrist, and Saffron did the same, locking their hands together as if they were about to arm wrestle. Baruti always put his left hand under his right elbow when he was shaking hands, which meant that he had to put down anything he was doing and engage both hands. In this way, it was more intimate than a Western handshake, focusing all the attention on the person being greeted. He always looked directly into Saffron's eyes, really acknowledging her presence, and she'd learned to do the same. After an earnest moment, they would slide their hands back to a western handshake and begin their business.

"Le kae?" Baruti asked, *How are you*? He grinned widely, "I saw you driving through town the other day with a surfer?"

Saffron blinked. Of course, they'd seen her. Who else had seen her? Living in a small town took some getting used to.

"I'm fine. I'm fine. Yes, that was a friend of mine. We'd gone snorkeling."

Tale smiled and bumped Saffron with her hip. "Is it? Friends, eh? You two were pretty close in that car."

Saffron turned her attention to unpacking the cooler full of eggs she was delivering. She felt her cheeks burning. This made Tale and Baruti laugh heartily.

"Don't worry. We're only joking," Baruti said. "We like seeing you out having fun." He patted her lightly on the arm.

Saffron set the eggs, carton by carton, into the refrigerated display, glad to have something to do.

"You've had a difficult week," Tale said. "I heard about the wedding, and that Dorah—oh, that Dorah—" Tale shook her head.

"Awful, isn't it?"

"Oh, not surprising, though," Tale said.

Baruti laughed, but it was a rueful sound. "Tale had a story or two about that Dorah."

"Oh?" Saffron asked.

"Oh. Yes. Oh." Tale was shaking her head, "She came in here and didn't like the look of some of our produce, so she threw three tomatoes right at me. I'll tell you," she closed her eyes and shook her head. Saffron saw the memory of each tomato in the fleeting grimace that crossed Tale's face. "Eish! I'll tell you if I could have reached anything more deadly than a banana I would have rid the world of her that day right here."

Hearing the usually warm Tale speaking of murder was a stark reminder to Saffron that Dorah was no ordinary case. The woman had treated people terribly. Saffron stepped back from the display and reached into her pocket.

"Is this familiar to either of you?" Saffron asked, pulling the bag Bradley had given her from her pocket. Baruti took it and inspected the fish necklace inside. "Mmmmm," he said, his flat-top bobbing. "It's carefully made. And the lashing is very intricate." Baruti handed it back, "Someone worked hard on that. But I don't know anything about it."

Saffron tucked it away. "Well, thanks anyway."

"You have fun with your surfer . . . Friend." Tale's voice inflected up on the last word in a light, teasing way and Saffron said goodbye before her cheeks got any hotter.

Saffron had so many errands. She thought through the list in her head:

-Kukku Kitchen Appliances for a classic punch bowl
-Coconuts and Bolts Hardware store to make a giant photo frame
-The Oceanside Cafe for some lunch

Heading down the street to Kukku Kitchen, she nearly ran into Mrs. Jones, who was standing smack in the middle of the boardwalk snapping photos of the shops along Holoholo Street.

Saffron didn't stop, just sidestepped and called a quick hello as she headed for the kitchen store.

That didn't stop Mrs. Jones from getting a complaint in, "There's too many people here!" the old woman fired at Saffron's back as she ducked into the store.

Kukku Kitchen Appliances was slow today, and Fumi was trimming her extensive herb garden that stretched across the front window, turning the streaming sunlight a brilliant green.

"Look at those!" Saffron pointed at the boxes. Though Fumi had been growing mint, dill, cilantro, and basil, she had a new tub full of oregano that she had just planted when Saffron had been here a few weeks ago. The little plants were several inches high now. Fumi smiled as she misted them with a spray bottle.

"They've come along well," she said.

Saffron pulled a box from her big handbag and held it toward Fumi. Fumi set down the spray bottle and came out from behind the counter. She took the box with delight in her eyes. When she opened it, she revealed a new hard boiled egg peeling device that Saffron had seen in an internet ad. Nothing pleased Fumi more than new kitchen gadgets to try out.

"Thank you!" She held the glass cylinder and cranked the little handle on the side. "Does it work?"

"I don't know," Saffron said, reaching into her handbag again and extracting a dozen eggs, "You'll have to test it out."

Saffron had met Fumi right here in her store just days after arriving in Maika'i, and Fumi always made her welcome. Lately, too, she and Fumi had worked out a rental arrangement for some of the lesser-used items in the store. Especially the service ware and dishes. If Saffron had an event, she used Fumi's display models and set Fumi's kitchen store business cards on the tables. It kept Saffron from having to buy everything for serving and got new customers into Fumi's shop. Everybody won. As an extra thank-you, Saffron tried to drop by some eggs from time to time.

"I've got something for you, too," Fumi said, reaching behind the counter.

"Oh?"

"Yep." Fumi held up what looked like a sock. "The Snooza-roo."

Saffron raised her eyebrows. "Oh-kay." Taking the item, she saw that it wasn't a sock, rather a fleece headband.

"A vendor sent it to me free. It has 'sound-blocking' technology that's supposed to help you sleep." Fumi said. "I can't stand anything on my head when I sleep, and I don't have any use for it here in the store—I just sell kitchen items. So I thought I'd give it to you."

"Thanks," Saffron said, tucking it into her pocket. I'll let you know how it works."

Fumi smiled, pleased as always to share a gadget. "How's the planning coming?" she asked, finally taking the eggs with a slight bow of thanks.

Saffron shrugged. "I've got the venue booked—the Piscine Lodge."

Fumi raised an eyebrow. "Glamorous."

The Piscine Lodge was not glamorous, though it had been at one time. It was, in fact, somewhat worn. Decorated with carved stone fish to coordinate with its name, it had seen better days. "They were married there," she explained, "and they want to renew their vows there."

"Can they use it? Don't you have to be a member or something?"

"Mr. Letoa—Claude—is a member, though it doesn't look like they've had many meetings there for a long while. It's pretty run-down."

Fumi nodded. "I guess the bride and groom probably don't look like they did fifty years ago, either. I guess it fits."

"Is it still okay if I use the punch service?" Saffron asked.

"Of course," Fumi said, "I'm glad I have it. A full punch set is hard to come by nowadays."

"It's been interesting doing this anniversary," Saffron said, "I think I've been to every antique shop on the island trying to recreate their wedding day."

"I'm sure, like all your events, it will be utsukushii—lovely."

"It will be like stepping back in time," Saffron said, the dreamy flower-child theme floating through her mind. "They were hippies, and their wedding was charming. It will be a fun recreation."

"This punchbowl will be perfect," Fumi said. Saffron followed her to the storeroom at the back of the shop. Inside, tall shelves kept the inventory away from careless shoppers and kept the front of the shop tidy.

The punchbowl and cups were set out in a big cardboard box, gleaming clean and ready. Saffron thanked Fumi again as she picked it up.

"I'm surprised it never sold," Saffron said, examining the cut glass handle of one of the cups that was sticking out of the wrapping paper. "It's got great style."

"Not anymore, it doesn't. It did when I special ordered it in. But then the person who ordered it came to pick it up and wouldn't pay for it because she'd just seen a different one in a magazine. When I told her I couldn't return it, she went crazy, smashing one of the cups and insisting she wouldn't pay for an incomplete set." Fumi shook her head, "I was shocked at first, but oh, after she left, I wished I had been growing hemlock in that herb garden. I'd have given her a handful of it."

Saffron blinked. Fumi was usually so calm. The little woman stalked back around the counter and snatched her spray bottle, raining droplets on the plants with fury.

Saffron figured she'd better leave before Fumi herself started breaking cups. But she suddenly remembered the necklace. She set the box on the counter and fished the necklace out of her bag. Holding it out, she asked the same thing she'd asked her friends at the market.

Fumi calmed as she studied the fish. "Well, it's not from the BlueWater Emporium," she said, referring to the big tourist shop that had opened on the other end of the main street. "Theirs are all plastic. This looks like real stone. And it's carved," she pointed out, running a fingernail along some obvious knife marks on the piece's edge, "which is more effort than they put into anything over there." There was a ripple of bitterness in Fumi's voice, as the BlueWater Emporium had cut sharply into the revenue streams of the other downtown shops.

"You don't recognize it, though?"

"No, sorry. I haven't seen one before."

Saffron put it back in her pocket and lifted the box of dishes. "I'll take good care of these," she said, "Thanks again!"

"I'll let you know how the egg peeler works," Fumi said brightly. Saffron got the feeling that the woman couldn't wait for her to leave so she could try out the new gadget. Just as Saffron reached the front door, she turned.

"Fumi," she asked, "just out of curiosity, who was the woman who ordered this punch bowl?"

Fumi's eyebrows drew together in anger, and she snatched her spray bottle again. Saffron knew what she would say before she said it: "Dorah Harrison."

Dorah's death was still big news in Coconuts and Bolts, Mai-ka'i's hardware store, too. Saffron shuddered as Jerome, the steady, slow talking proprietor, looked her in the eye.

"After that woman pulled over a whole rack of garden stakes out of spite because her order was late, I told her if she ever came back into my store I'd put one of those garden stakes through her heart."

Saffron had never seen such vehemence in Jerome Wiley. Even at his most agitated, Saffron would have described him as lethargic, and he had all the fierceness of a panda. Dorah's special gift seemed to be to glean the hatred of the people. And for good reason. It seemed she went around antagonizing them and attacking them.

Jerome hadn't seen the necklace before, either.

"Nope," he said, scratching the gray stubble on his chin, "But if you'd like, I'll getcha a new piece of twine for it." He waved a hand toward the wall of ropes, twine, and string on spools.

Saffron peered into the bag. Jerome was right—the licorice-colored cord was frayed where it had broken. Saffron had been so focused on the fish that she hadn't noticed the break in the bundled cord. It made her wonder if the necklace had been snatched off of whoever was wearing it.

Saffron stopped at the Oceanside Cafe for lunch. It wasn't the only eatery in Maika'i, but it was the best, and its proprietor, Bernadette, insisted that Saffron eat for free. So, Saffron always brought some extra cartons of eggs which Bernadette pretended she wouldn't accept, then did.

Seated in her favorite booth by the window, Saffron watched the sea. It was turbulent tonight, the color of spun steel, and Saffron felt the same way. She wished she could keep from thinking about Nik, or that she had the courage to call Keahi back, but both seemed beyond her current abilities.

She'd come for a hot bowl of saimin, the Hawaiian noodle dish that she'd come to love. There were countless variations, and here at the Oceanside Cafe they'd make it just about any way you wanted it, but tonight Saffron had gone with the standard menu style. It was a wonderful mix of the various cultures that had shaped Hawaii: rich Chinese egg noodles, Japanese dashi broth that gave it a sweet and savory flavor, a hard-boiled egg (one from her own egg farm, she thought with satisfaction), thick chunks of ham, chewy shiitake mushrooms, and a finishing crunch of bok choy, scallions, and bean sprouts.

Bernadette, standing beside the booth, watched Saffron with satisfaction. "I like a customer who enjoys my food."

"Well that's me," Saffron said around a bite of noodles. "These are sensational."

"We make them ourselves," Bernadette's pride was evident in her voice. "Only one person has ever complained."

Saffron heard the name coming, but she waited until Bernadette said it anyway.

"Dorah," Bernadette shook her head and clucked in dismay like one of Saffron's hens.

Saffron shook her head, "Well, I can't find anything to complain about."

"*She* said," Bernadette leaned her considerable bulk onto the table, "that the noodles were," Bernadette's face contracted into an expression of disgust, "gummy."

Saffron raised her eyebrows. Bernadette only got annoyed about two things: when customers disparaged the food, and when they didn't pay.

"It was a humid day, last summer. She was eating here with an old lady who had to have her drink refilled every five minutes, and she was wearing the most ridiculous wetsuit—Dorah, not the old lady. And did I say anything about that? Or about the fact that I had customers waiting lined up around the block and they sat in a prime booth for two and a half hours? No, I did not. I was perfectly welcoming and professional, and she still stood up and dumped my noodles on the floor, saying they'd match the sticky tile."

Bernadette closed her eyes, her cheeks twitching with anger at the memory.

"I'll tell you, I could have smothered her with her own noodle bowl myself that day."

She turned her attention back to the little bag Saffron had handed her and studied the necklace carefully. "Doesn't ring any bells. I've never seen one exactly like this before."

"Any idea where it might have come from?"

Bernadette shook her head. "No idea. But you could ask over at the jewelry store. They work with some of our local carvers, and they might know something."

Saffron slurped the sweet noodles and nodded. She hadn't thought of Pacific Gems, but they would be a great place to continue her search. If she didn't find something out soon, she'd have to give the necklace back to Bradley with no more information than he'd had before, and if she didn't prove useful, he might not loop her in on future developments.

Saffron had always liked things in their places, and she'd never liked unanswered questions, though she'd certainly had to live with plenty of those. She enjoyed working with Bradley on these cases because she enjoyed finding answers.

CHAPTER 7

Pacific Gems was empty when she went in. The bell on the door jingled, and she knew that the owner, Evan Stephens, would be out soon. He was likely in the back setting a dazzling stone in his signature fish setting: the humuhumunukunukuapua'a, the state fish of Hawaii. He made necklaces, bracelets, and incredible rings.

Saffron gazed at the rings in the case now. Yellow and white gold, they sported finely filigreed fish encrusted with yellow and black diamonds. Next to them, engagement rings with humuhumunukunukuapua'a, etched into them, set with princess-cut diamonds. She tried not to think of Keahi or the time they had come in here to drop something off for his grandpa. They'd lingered, just a moment, over this case, and though neither of them had said anything, there had been an unspoken excitement in the air.

Evan wandered out, his jeweler's glasses magnifying his eyes like an owl's as he peered through them. His expression changed to delight. Saffron had pointed many a client and many of her cottage renters in the direction of Evan's store, and he remembered things like that.

"How are you? Got any weddings coming up?"

Saffron did, in fact, have several weddings she was organizing over the next couple of months, but that wasn't what she'd come for this time. "Evan, I've got to rush back to the farm for my evening chores, but I wondered if you'd take a look at this." She extracted the bag and offered it to him. He took it, opened it, and slid the fish necklace into his palm.

"Hmmm," He said as he examined it. "I hear you've been working with Bradley on some of his cases."

Saffron was non-committal. "You helping on this drowning of the woman out at Uwē Beach?"

Saffron didn't answer, but Evan went on anyway.

"Doesn't surprise me. I nearly choked that woman with a twenty-four-carat gold Cuban link chain. She was in here buying one for her mother, and she didn't have one nice thing to say about anything. She said my fish rings were *inaccurate*." Evan looked like a hen with its feathers fluffed up in anger.

Evan was engrossed in the necklace. "Made from lava rock. Kind of unique material for carvers to use for these." Saffron wasn't sure if he was talking to her or to himself. "Interesting. Linen cord, not hemp. He glanced up and caught her eye. "Probably means it's not just a malihini piece. Those are usually made with cheap hemp cords." He flipped the fish over. Reaching under the counter, he extracted a polishing cloth.

"It's been in the ocean," he said, rubbing the necklace. "It's got salt and crud here over the maker's mark. And what's with these little red threads?" Evan didn't expect an answer, so Saffron didn't give one. Maker's mark? She waited expectantly.

"Its a backward E merged with a capital B. EB," Evan peered at the back of the fish for a long moment before looking up with a shrug. "Sorry, Saffron, I don't recognize it. There's definitely a carver's mark here, but I've not seen it before. That could be because the carver's not from here. It could just be because he or she is new at carving, or long dead, or a hobbyist. But probably not long dead. It looks like relatively new work, maybe within the last few months, even."

Saffron let out her breath. She hadn't realized she'd been holding it. Another dead end.

"You know who you should ask?" Evan squinted through the jeweler's specs, "Mano."

Saffron's stomach twisted. *Mano.*

Evan slipped it in its bag and handed the piece back. "He knows all the carvers around here—he trained a lot of them. Mano would know if anyone would." Evan grinned, "And you have an in with him, dating his grandson and all."

Saffron felt her throat get tight, but she nodded. Backing toward the door, she pushed out the words, "thanks, Evan. See you soon."

"Not if I see you first," he chuckled, his eyes huge behind his specs.

Saffron ducked out the door.

• • • •

SHE WAS IN THE MIDDLE of chicken chores when her cantankerous guest charged into the egg house.

"I have had it! I have had it! I want a refund!" It was the ancient woman staying in the Coral Cottage.

"How can I help, Mrs. Jones?" Saffron turned from her egg cartons to see the woman standing, hands on hips, in the doorway.

"You can do something about all this sand!"

"Pardon me?"

"Every time I go down by the water, there's sand all over my shoes, and my towel, and when I come back to the cottage, there's sand anywhere I walk."

"Sand?" Saffron said, "On the beach?"

"Yes. Too much of it. And it's too fine. Nobody told me it was going to be so sandy here."

Saffron had heard complaints before. The water drained from the cottage sink too slowly, the view out the window was obstructed by a palm tree, there was a rooster on the loose, but this was the first time someone had complained about the beach being too sandy.

"Well, Mrs. Jones, if you'll look in your hall closet, you'll see a handheld vacuum on the shelf above the regular one. That can help a lot with the extra sand."

"I didn't come here to vacuum!" The woman spun and stormed out. "I rent a cottage, I expect it to be clean!"

Saffron stood staring after her. The sound of Bossy's annoyed clucking was like Mrs. Jones' echo ringing through the egg house.

• • • •

MANO WAS ON HIS PORCH when Saffron drove up. She didn't look at the big silver SUV, parked in front, waiting for Keahi to come home.

Mano greeted her warmly, and she sat on the swing on the lanai where she had Keahi had sat the night before he'd left for Boston. She tried not to feel his arm around her.

"I wondered if you knew who'd made this?" She said, holding out the bag.

Mano raised an eyebrow and reached a work-worn hand toward her. He slid out the necklace and hummed as he looked it over.

"Oh, sure," he said, "I know who made it."

Saffron heard herself suck in air. "What? Really?"

"Sure. Student of mine couple years back. Ekewaka Bello. He's an okay carver, but he's not making a living at it."

"What does he do? Where can I find him?"

"I've seen him hanging around Barkadoodle the last couple of times I've been in there." Mano gestured vaguely in the direction of town and the little pet shop there.

A sound like a choking engine caught Saffron's attention. She turned to see Keahi's mother, Iolana, standing in the doorway. "Time for lunch," she directed her words to Mano, her father-in-law. Saffron could see by her stiff shoulders and the line of her lips that she had heard about Saffron spending time with Nik.

She wished she could explain, wished she could tell them about Evelyn and the uncertainty she felt. She wished she could assure them that she and Keahi still felt everything for each other that they had felt before he went away.

But none of those words would come. All she managed was a weak, apologetic smile. Iolana did not return it.

Mano noticed and clucked at his daughter-in-law. "I'll be there in a minute," he said, "when I'm done talking to *our friend*."

He stressed the last words, and Saffron tried to take a little comfort from it.

"Your lunch will go cold," Iolana said roughly.

"We'll warm it back up," he said.

Iolana looked pointedly at Saffron, "You can't warm something up once it's gone cold."

Mano scoffed. "In the heat of the island sun, hunona wahine," he said the words for *daughter-in-law* distinctly and slowly, "anything can find warmth again."

Saffron picked up on the subtext. Her cheeks were burning, and the island sun had nothing to do with it.

"Now," Mano asked, dismissing Iolana with a wave, "Tell me where you got this necklace."

Keahi's mother stomped back into the house, shutting the door hard. Mano leaned forward, and in a low voice asked, "Are you mixed up in anything? I thought you pau sleuthing."

Saffron considered that. Pau meant finished, all done. He thought she was all done sleuthing? She may have led him to believe that after her last nearly fatal case. But she hadn't meant to get involved with this one. It had just kind of pulled her in. Nevertheless, Mano's eyes shone with tolerant affection.

"Not exactly pau," she said. "But I'm not seeking these cases out. Bradley just thought I might be of some help in this one because he's kind of stuck."

Mano nodded, then eased himself forward and stood. "Okay. Let's go."

"Go?"

"I'm going with you to meet Ekewaka. You won't know him if you see him."

Saffron was torn. She loved being with Mano. She loved his steadiness—something Keahi had inherited from his grandpa. She loved his wisdom, and she loved his practical approach to life. He was always an asset in her investigations. But she also squirmed at the thought of the quiet ride into town, the questions he might ask that she wasn't ready to answer.

Mano wasn't asking questions now. At least, he wasn't asking permission. He was climbing into the passenger's seat of her car. Saffron couldn't stop her own smile as she stood and followed him.

The ride into town was not quiet. Mano chattered about his newest carving techniques and about the weather on the island. When they pulled up in front of the pet store, he hopped out of the car like a twenty-year-old and charged up the steps. As Saffron scrambled after him, it occurred to her that perhaps he enjoyed sleuthing as much as she did.

Saffron's attention was arrested on her way in by Echo, a scarlet macaw that belonged to the owner of the shop.

"Hello, hello!" Echo called. She was upside down, swinging on a hoop underneath her perch.

"Hello, hello, Echo!" Saffron called back. Before she could mount the last stair, Echo had launched. Saffron braced herself as the nearly three-pound bird sailed toward her and landed noiselessly on her shoulder. Echo tucked her wings and began nibbling at Saffron's hair.

"Must be a redhead here," called Bernie, the shop owner, from inside the door. Saffron walked in and tossed him a smile. "Echo loves redheads. She thinks your hair is a flower. Or a fruit."

"Very flattering, Echo," Saffron said as Echo nibbled her ear. The beak was sharp, but Echo was gentle. Mano stood smiling, his white teeth flashing against his tawny skin.

The greetings were over, and Saffron got the feeling that Mano had already asked if Ekewaka was there, because the men were angled expectantly toward the store-room door. It was only a moment before a young man glided through it, his grace evident in every movement. He moved as if he were as weightless as the fish in the bag he was carrying.

He had a close-shaved head, large brown eyes, and skin the color of coral.

"Eke!" Mano cried, greeting him with the warm smile and hearty handshake he seemed to save for all the town's young men. Saffron noticed their confidence increased visibly whenever he looked them in the eye and made them feel seen.

Eke smiled back, a bright expression.

"Hey," Mano teased, "you didn't invite me to your hukilau the other night, brah?" Saffron knew that Mano loved a beach party.

Eke ducked his head. "You're always invited."

Mano lowered his voice, "I hear it got a little too wild."

Raising his hands, Eke defended himself. "It was not my fault. This crazy malihini was the one. He was loud and obnoxious. But you feel bad for him, cuz his aunt just died."

"Wait," Saffron said, stepping forward with the big bird on her shoulder, "are you talking about Dylan?"

Eke eyed her suspiciously, but a nearly imperceptible nod from Mano must have convinced him that she was okay. "That's right," the young man said.

"When was this party?"

"Couple nights ago—when we had the big full moon."

That was the night of Dorah's murder. "How long was he with you?"

"All night, man. We just barely got him cleaned up in time to go to his mom's wedding the next morning. He spent all night with us." Eke rolled his eyes, "that's a night I'll never get back."

So Dylan couldn't have killed Dorah. His timeline was wrong. It was possible that Eke was lying, but he'd have no reason to.

Mano gestured for Saffron to hand him the necklace, and, with Echo still balancing on her shoulder and sifting through the strands of her hair, she did.

"Is this yours, brah?" Mano asked.

Eke's eyes widened. "What? Where did you find this?"

Mano looked at Saffron. She had to make a decision. Should she veil the truth, hoping he'd give away more information? Or should she tell him everything? "Uh," she stalled.

The kid didn't wait for her answer. "I carved this a couple months ago. It was a commission. I had it in here, on that counter—" he waved a hand, "and it disappeared."

"Disappeared?"

"Yeah. Just vanished. We looked everywhere, huh, Bernie?"

"Sure did."

"Do you think it was stolen?"

"I guess, but it's funny because the only person who came in here during that time was Crazy Milo."

Saffron exchanged a glance with Mano. "Who now?"

"Crazy Milo. He's a fish collector. He's the guy who's wife was killed the other night."

"He was here when the necklace went missing?"

"Well, he came that day. We don't know for sure if it was already missing before he came, or if it went missing after he came." Saffron thought of her bracelet. Maybe Milo was a kleptomaniac as well as a kidnapper.

Bernie spoke up. "Milo's our best supplier, so I don't like to think that he might be a thief."

How about a murderer? Saffron thought but didn't say.

"I guess I should ask him about it," Eke said, "I should have asked him this morning."

Saffron straightened. "You saw Milo *this morning?*"

Eke held up the bag in his hands. In it, a saucer-sized fish was swimming. Its delicate slate body was adorned with daffodil-colored stripes. It was outlined in onyx and bright lemon yellow that continued in bands across its face. It had an intelligent and searching expression, and it barely moved as it hovered in the bag Eke was holding. "He brought this in," he said.

"What kind is it?" Saffron breathed. Even Echo seemed to be entranced with the fish. She stood still and silent, her weight and a silky wing against Saffron's cheek the only reminder to Saffron that she had a passenger.

"It's an ornate butterflyfish," the kid said.

"Milo's really off his game, bringing that in here," Bernie grumbled.

"Why?"

Bernie scoffed. He was so knowledgeable about animals that he sometimes seemed to forget that not everyone was. "Because it's an obligate corallivore, obviously."

Saffron narrowed her eyes, "I thought Eke said it was a butterflyfish."

Bernie closed his eyes as if trying very hard to control his disgust at her ignorance. He kept his eyes closed while he explained. When he spoke, he spoke very slowly. "*Ob-li-gate* it means restricted to. *Co-rall-i-vore*: eating coral. Ornate Butterflyfish ONLY eat coral polyps. Live ones. You can't keep 'em. They're impossible fish to keep alive. I kept one alive for a month, once, but that was only by spending every waking moment finding polyps for it. They're best left in the ocean."

"We're going to have to put this one back there before it gets too hungry," Eke said. "I was just on my way to do that."

"He took it from the ocean? Can he do that?"

Bernie growled, "of course he can. He's got the proper permits. But it is surprising that he would take any from the ocean, cuz he's got a pretty good operation going at his house, and his specimens are excellent."

This was all very fascinating, but Saffron snapped back to the real issue. "Milo was *here*?"

Bernie opened his eyes and stared as if Saffron had sprouted gills herself, "that's what I said."

Mano stepped in, "Milo's in some trouble."

"Trouble?" Bernie's voice was alarmed. "What kind of trouble? Something with the DAR?"

"DAR?" Saffron asked.

"Division of Aquatic Resources," Bernie snapped. "Milo has always been responsible—had his permits in line and everything, but if he starts messing up, this whole place is in jeopardy!" He waved his arms wide, causing the parrot on Saffron's shoulder to flap wildly and smack her in the face repeatedly with a berry-colored wing.

"Jeopardy!" Echo echoed.

"This trouble is a little bigger than the DAR," Saffron said. "Milo's wife was murdered."

There was a stunned silence in the shop. Bernie closed his eyes again as if blocking out the world.

Eke breathed out, breaking the silence. "Heavy," he said.

"This necklace was found on his wife's body," Saffron said. "We're trying to figure out how it got there."

Bernie, eyes closed again, spoke with finality, "Then I guess you're going to have to ask Milo."

CHAPTER 8

Bradley came and questioned Bernie and Eke, but they had no idea where Milo had gone after he delivered his bags of fish to them. Saffron shared the information she'd learned about Dylan, and they scratched him off their "suspects" list.

She was still thinking about the encounter late that evening, in the bright glow of the Hawaiian moon. Saffron sat on her lanai tossing grains of rice from her poke bowl to Curry, frustrated at finding another wall.

"I thought we were so close," she told the rooster, "but they had no idea he was even a wanted man. They said they'd watch for him, but they didn't have any helpful information."

Curry rattled sympathetically. Saffron appreciated it, though it didn't solve anything. She scooped the last sweet spoonful of rice, fish, and thick brown sauce into her mouth.

In the next moment, several things happened simultaneously in the next moment. Curry stretched his neck, stood tall, and started making a popping cluck that Saffron recognized as a warning. A shadow fell over Saffron's shoulder, and she spun around. And Milo Harrison climbed over the railing of her lanai.

Saffron was on her feet, her bowl crashing to the lanai. She held her fork like a weapon, wondering if the guests in the cottage would hear if she screamed. With her other hand, she pulled out her cell phone from her pocket. She tapped the numbers 9-1-1, but Milo's voice interrupted her before she hit *send*.

Milo's voice was quiet in the dim moonlight, "I—I'm not here to hurt you. I'm returning something." His breathing was ragged.

In his extended hand was the glint of Saffron's gold plumeria bracelet.

"I just came to bring this back," Milo said. He laid it on the arm of the chair Saffron had been sitting in. Behind Saffron, Curry was making an aggressive bawk and strutting back and forth. She stepped closer to the rooster. She'd seen him attack before, and he had pretty good aim. Looking at Milo's scrawny arms, her money was on Curry. "It looks expensive. I thought you might be looking for it."

Saffron's keen sense of color was flagging something unusual about Milo tonight. He was wearing a dark blueberry-colored shirt, but it wasn't a uniform hue. Across the shoulders and his paunch was a grainy pattern that was lighter than the rest of the fabric. The color was dusty, more denim than the deeper indigo of the rest of his shirt. It was an ordinary work shirt, and it made no sense for it to be two-toned. Saffron pulled her attention away and peered at him through the darkness. "Why didn't you just keep it, or sell it?" her voice was accusatory, fueled by her memory of being trapped in the garage and from her fear of what he was capable of.

"It's not mine," he said softly.

"Well, you certainly have high ethics for a kidnapper and a murderer." Saffron's voice was shaking.

Milo winced. He certainly didn't seem like a hardened criminal. She almost felt bad for speaking so harshly, but then she remembered the terrible thing that he was accused of. And he didn't deny what she'd said.

"There's something else," Milo said, his voice small.

Here it was. What was his ulterior motive for showing up at her house? Saffron glanced down at her phone and tapped the "send" button.

"I need you to give my wife a message," Milo said. His voice was lost in a racking cough that made his shoulders shake. A soft shushing sound followed the attack, and Saffron tried to figure out if he was making it with his coarse breathing.

Saffron held her breath. Was he going to kill her, too? How else could she give Dorah a message?

"I need you to tell her that I sold the butterflyfish. They haven't paid me yet, but I dropped it off with the Barkadoodle fish order, and when they pay me, I'll have the money to get her a good lawyer."

Saffron didn't know which part of his message she should address first. Milo obviously didn't realize that the pet store wouldn't be paying him for a fish they were setting free, but that seemed secondary to another fact that was becoming clear: Milo didn't know Dorah was dead.

Saffron heard the tinny voice on the cell phone in her hand. She didn't hang up, but she did slide the phone into her pocket. "Milo, where do you think Dorah is?"

"In jail, of course. For kidnapping you. I went for a walk after you left, and I was walking up to the house when the sirens of the police car came screaming down the road. I panicked and ran." He hung his head. "Sirens just push me over the edge. Ever since that terrible night that I—" he stopped, and Saffron knew he was talking about the murder of Rachel's first husband. Milo drew a shaky breath and went on. "I should have gone in to wake her up, but I didn't want to go back to jail. I just freaked out and ran. I guess they arrested her. I've been hiding out."

"Oh, Milo," Saffron tried to keep her voice kind, "I'm so sorry I have to tell you this." She tried to think of the right words.

"Tell me what?" His voice was puzzled and also apprehensive. He looked at her expectantly.

"Your wife—Dorah," Saffron hesitated, "Dorah is," she couldn't say it, "isn't, in jail." She finished lamely.

Milo looked relieved, and Saffron's stomach twisted. "She's not in jail. She's—she passed away, Milo."

It sounded wrong, sounded like Dorah had just slipped away while dreaming in her soft bed. But "dead" sounded so harsh.

She watched him take the news, watched his eyes widen until they were perfect circles of white in the night. She watched him stagger backward and sink to the worn boards of the lanai with a hurt and mournful sound.

Saffron moved toward him.

"How do you know this?" he asked. "Are you sure?"

Saffron tried not to think of the matted hair, the bruised skin. "I'm sure. And I'm sorry."

"Where is she? Where is Dorah?"

This was a question that had not occurred to Saffron. "Well, I think she's at the hospital," she said. She did not add that Dorah was in the hospital's morgue. The word was too cold, too cruel.

"What happened?" Milo was sitting with his knees pulled to his chest, his thin arms wrapped around his bent legs. He looked impossibly fragile.

Saffron tried to think of a gentle way to tell him that Dorah was killed. The way he was responding, it seemed unlikely that he had done it. There was no way to say it. Instead, she told another truth: "They're not sure yet what happened."

It was at that moment that the lanai was washed with hot blue light, followed by a flash of red. The piercing cry of a police siren exploded in the night, and Saffron spun to see Bradley's police cruiser turning off the main road at the end of her long driveway. Dust billowed in the wan illumination of its taillights and Saffron remembered the phone in her pocket.

"Milo, I—" she turned back to explain, but she was alone on the lanai. The bracelet, glinting in the flashing lights, was the only indication that the fish keeper had been here at all.

Bradley was at her side almost impossibly quickly. All she could do was blurt an explanation and point in the direction she thought Milo must have gone.

Gun drawn, Bradley followed him.

Saffron watched the beam of Bradley's flashlight swallowed up in the vegetation past the driveway. She had to turn on more lights. Curry continued his warning cluck as she crossed the lanai. She paused at the chair where her bracelet was. She wanted it but wondered if Bradley needed to check it for fingerprints. She supposed it was evidence now.

As she stood looking at its dull gleam, Saffron's bare feet felt gritty on the lanai. Where Milo had been standing was a ring of fine sand. Absurdly, she thought of Mrs. Jones' complaint that the beach was too sandy. But it wasn't exactly like the sand from Saffron's beach. This felt slicker, smaller. Saffron wondered if it came from wherever Milo was hiding. She'd have to tell Bradley about it. Saffron tracked the sand with her across the lanai to the bristly mat outside her door. There she dusted off her feet and went inside to switch on every light inside and outside the house.

It was hours later, in the dead of the night, that Bradley gave up looking. They sat at Saffron's kitchen table and drank cold sodas to defray the sticky heat of the night.

"Did he say anything about where he was hiding out? Anything that would help us find him?"

Saffron ran over their conversation in her mind. "Nothing."

"So what do we got? The bracelet, the sand on the lanai," he ran a hand through his thinning hair. "That sand he left is so fine. I don't know any beach that has such powdery sand."

"It's so white, too," Saffron said. Most of the sand on the beach by her house was golden and amber.

"Maybe some little beach on the far side of the island?" Bradley mused.

"It feels surreal that he was even here," Saffron said, holding her soda can to her forehead.

"So, what're we thinking here?" Bradley asked. "He came to give this back," he poked at the little evidence bag containing Saffron's bracelet, "and to get a message to Dorah?"

"That's what he said," Saffron acknowledged. "The bracelet could have just been an excuse to come here, or a peace offering so that I would do him the favor of passing the info on to Dorah."

Bradley shook his head, "He didn't know she was dead, so it seems less likely that he killed her."

Saffron had been thinking the same thing. She nodded.

Bradley kept talking, "Unless she died afterward. I mean, maybe they fought, he got angry and hit her with something, then she ran out and died later."

"I suppose that could have happened," Saffron admitted. "He just seems so . . . Meek. Do you think he could really do it?"

Bradley shook his head knowingly, "Listen, Gumshoe. I've seen enough unlikely criminals to know that it's just a matter of motivation. Properly motivated, *anyone* could do *anything*."

That was a chilling thought. "We won't rule him out then," Saffron said.

"That's the problem with this case," Bradley complained, "I haven't been able to legitimately rule anybody out yet, except the kid—at least he has an alibi."

Curiosity prickled in Saffron's mind. She leaned forward. "Any new info?"

"Not as much as I'd like. I've interviewed the others, but other than their animosity toward Dorah, I can't find any reason to really suspect them. They're keeping pretty quiet. "Have you talked to the sister yet?" Bradley asked.

"No," Saffron said, "But I'll do it tomorrow."

• • • •

RACHEL WAS STAYING at the Sweet Pineapple Bed and Breakfast. Run by a jolly woman whose life's purpose was to feed people, the establishment was bright, clean, and inviting. The proprietor, Bunny Monroe, carried in a plate of finger sandwiches and bowed out. Saffron sat in a wingbacked chair in the parlor facing Rachel.

"Nothing has gone as planned," Rachel was lamenting. Her eyes had dark circles under them, and her skin had the dull pallor of someone who hadn't slept in several nights.

"Like what?" Saffron asked. As an event planner, she knew the importance of things going according to plan, and she knew the chaos that ensued when they didn't.

"My sister is dead. My son's a suspect."

Saffron laid a hand on Rachel's arm. "Actually, that's a little good news. Bradley has taken Dylan off the list of suspects. He has an alibi."

Rachel's eyes fluttered closed briefly. "Thank goodness. I don't know if I could stand losing him."

Saffron looked around. "Where's Blake?"

Rachel drew a ragged breath, "He left. He left before we even made it back here to the B&B on our wedding night."

"Left?" Saffron was startled. Hadn't Bradley told them to stick around?

"He said he had to go back to work for a few days. He only had so much time off. But I think he was just overwhelmed by the," Rachel paused, and Saffron could see that the woman couldn't stand to say the word *murder*, "by what happened. I'm trying to be understanding, but it means I'm stuck here and handling all this alone. Is that what a marriage is supposed to be like?"

Saffron heard her despair in the last sentence. She shook her head. "I'm sorry. Will he be back soon?"

"He said he'd be back as soon as he could," Rachel said. "But I don't know. Ever since we got to Hawaii, he's been," she paused and ran a trembling hand across her forehead, "different."

Saffron leaned forward, "How so?"

"I don't know, just distant. Nervous. I assumed it was because of the wedding. I mean, most people are nervous before their wedding."

"That's true." Saffron looked around the little parlor and ate another finger sandwich, giving the woman a moment to breathe before easing into another question, "Tell me about how you met Blake."

Rachel ducked her head and gave a half-guilty smile. "We met online."

"Oh?"

"Yes, I'm embarrassed about it, but I was just at the end of my rope. I'd tried the dating scene around my town. I'd been set up, stood up, let down, and I had decided to forget about the inheritance and live my life alone. But then I opened my email one day, and there was an ad for this lonely hearts app, and I just downloaded it on a whim."

Saffron knew the feeling. She'd thought about going online a time or two after breaking up with her first serious boyfriend, Reggie, back in Washington, DC, before she came to Hawaii.

"I found Blake just a few days after joining. He flagged me down," she shook her head and explained, "there was this function on the app where you could send little waving flags with different icons on them, like a heart or a smiley face or a kiss. He sent me a question mark, and when I looked up his profile, I couldn't believe how perfect he was."

Alarms were going off in Saffron's mind, but she didn't voice them. "How romantic! What made him perfect?"

"Well, I guess not everyone would think he was," Rachel said, "but I did. First, he had this strong, single syllable name. My first husband was named Rob. I loved that. And Blake has these beautiful horses—a horse ranch out in Missouri."

Saffron could see the draw of that. She'd become more of an animal lover since taking over the egg farm. But there was something off. She tried to remember what Blake had said that morning in the minivan. It came back to her: the petals and plates campaign, "Wow," she said carefully, "but, I thought he was in advertising."

"Advertising?" Rachel looked at her quizzically. "No, I don't think so. But, he did mention that he'd recently switched jobs. Maybe he was in advertising before." Her expression was chagrined. "I should know that, huh? But we have plenty of time to get to know all each other's stories."

"So, he had to get back to the ranch?"

"No, his brother really does most of that. Blake's 9 to 5 job is at a bank."

Saffron considered that. A bank. "So he has to do that as well. He must not be making a lot at the ranch. Is it a big operation?"

Rachel shrugged. "It looks big. I haven't actually been out there."

Another alarm. "Oh?" Saffron had found that, in general, people's lives followed a pretty set pattern. Blake's seemed convoluted and complicated. It made Saffron feel uneasy.

Rachel picked up on the doubtful tone and rushed to explain, "Well, see, he runs it with his brother Chas, and Chas doesn't really like people visiting, so he said, I mean, we decided, that it would be better to go out there later, after the wedding. But he came to see me in Wisconsin!"

Saffron didn't like that Rachel hadn't seen Blake's life with her own eyes. But his story, she supposed, was plausible. Saffron wondered if she was just being too suspicious. "How long did you date?"

Rachel's cheeks colored. Instead of answering the question, she clarified, "I would usually insist on getting to know someone much longer, I mean, I dated my first husband for two years. It's not like me . . ." She trailed off, then said, "we did get to know each other for several weeks. And there was such a connection," she insisted, leaning over and putting a hand on Saffron's arm. "He wasn't just perfect because of his name, or the ranch. He likes the same movies as I do, loves pasta, sleeps late. He has no children so there wouldn't be the complication of dividing the inheritance between them and Dylan. He went to Africa with the Red Cross last year to help dig latrines for villages. He cooks these amazing gourmet meals. He loves the beach."

Saffron tried to squash the cynical thought that *everyone* loved the beach. And the Red Cross? Saffron just couldn't see Blake making that kind of personal sacrifice. But maybe she was wrong.

"We were such a good match that the site flagged us! It has this function, where if enough of your interests match, it says you should be together. Once we started dating, the app would suggest activities based on our compatibilities, and when we got engaged, we got our own "Flag of Fame" with our love story and our profiles. The app uses it for advertising now!"

"You had all that in common, huh?" Saffron tried to think of any time she'd had half so much in common with a boyfriend.

"And he was looking for a serious relationship," Rachel finished. "I knew if I was going to get married, I should probably do it quickly."

"Because of the inheritance?" Saffron asked.

"Right," Rachel rushed to say, "I wouldn't have gotten married just for that, of course, but if I was going to get married anyway, I figured, why wait when I still had a chance to fulfill the stipulation of the will and get the money?"

The way she said *get the money* bothered Saffron. Under Rachel's light tone was a steel edge of greed that couldn't be ignored. It seemed to be genetic.

"You've been waiting a long time for that money, haven't you?" Saffron asked.

"At least it feels like a long time. For a while, I was sure that Dorah had made off with it, but that was another thing that Blake did for me—" Rachel lowered her voice. Her eyes darted sideways as if checking the door, "he looked it up."

Saffron didn't understand. "Looked it up?" She shrugged, "I don't understand."

"Well, I told you. Blake isn't just a rancher. He's also a banker." The professions seemed at odds in Saffron's mind, but she suspended her disbelief as Rachel went on, "and, even though he wasn't supposed to, he sent a request and checked on the account for me. He was shocked by how much money was in there. I knew that the lawyers had kept their word and held onto it and that Dorah hadn't gotten her hands on it. So, if I was vacillating about getting married, all those zeros made up my mind."

And probably his, too, Saffron thought.

"And Blake was okay with the speed of your courtship?"

Rachel laughed, a short, explosive sound. "Blake asked me to marry him thirty-five hours after we met for the first time in person! He was moving a lot faster than I was!"

Saffron tucked a piece of her hair behind her ear. Maybe it was because her father had walked out when she was a baby. Maybe it was because her mother had died. Maybe it was because Reggie had left Washington and broken her heart. Whatever it was, she was more than a little suspicious of things that looked too perfect, of things that just seemed to work out. Life, in her experience, didn't usually just work out.

She was about to ask a follow-up question when Dylan slouched into the room and gave her a nod in greeting. The kid moved in a jerky, hunched way, as if he could flee at any time.

He looked at his mother, "Any sign of Blake yet?"

She shook her head, and Saffron saw the crimson flush of anger around Dylan's nose.

"I can't believe he'd just leave you here in the middle of all this."

Saffron couldn't either. But Rachel and Blake had only known each other a couple months. Maybe they hadn't fully developed their relationship yet. Saffron knew it could be hard to lean on someone. She was filled with a deep longing for Keahi. They'd been able to lean on each other from the beginning. She resolved to phone him as soon as she was done here.

"He's just dealing with a lot, too, honey."

Dylan shook his head, and his dark hair sifted across his eyes. "I told you not to marry him."

"Honey," her tone was a warning, and Saffron saw the almost imperceptible jerk of Rachel's head toward her. Rachel didn't want Dylan saying too much in front of her.

He pressed his lips together, the strain of keeping quiet evident in his eyes.

"It's okay," Saffron said, "You can speak freely. I'm just trying to figure out what happened here, and to keep everyone as safe as possible."

Dylan started to speak, but another glance from his mother shut him up. It was evident that if Rachel wasn't going to let him speak freely.

He rushed to change the subject. "Did you get your money?" He asked his mother. "When the lawyer came earlier?"

"Not yet," Rachel said. Saffron recognized the soothing tone in her voice. All mothers had it, and all of them used it when they knew their children weren't going to like what they were saying.

Dylan did not like the news. "What do you mean?" he fumed. "You were supposed to have it days ago!"

"Mr. Cutler said it was just going to take a little longer," Rachel said.

Dylan rolled his eyes. "It's never going to happen, is it?"

"Now, Honey," Rachel said, and her tone was half calming, half warning.

"But really. Do you think it's going to actually happen? You've been waiting years, and now it seems like one more roadblock."

Rachel closed her eyes against the barrage. Saffron was surprised that she hadn't yet received the money. The lawyer, Cutler, had seemed very efficient. She decided that the law offices of Bellevue, Kwan, and Cutler would be her next stop.

CHAPTER 9

The law office was situated in a quiet corner of Maika'i. It was a relatively new building with floor-to-ceiling windows looking out over the town and the ocean beyond. The waiting room had a magazine rack, a circle of comfortable chairs, and a long saltwater aquarium bisecting it.

Mr. Cutler was with someone, the receptionist explained, but would be free within the hour.

"He has just been running this whole week," she said. She was a pleasant, middle-aged woman. The plaque on her desk said *Phyllis*. She had come around to feed the fish in the big tank. She was carrying a plastic container with chunks of something floating in a sickly brown bath. When she opened it, Saffron put a hand over her nose. The smell of rancid garlic and seaweed emanated from the container.

"Whew!"

"Oh," Phyllis said, "sorry. I forget. I don't notice it that much anymore."

"What in the world is it?"

"It's fish food. It comes in these frozen blocks, but then you add garlic-infused liquid and let it soak."

"Why?" Saffron asked, watching the woman slide back a panel on top of the aquarium, "why would you do that?"

"Tropical fish are apparently very finicky eaters," Phillis said, reaching in with a bare hand and scooping up some of the chunks. She squeezed the liquid out and then dropped them through the hole. "They like garlic, though, and the parasites that want to live on them don't like garlic, so it works both ways."

"It's terrible," Saffron said. She noticed now that Phyllis' fingers on that hand were tinged a brownish-green, just like Milo's had been. Maybe he wasn't a smoker after all. Perhaps it was from his fish-keeping hobby. That would explain his garlicky aroma as well. She was relieved when Phyllis snapped the lid back on the container, slid the top of the aquarium closed, and bustled back behind her desk to fetch a hand wipe scented with lemon.

Saffron breathed again. "Lots going on in the Maika'i legal realm, huh?" She asked absentmindedly as she watched a big flat-faced fish dart out from under an overhanging rock and slurp up one of the cubes.

"Oh, yes. It's always busy. Divorces, people suing people, land feuds," Phillis sighed almost happily. A glance at her warmly flushed face told Saffron that she liked being in the center of all the conflict in Maika'i. Perhaps Saffron could use this to her own advantage.

"So, you guys handled the inheritance case for that woman whose body was found the other day, didn't you?"

Phyllis nodded sagely, "Oh, yes, that has been an open sore for decades!"

Saffron tried not to sound eager. "That long, huh?"

"Oh, yes! I remember exactly when it started. That mean old man came in on my first day of work!" Saffron tried to think of a follow-up question but found no need for one as Phyllis dove into the tale with no further prompting.

"I was a new bride, and I had just started working for Mr. Kwan. I was trying to get everything right, and that man—Leon Cole, he was the dead woman's father—would not even sign in for his appointment because I had the wrong color of pen at the desk!" Saffron shook her head. It was easy to see where Dorah had inherited her winning way with people. "He said he only wrote in black ink. Can you imagine? I had blue, I had red, I even had green, but he made me go to Mr. Kwan and get a black pen. I was so humiliated. Mr. Kwan said he treated everyone that way, and he passed him off to the junior associate as quickly as he could. I always figured that was because even Mr. Kwan couldn't stand him."

"Poor junior associate," Saffron said, shaking her head.

Phyllis leaned over the desk, the excitement of a little-known fact lighting her eyes. "You'd think so, but Mr. Cutler got on fine with the old man! After that, he was the only one the old man would work with! They just seemed to enjoy each other's bad moods, and they seemed to speak the same language."

"So he worked with Cutler a long time?" Saffron said, tapping on the glass to rouse a sleepy-looking fish into nibbling at the food in front of it. She wondered what it was. It had intricate patterning—stripes and pencil-edging around its fins.

"Years. Cutler made partner mostly on the work he did with the old man's estate. He was set to become quite the celebrity around here if the disbursement of the funds had gone off more smoothly."

"Hit some hiccups, has it?" Saffron glanced up.

"Oh, yes! With that woman's death, the final disbursement could be tied up in the courts for years, and the firm won't get paid until it's all settled. Mr. Kwan and Mr. Bellevue are livid."

A dry voice rasped through the room, and Saffron looked up to see Cutler standing in the hallway behind Phyllis. Behind him was a fierce-looking woman with steel-gray hair and a confident carriage.

"I'm livid myself, Phyllis," he said.

Phyllis blushed a deep crimson under her pasty make-up. "I'm sorry, Mr. Cutler, I didn't see you there."

He waved a dismissive hand, "Mrs. Lawrence and I have finished her divorce settlement. Please collect her signature as she leaves." He gestured the woman toward the desk, caught Saffron's eye with his own, and jerked his head toward an open door down the hall. "If you'll step this way, Miss Skye," he said, "I assume you are here to see me?"

"Y—Yes," Saffron said, following him, "I am."

Cutler's office was smaller than Saffron would have imagined, but every paperclip was in its place. The office was decorated in rich ebony and chrome. Stainless steel fish dotted the walls and the shelves behind his desk. The pencil sharpener held no shavings, the tape dispenser was full, and every file folder was sharply creased.

"Phyllis has apprised you of the situation?" He asked.

"Well—sort of," Saffron said, "She was just getting started."

"Stop acting chagrined. There's no secret. Dorah's death has caused some . . . Complications," he said. "The law firm was prepared to disburse half of the estate to each daughter, as the will stipulates, but now . . ." Saffron heard a tremor of annoyance in

Cutler's voice, "some adjustments have to be made. We have to re-do some of the paperwork."

"Well, that seems manageable." Saffron tried to sound encouraging.

"Everything is manageable with the right information and the right process," he said confidently. "Well, now you know my business. What, may I ask, is yours?"

His directness caught Saffron off guard, "I just, well, I came to see why Rachel hadn't received the money yet."

"Which you now know." He gave her a slight nod and looked down at some papers on his desk.

It took Saffron several seconds of silence to realize that he thought their conversation was over. She shifted and cleared her throat. "I suppose I have another couple of questions for you, while I'm here."

She saw him close his eyes, saw his upper lip curl in disgust before he raised a blank face to her. "Listen, I'm not a man used to idle chit-chat. My fee is $325 an hour, so people usually don't waste my time."

Saffron wondered if he would bill her for this visit. The thought made her speak faster than usual, "I'm just curious about one more thing: you have been involved with this weird situation for a long time. I'd like your insight. I think you know I'm not responsible for Dorah's death, even though you insinuated that I was. So, assuming that I'm not the one, who do you really think killed Dorah?" She asked it directly but calmly, crossing her legs as she did so in an effort to appear as if she'd stay as long as she needed to hear his answer.

"I don't think it's a difficult case," he said. "Ruling out the kidnapped wedding planner, you can almost guarantee that it was the hen-pecked husband." He peered at her, and the rims of his glasses looked sharp and dangerous glinting in the fluorescent overhead light.

Hen-pecked. That made Saffron think not of Milo, but of Bossy, her hen, and the feral rooster that kept coming to visit Bossy. He wanted her attention, had brought her mice and berries all week, even though she rapped him viciously on the head or pecked his comb whenever he got in range of her sharp beak. He did that funny dance whenever he saw her. She tried to imagine him attacking Bossy to get revenge, but it just didn't fit. He was doing all he could to impress her, to get her to notice him.

The rooster wanted Bossy's attention, not her ruin. And that, Saffron felt sure, was true of Milo, too. But how to explain that to Cutler? He would be unlikely to lend any veracity to a chicken analogy. He seemed more like a hard facts guy.

"Just because of the way she treated him?" Saffron asked.

"That's right. A person's psyche can only take so much," Cutler said. "And Milo had spent time in prison. He likely just snapped."

"I don't know," Saffron said, "he doesn't seem the type."

Cutler sighed. He looked at her, his pen-and-ink eyes piercing, "What is it you want me to say, Miss Skye?"

"I just don't think it's Milo."

"Have you developed some sort of Stockholm syndrome?" he asked. "It seems irrational."

Saffron considered that. "No, I still want him caught. He still needs to do time for the kidnapping. I just don't know if he's the one who killed Dorah. And it's upsetting to me to think about a real killer out there walking free."

Cutler swept his glasses from his face and rubbed the bridge of his nose where they had been sitting. He suddenly looked very tired. His heavy lids closed briefly, and Saffron detected a crimson rim around them. His skin had a slightly gray undertone, and four dark freckles made a little track along the left side of his nose, where the glasses had been sitting. He needed more time outside, Saffron thought.

"Alright. If I had to think about it, which I wouldn't if you would leave," he looked at her pointedly, "I would come to the same conclusions you've already reached: Milo is circumstantially likely, but not practically. The sister is both capable and motivated. The nephew doubly so. Then you have to just assume a certain probability that it wasn't any of those people at all, that it was the neighbor who the victim berated daily or one of the many people in town." He sighed. "I don't know any more than you do, but I'm flattered that you think I might."

Saffron wasn't being put off so easily. "What do you mean the sister is capable? I can see that Rachel has the strongest motivation, but I wouldn't think she would have the temperament, or the strength, to hit Dorah that hard."

This seemed to interest Cutler. "So it was blunt-force trauma that killed her?"

Saffron knew that should probably be confidential, but Cutler was used to dealing with attorney/client privilege. He should be discreet.

"It looks that way."

His lids fluttered closed briefly as if he were momentarily overcome by emotion. Saffron was surprised: he hadn't seemed like the type to be bothered by the grisly facts of a case. She tried to think of something comforting to say, but before she could think of anything, he straightened his shoulders, put his glasses back on, and cleared his throat. "So, if physical strength is a key feature of your suspect, you're likely looking at the kid."

"Dylan?"

"Right. He's strong enough to do it. And he certainly has that resentful vibe that many criminals display."

Saffron didn't tell him that she knew it wasn't Dylan, that he'd been with Eke and his friends all night the night Dorah died. But she also couldn't argue that Dylan had a resentful vibe. She used the opening to fish for a little more information. "But his father was killed. I can see why that would leave behind some resentment."

"Oh, I'm not making a judgment," Cutler said, "I'm just saying."

"What do you know about the father's death?" Saffron asked.

Cutler shrugged, "From my discussions with the Harrisons over the last several years working on this case, I know that many years ago, when Rachel and her husband and a very young Dylan were here on the island vacationing, there was an argument between the father, Leon, and the two sisters. It was about the will. He had written it out," here Cutler tapped a worn file on his desk. Reading upside down, Saffron saw that it was marked "LEON COLE WILL." Cutler went on, "and the sisters were upset by his stipulations. But they turned on each other. Apparently, they fought, and the husbands broke it up. Everyone went to bed, but the next morning Rachel's husband was found washed up on the beach. He'd been beaten to death."

Saffron closed her eyes against the words and the image they brought with them. She couldn't help but see Dorah's body on the sand.

"Milo confessed to fighting with him about the will and pushing him off the rocky point by Uwē beach." Cutler finished. "Because of the emotional circumstances, they reduced the second-degree murder charge to voluntary manslaughter. He received a sentence of 20 years, but shaved off a few for good behavior and service hours rendered while in prison."

Saffron opened her eyes. The faded file seemed to call to her, its ragged edges beckoning. "Can I see the will?" she asked.

At this, Cutler stiffened. He laid a protective hand over the folder. "No, no," he shook his head vigorously, "attorney/client privilege would certainly preclude that." He straightened his glasses. "Everything I've told you so far is public knowledge, easily retrieved from the archives of the local newspaper or public court documents, but I draw the line at divulging the details of my client's file."

Saffron couldn't blame him. In fact, amid all the talk of deception and manslaughter, it was strangely comforting to encounter a firm ethical position. "I understand," she said. "Sometimes I have to keep things quiet, too."

"Like the wedding?" Cutler asked. It made sense he'd bring it up. After all, he'd been invited to the wedding as a witness, but only under a promise of secrecy.

"Yes. Like the wedding." Saffron nodded. "Sometimes a client requires discretion."

Cutler's face was slightly pink around the nose and cheeks. Saffron recognized that as annoyance. He was ready for her to leave.

"Well," she said, sensing she wouldn't get much more out of him, "Thank you for seeing me. If you think of anything else that might be relevant, don't hesitate to contact me."

"I will," Cutler nodded curtly.

Saffron's phone buzzed. Nik was coming to take her snorkeling again this afternoon. She remembered the pretty fish she'd seen in the waiting room. She wanted to look for some of them in the wild. "Before I go, I wanted to ask you a question about your fish tank."

Cutler's eyes narrowed, and his nostrils flared. "It's not a fish tank," he said indignantly. "That's a reef tank."

Saffron arched her eyebrows and shot him an incredulous look. "Those are different things?" She asked.

Cutler stood and leaned on his fists over the desk. "Of course they are."

She waited for an explanation, but none came. His impatience with her ignorance was palpable.

"And they're different . . . How?"

"In so many ways. But I suppose the easiest thing is simply to tell you that there are three types of saltwater aquaria." Saffron assumed that the word aquaria was the proper plural form of aquarium, but it sounded unnecessarily pompous anyway. She would have just said aquariums. Cutler was going on, "There are Fish-Only Tanks, as you assume mine is, but the only organisms in those tanks are the fish themselves. Gravel, decor, everything else, is artificial. Then you have FOWLR tanks, which stands for Fish Only With Live Rocks, where hobbyists add chunks of live rock—rock inhabited by bacteria and microorganisms that both give the fish somewhere to hide and also give them opportunities to feed. Live rock keeps the marine environment more natural and diverse. But the most difficult aquarium to set up and to keep is the Reef Tank, which describes my tank in the waiting room. These tanks are full of not only fish and live rocks, but coral and corallivores, as well as anemones, starfish, and other organisms. They are, by far, the most challenging aquaria to do well, and mine is a particularly stunning example. It nearly perfectly mimics the wild reefs around the island."

"Wow. It does look like the reefs I saw snorkeling. Is that how you make it so realistic?"

Cutler scoffed. "I don't snorkel."

This surprised Saffron. He obviously had a passion for reefs. "Why not?"

"I am not a swimmer. I know far too much about the ocean to want to go into it." He paused. "Ever."

Saffron wasn't sure how to respond to such adamance. She obviously wouldn't get far trying to convince him that snorkeling was magical. She went back to the aquarium. "I had no idea there were such an array of tanks." Saffron said apologetically. "I was really just wondering about one of the fish—the yellow one."

His mouth bunched to one side in annoyance. "There are six specimens that are some degree of yellow," he said, pushing his glasses up on his nose, "and they are varying shades of the color."

Really? He was going to try to play the color card with Saffron? Because of her superb sense of color, she not only knew 'varying shades,' but she had words for the shades. She was more than a little tired of his air of superiority.

"I guess the one I'm wondering about is not the sunflower one, or the canary one, and not the one with the mustard stripes. It's not the fulvous, dull-yellow one or the jessamy one," she saw, with some satisfaction, that she had lost him, and she liked the baffled expression on his face. "Jessamy," she explained, "is a pale, whitish yellow—the color of the center of a jasmine flower. No, the one I'm interested in is the one with the citreous stripe along the back, the watchet stripes, the onyx blotch on its back, and the gamboge accents on its jaw and fins."

"Watchet?" He managed.

"Yes. The stripes are the precise color of the cliffs off the coast of Somerset, England, near the town of Watchet. Their pale blueish greenish gray comes from a kind of alabaster." It was one of her favorite words, as it mixed three shades into one.

"G-gamboge?" Cutler was shaken. He was obviously unused to not knowing everything.

"It's a deep, orangy-yellow," she said, again using the imprecise color language everyone else seemed more comfortable with.

"Oh, oh, yes," he said, "gamboge. Well, what you're describing seems to be the saddleback butterflyfish."

Saffron's ears perked up. "Butterflyfish? The owner of the pet store said you couldn't keep butterflyfish. He said they were too hard to feed."

Cutler's eyelids fluttered closed just in time to cover an eye-roll. "He should have said *most people* can't keep them. Most people are not dedicated aquarists. Most people don't provide them with the specific coral polyps they need. I, on the other hand, cultivate several species of coral specifically for feeding my butterflies." This was a topic he enjoyed. Saffron could see it in the tightening of his features, the way he leaned even more forward on his fists over the desk. "Even many advanced aquarists will tell you that you can't keep a butterflyfish in a reef tank. But those aquarists rarely take the time to provide butterflies with the precise species of coral they want to feed on. Instead, they try to convince the fish to eat prepared foods that provide convenience. But extraordinary things are rarely convenient."

"Wow," Saffron said. "I've learned a lot about keeping fish in one afternoon."

Cutler eased back on his heels and took a hand from the desk to straighten his glasses, then his tie. "The proper keeping of fish," he said curtly, "is a lifelong pursuit."

CHAPTER 10

Sitting in the car outside the law office, Saffron's train of thought was interrupted by another buzz from her phone. She picked it up lazily, expecting a message from Nik.

But the message was from someone else. Saffron's heart swam when she saw Keahi's face on her screen.

The message was brief. "Miss you. Surgery tomorrow. Wish me luck."

And before she knew it, she was dialing. She had been avoiding his calls and his messages. At first, she'd been mad at him. But now, she was mad at herself. What did she want? She knew she was excited to go snorkeling with Nik, and she knew that she still longed for Keahi's company. Both seemed equally valid emotions. And she was going to have to tell Keahi eventually that she'd kissed Nik. She didn't know how to do that given the stand she'd made about him spending time with Evelyn.

There was a smile in Keahi's voice when he answered the phone. "Hey. I was beginning to worry that a tsunami had swallowed the island and carried your phone out to sea."

She smiled, too, at the sound of him. "No, just been . . . Busy."

His voice was tighter when he asked, "More detective work?"

"Oh, just asking a few questions here and there."

His voice was so strong, so caring, when he said, "Saffron, be careful. I know how close I came to losing you on the last case you got mixed up in."

He was right. Her number had nearly come up. "This one's different," she assured him, "just a little local mishap. I'm just asking some questions for Bradley."

"Bradley can ask his own questions," Keahi said stubbornly. Then, when she remained quiet, he said, "I just want you to be safe."

"I know," she said. "I will be. I'm not hunting down anyone. Just talking to reasonable people in well-lit locations."

He grunted noncommittally.

She made her voice bright, "I'm glad you called. I'm sorry about the other day."

He was quiet. "I'm sorry about Evie," he said, and there was genuine turmoil in his voice. "I'm sorry I can't promise never to see her."

It wasn't what she wanted to hear, but Saffron understood better now why he couldn't. She knew that she, herself, couldn't promise to never see Nik again, and though Keahi didn't know about it, she still found herself saying, "I'm sorry too."

There was a long silence. Saffron broke it. "You're going to do great on this surgery. You are a talented surgeon."

Keahi didn't argue, but he didn't affirm what she'd said, either. "I hope so," he said somberly. "I really do."

There was no more to be said. She couldn't tell him about Nik right now, before such an important event. He needed to be thinking clearly, couldn't afford any distractions. Saffron refused to be one.

With as much conviction as she could summon, Saffron said, "Everything's going to be just fine."

• • • •

SAFFRON STAYED ON HER own side of the station wagon as Nik drove them out to snorkel. He didn't seem to mind, just draped an easy arm across the back of the seat between them and brushed her shoulder with his fingertips occasionally as they talked.

"So," he said, his voice humming with excitement, "I did some searching, and I found a better place to snorkel. It's harder to get to, so not so many tourists find it."

As soon as they hit the water, Saffron was immediately absorbed in the reef world once more. Underwater, the distracting sounds of the surface were eliminated. All she heard was the whoosh of the waves hitting the reef beyond and her own breathing, the two sounds in sync.

It was peaceful, a silent world of diverse hues and shapes still unlike anything that land had ever shown her. A school of ebony-striped fish grazed along ridges of opaque coral and sea cucumbers the color of a stormy sunset wound their way through a school of tangerine fish wearing fuchsia lipstick.

After seeing Cutler's fish tank—*reef tank*, Saffron corrected herself—she had a better idea of what she was seeing down here. It was a complex ecosystem: microscopic bacteria and other organisms lived in the sand and the rocks, feeding on waste and on the tiny plants and algae that grew on them. Coral was constructed on top of the rocks, providing more food and places for other organisms to live and hide. Fish fed among and on this coral. Spiky urchins nestled among its crevices, and sea stars embraced its outcroppings. Though she didn't see another, she knew that there were octopus here, too, and as she watched the jewel-like fish swaying and nibbling, she wondered how close they were to being a meal themselves.

It was, as she had first thought, a complete city in miniature, with its stern police-looking fish, its bright performers, and even its garbage collectors. Between the jutting coral, golden sand glowed in the filtered afternoon light.

Saffron's shadow kept pace with her, gliding along the bottom of the ocean floor, causing fish to dart away. Ahead of it now, a field of waving color caught her attention. Here, the sea floor fell away and rose again in a stark wall. Brilliant aqua sea sponges were scattered about the wall, interspersed with the branching strawberry arms of an organism Saffron guessed was either a coral or an anemone. A bouquet of feathery peach animals suddenly disappeared, retreating into stony tubes as Saffron's shadow passed over them. Something that looked like marmalade-colored cauliflower sat gently swaying with the tide. And across the whole wall, in brilliant shades of lime, sky, and watermelon, were creatures Saffron could only guess had come from another planet.

They clustered in groups, each standing on a thick stalk. Their tops were disks surrounded with transparent, fleshy nubs, like short tentacles. They looked like alien eyes: brilliant, fluorescent, with rings of waving lashes around their edges.

The clumps varied in color, making a rainbow of the animals all over the rock wall.

The rock wall fell away to a depth of fifteen feet or so, and Saffron treaded water in the swell and ebb of the waves, trying to take it all in. As she drifted along the wall, looking at the alien eyes and the coral beside them, she noticed some divers at the bottom of the wall. They had full scuba gear on, and, most interestingly, a bucket with holes drilled all around it, just like the one she'd seen in Milo's garage.

They also had nets. Saffron glanced around for Nik, but he'd left her to explore and had drifted away to peer at another outcropping thirty feet away so Saffron couldn't ask him the questions buzzing in her mind.

Instead, Saffron drifted and watched the divers, trying to determine what it was they were doing. They looked to be a man and a woman. The woman's silver ponytail waved in the tide behind her like a flag. The strap of his mask sat tightly around cropped black hair, and he turned a chiseled face to the woman and nodded.

She had a mesh bag fixed to her hip, and she extracted from it what looked like a used water bottle and a net. Her partner took the bottle and leaned close to the reef, pointing the end of it at an isolated little group of the alien eyes. The woman stood holding the net up near his shoulder.

Saffron watched as the man squeezed the water bottle, causing it to spew a cloudy liquid onto the strange organisms. It rose in a plume around them, and an apricot clownfish darted out of the coral and swam directly into the cloud. Saffron had to remind herself to keep breathing as the palm-sized clownfish froze in the water, his oscillating fins stilling and his forward momentum diminishing. He was stunned, still, frozen in the water. The woman took her net and scooped him up, peeling back what seemed to be a fine mesh net stretched over the top of the bucket with the holes and slipping him inside before replacing the net over the top.

The alien eyes that the man had enveloped in the cloud were doing something amazing. They were pulling their stubby lashes over their centers and closing up like fists at the end of their thick bases. The man was peering at them, snapping photos with an underwater camera, and as Saffron watched, the woman with the silver plume of hair collected at least three more stunned fish.

She turned and stroked toward Nik, who was paddling lazily along a very shallow area of the reef. Tapping him, Saffron gestured toward the beach, and he followed her.

Sitting on the warm sand, Saffron rubbed her scalp where the straps of the snorkel mask had been and told him what she had seen. Nik nodded and patted her arm. "They're probably just collectors." He said.

Saffron didn't think that was quite the right tone. Nik, as always, was unconcerned. "But they froze those fish. Did they kill them?"

He waved a hand. "Oh, no. They wouldn't kill them. They're probably going to put them in their own aquarium or sell them. It's perfectly legal, as long as they have the right permits. Don't worry."

"It looked awful," she said.

"Yeah, but it probably doesn't hurt the fish. Maybe stresses them out a little. But most collectors are pretty gentle with them."

"What about the alien eyes?"

Nik blinked. "Come again?"

"You know, those weird animals with the one fat leg and the circles on top?"

"You mean coral?"

"No, I don't," Saffron said, though she suddenly doubted what she knew, "I don't think I do, anyway. Aren't coral the hard, branchy ones?"

"There are lots of kinds of coral. But I think you're describing the pal—," Nick hesitated, "paly—, well, I'm not really sure what they're called, but somebody pointed them out to me once and said that they are a kind of soft coral. They're called polyps or something."

"Well, whatever they sprayed got on that thing, too. And it started closing up, so I don't think it liked that very much."

"Probably not," Nik granted. "But maybe they were trying to get a fish that was back behind the coral?"

"Maybe. But you've seen this before?"

"People collecting fish? Oh, yeah. Tons of times. It's a huge hobby around here, and a huge business."

Saffron tried to calm the alarms in her head. "Okay then. I guess if you think it's okay."

"I was going to suggest a break anyway," Nik said, laying a hand on her upper arm, "I brought a picnic."

His touch was warm. Saffron felt every grain of sand between his skin and hers. She could only nod. Walking beside him to the station wagon, Saffron felt a cocktail of emotions. The excitement of the day mingled with the new rush of attraction she felt for Nik, making the sun's glare seem brighter and the sound of the waves more intense. At the same time, she still ached for Keahi, and an umbrella of guilt over not having told him made her stomach twist. She still felt uneasy about Dorah's death, and the divers with their water bottle, and she felt the familiar edginess of being overly hungry.

At least that feeling promised to be short-lived. Nik had brought a feast.

They spread a blanket on the sand and began extracting things from Nik's cooler. Pillowy steamed pork buns called manapua were the first thing he removed, followed by little cups of sliced pineapple. He pulled out a container of mac salad, the thick, salty/sweet complement to every island plate lunch, and a big jug of POG—passion fruit, orange, and guava fruit punch. Last, he extracted a little snap-tight container with white squares in it.

Saffron had seen these at luaus and family parties with Mano and Keahi, but she wasn't sure what they were.

The manapua stole her attention, though, and she started her lunch with a bite of the sweet, chewy bun. Inside, it was filled with bright red barbecued pork. It was one of her absolute favorite foods here in Hawaii.

Nik was plowing through his third, and he smiled at her. "You know, one thing I love about you is that you enjoy good food," he said around a bite.

She could say the same thing about him. Spending his days surfing, Nik seemed to always have a hearty appetite.

Saffron shrugged. "I love Hawaiian food. And it's fun eating with you. I never feel like I'm eating too much."

"Lotta girls," he said, "just pick at their food. They think it's attractive for them not to eat. I find it the opposite," he shook his head, "if someone doesn't like food, they just don't have the kind of passion for life I'm looking for."

Saffron took another bite of her roll. "I've got a passion for life *and* for manapua," she said.

He scooted closer. "You have passion for a lot of things." Saffron wondered if he would kiss her again. This set off a tumbling turmoil inside her about whether she should let that happen.

But he was just reaching for the POG to fill her a cup. He kept talking. "You have passion for your parties. How's that anniversary party coming along?"

"Everything's ready, I think," She said. "Invitations are out, the RSVPs are rolling in, catering's on track, decorations are ready. I think it's going to go well, as long as we can fit everyone in the Piscine Lodge."

"Piscine. Funny word. What does it mean again?"

"It's an adjective form of fish. Fishy, I guess you could say."

"Do they even still use that place?"

"Not much. A party or a wake now and then."

"Lots of people coming then?"

"Yes, frankly, more than we thought would come. They invited everyone in their family, all their old friends, even some neighbors from years ago, but they didn't think too many people would actually make it. They were wrong."

"Should be fun."

"Yes. We've had to shrink the dance floor because we need part of it for more tables. But they'll get to see lots of the people who are important to them, so that's what matters."

Nik was gazing at Saffron. She took a bite of creamy mac salad as he spoke, "I admire your ability to pull all those details together. I can barely remember to put gas in the wagon."

"I like it. Planning events is like partying on somebody else's dime."

"And you have a lot of passion for your chickens. It surprises me how you know each of them and how you talk about them like people."

Saffron thought about that as she chewed her last bite of manapua. "I do know them. They're more like friends now. Some of them I like more than others."

Nik laughed. It was a clear, honest sound. "Really?"

"Sure. Some of them are jerks." Saffron took a sip of the sweet, bright punch, "like Bossy. She's always picking on everyone, telling them what to do and pulling their feathers. I have a hard time liking her. She's just grouchy."

"Sounds like Dorah," Nik said. Saffron stared. She loved that he'd drawn that connection, too. He saw her looking at him, "I probably shouldn't say that. Sorry. It's not nice to speak ill of the dead and all."

"Right," Saffron didn't follow up, but she liked that they'd both noticed the similarity. She and Nik had a lot in common.

"Ready for dessert?" he asked, peeling the lid off the box with the white squares.

"What are they?"

"Haupia." He grinned as he lifted a thick, white square from the box. "Coconut pudding."

It didn't look like pudding. It looked like gelatin. But Saffron took one of the squares and nibbled at it.

"Mmmmm," she couldn't help but close her eyes. This was divine. Thick and creamy and sweet, it was like a solid custard. It was smooth and cool.

"You like it?" Nik was polishing off a second square himself.

"*Love* it," Saffron said. "I think I have a new passion."

Nik laughed.

She took another square just as she noticed the divers from the reef exiting onto the beach not far from them. On their hips were attached clear plastic containers—like square bags—containing half a dozen bright fish. Water streamed from the bucket with the holes drilled in it as they hauled it up onto the beach. Saffron recognized the fish she'd seen them catch swimming in one of their bags. They must have transferred it from the bucket into the bag while still underwater.

The woman with the silver ponytail was hauling other gear, and she paced across the sand to a white pickup truck in the parking area and hefted the bucket and her tanks into it.

On the side of the truck was an emblem. Three squares, stacked diagonally, with extending lines that made them into fish and dots for eyes. Her companion tossed his tanks in the pick-up bed, and together they climbed in and drove away. Saffron thought back to the scene under the water: the bottle, the fish stilling and being caught. Something about it bothered her despite Nik's reassurances.

A light touch on her arm drew her attention away from the truck and back to Nik. Saffron saw from his raised eyebrows that he had just asked a question.

"I'm sorry?"

"I just asked if you've got any other plans tonight?"

The triple-fish emblem slipped from Saffron's mind. In its place was a warm voice reaching across a continent, across an ocean. Keahi's smile. Keahi's embrace. She blinked them away and stuttered, "Chores. I've got lots of chores tonight. It's the egg line tomorrow, and I have to get ready. And then, tomorrow afternoon, I have to set up for the Letoa anniversary party at the Piscine Lodge. It's the day after tomorrow, you know."

A flicker of disappointment crossed Nik's features. "Darn. Well, until I can go underwater with you again, then," he held up his plastic cup of POG, "I'll be holding my breath."

CHAPTER 11

S affron was glad she was tall. The key to the Piscine Lodge was hidden behind a carved stone lionfish three-quarters of the way up on the side of the big wooden doors. The doors themselves were covered with carved sea bass, angelfish, tangs, and sturgeons. She barely caught it with her fingers and pulled it from its perch.

The key, too, was decorated like a fish—Hawaii's state fish, the humuhumunukunukuapua'a. The oblong shape made the key easy to grip in Saffron's rain-slicked fingers. She jammed it into the lock, pushed the heavy door open, and picked up her big box of decorations just as the clouds opened and began to pour down.

She ducked inside. The door made a ringing boom through the big open hall. Saffron set the box down in the dusty half-light and fumbled for the light switch.

When she found it, though, it didn't do any good. She snapped it up and down a few times, but no lights came on. Saffron didn't know whether she wanted to cry or curse. She shuffled through the dark hall, feeling the worn hardwood under her shoes until she thudded into one of the eight-foot round tables that she'd come here to decorate. She lowered the heavy box onto it and set off for the far wall.

Saffron navigated through the room by keeping her eyes on the subtle bluing of the light near what she knew would be the windows. There were long, heavy curtains that covered the floor-to-ceiling windows at the back of the room, and only the barest amount of light edged around them. Most people would only be able to see some evidence of their existence if the morning sun was shining directly onto the windows from outside, but Saffron could detect the subtle sapphire hues even on this stormy afternoon.

She found the curtain cords and pulled the draperies back from the windows one by one. Outside, the ocean was a plate of gray-green glass. She felt cozy in the dusty old lodge. Though the light was pale and steely, it still brought clarity to the objects in the big room.

Saffron had to smile at the many and varied fish decorating the place. A tuna clock graced the far wall. Lionfish, their impressive fanlike fins spread around them, floated across the carved back of each chair and around each of the pictures arranged in a grid on one wall. Even the hardwood floor was patterned with the signature fins and scales of the creatures. From what Saffron understood, the Honorable Piscine Order was a local chapter of a once trendy social club focused on bettering its members and serving the community. It was a nice, if an anti-quated, idea, Saffron thought.

Saffron looked around the room and tried to picture the place as it would have been the day of the Letoa's wedding. Mr. Letoa's father had been a Piscine, and had, according to the Letoas, arranged the ceremony at the lodge as a kind of compro-mise between the bride and groom's desire to be married out in nature and their mothers' wish for them to wed in a church. The quirky, yet solemn lodge seemed just the right compromise.

It looked a little drab now, though. Its chocolate and cin-namon hues swallowed the wan window light. Saffron's hippie theme would solve that. Vintage lace, feathers, and daisy chains would go a long way toward brightening the place up.

It was nice working in the quiet of the lodge while the storm raged outside. The lights came on just when the outside light was disappearing, and Saffron liked the warm yellow glow of the bulbs on the ivory and cream lace tablecloths. She had made sev-eral trips to her car, and all the dreamcatchers, crystals, and bub-ble-gum colored peonies had joined the first wave of decor to transform the stuffy lodge into a hip bohemian oasis. She dug out her work gloves to arrange some garden roses in the center-pieces.

Saffron was arranging the last centerpiece when she heard the heavy door open and boom closed. Surprised, she turned to see Bradley stomping and shaking the drops of rain from his hat and jacket. His expression was somber.

"Hey, Gumshoe. Any news on the Harrison case?"

She shook her head, "nothing yet." It was strange for him to come find her. "What's going on?"

"Well," Bradley sidestepped her question. "We've had some," he chose his words carefully, "*developments*, and I wanted to make sure you were safe—especially after that visit from Milo the other night."

Saffron laid a peach rose down on the tablecloth and came toward him. She could see he was deeply troubled. "Has something happened?"

"Well, yes." He shifted uncomfortably. "And I just feel so bad about it, because I haven't been able to crack this case. Even after the autopsy report came back—"

Saffron grabbed his arm, "the autopsy came back? What did they find?"

"Same as we thought—poisoned."

Saffron closed her eyes briefly. "The cyanide?"

"It's consistent with cyanide. Apparently, cyanide can be hard to detect because signs of it more or less disappear after 2 days. They made a mistake when the body arrived, classified her as a drowning, so when they got around to the autopsy, they couldn't find evidence of cyanide exactly. But everything is consistent with it, and we have the bottle with Milo's fingerprints on it."

"And mine," Saffron said slowly.

"And yours. But yours aren't on the lid, so it's unlikely you opened the bottle."

Though Saffron knew she was innocent, it was still a relief to hear.

"So Milo, huh?" She said. On some level, she had suspected it.

"Yeah," Bradley ran a hand over his face, pushing back his wide-brimmed hat as he did so. "And now, he's tried again."

The words sucked the air out of the room. "What? He tried to kill someone? Who?"

Bradley was shaking his head as he said, "Rachel."

The news dimmed even the color of the flowers. The sunny gold ranunculus and the pearly dahlias hanging from the ceiling beams seemed suddenly less bright to Saffron. "Rachel? Is she okay?"

"Pretty shaken, but she wasn't hurt."

Saffron grabbed her coat and the key to the Piscine Lodge. "I'll follow you. Take me to Rachel."

• • • •

SAFFRON SAT ACROSS from the slim woman and tried to ask her questions with some restraint. The parlor of the Sweet Pineapple Bed and Breakfast was artificially cheery in the light of every lamp, light, and candle that Bunny Monroe, the owner, could find. It was as if she were trying to protect Rachel by the sheer wattage in the room. She had laid out a spread of sliced fruit and baked goods for the guests, but nobody besides Dylan was eating.

"What happened?"

"The brakes in my rental car went out, just as I was leaving here."

Saffron nodded. The bed and breakfast sat on a steep hill that ended in a lookout over the sea. It would be a bad place to lose your brakes.

"What did you do?"

Rachel's eyes suddenly cleared. "I downshifted, of course."

"Downshifted?"

"Yeah. My first husband, he always said that movies where people lose their brakes are ridiculous because you could just shift to a lower gear to slow down the car. As soon as I realized I had no brakes, his voice came perfectly back to me, and I threw the car out of drive to second, then first gear. Then I was going slowly enough to steer off into a bush."

Saffron let out the breath she didn't realize she'd been holding. "That was smart."

"It would have been smarter if I'd never come here in the first place." Rachel said. She was wringing her hands, and Saffron noticed the skin on them was beginning to chafe. It brought her back to the night she was kidnapped—Dorah's raw, red hands, the color of crab claws. The sisters were more alike than Saffron had previously thought.

She glanced at Bradley. "Any chance it was a freak accident?"

He shook his head. "Brake line was pretty obviously cut. Messy job. Obviously didn't care if there was evidence, probably because he figured the car would go off into the ocean."

"Fingerprints?" Saffron asked.

"None. Old Milo must have gotten wise and worn some gloves this time."

"Why would he want to kill Rachel?" Saffron asked. "He doesn't have anything to gain, now. At least, not money."

"Unless he thought I'd gotten the money and was hoping to steal it after he'd killed me," Rachel said. "That money isn't a gift. It's a curse."

Saffron patted the shaken woman's shoulder. "He couldn't get to it even if you had it. It would be in your bank, right?" Rachel nodded. "I don't think he was after the money." Saffron listened to the rain.

"Wait," Bradley said, "there is something. It could be revenge for all those years in prison," Bradley shrugged. "Rachel testified at the trial."

Rachel sunk her head into her hands.

Saffron offered a few words of comfort to the shaken woman, then stepped out into the rainy night with Bradley. The air on the lanai was a warm mist that tasted like fruit and flowers. Saffron breathed it in.

"We've got to find him," Bradley said, "before he tries again."

"Is she going to be safe?"

"I've got some back up coming in from Laie to be with her," Bradley said. "I'd like her to head on home, just to keep her safe, but she won't leave until they've had Dorah's funeral. With the hold-up on the autopsy, that will take a few more days.

There was something exquisitely sad about Rachel wanting to be at her sister's funeral, especially in light of the fact that days ago she was trying to keep Dorah from even knowing about her wedding. The inheritance feud seemed so small now, so petty. Saffron thought again about the scrub brush, about Dorah's matted hair. She couldn't bear to think of a similar fate for Rachel.

"Where do you think Milo could be hiding?" She asked, as much to push the image from her mind as anything.

"I honestly don't know. I would have thought he'd have gotten off the island by now, but the FBI is helping us keep an eye on the airports and the docks. I don't think he's left." Bradley went quiet. Saffron wondered if he had once been a smoker, the way he blew out a long breath, then drew in the sweet air and held it a moment before he continued speaking, "Hawaii is wilder than most people realize. You could hide out in these mauna—these mountains," he translated for her, even though Saffron was getting used to many of the more common Hawaiian words. "I guess he could be anywhere."

"Officer," a voice from behind them interrupted. It was Dylan, looking more like a child and less like an angry teen than Saffron had ever seen him look. "Can you come back in? My mom says she feels safer when you're here."

Bradley nodded, though Saffron could see that his mind was still searching for mountain hideouts. "Sure, sure," he said. "You be okay heading home?"

"Oh, of course," Saffron did need to get home. The party was tomorrow, and it would be a long day.

Saffron should have turned right when she got to Holoholo street, the main street in Maika'i, but she didn't. She turned left. Before she knew it, she was standing in the rain in front of the little house on Uwē Beach.

What am I doing here? She slipped on her work gloves from the party box. Bradley wouldn't appreciate her leaving fingerprints all over the active investigation. She sat for a moment in the car, staring at the little house.

The lights in the aquariums inside were on, and they sent a blueish glow emanating from the windows. Saffron thought through the last time she'd been here: the kidnapping, the hours in the garage, the unexpected release. It had been a weird night. As she left the safety of the car and ducked through the rain, she tried to calm her hammering heart.

The front door was unlocked, and she slipped inside. The living room was just as she remembered it: a long, narrow room the width of the garage, with the entrancing tank along one wall. The desk where Milo had sat was there, opposite the couch where

Dorah had sat. The room was still misty, the whoosh of the water filter a dull roar behind the wall.

Saffron walked to the aquarium and peered at it. Floor-to-ceiling, it contained multiple sizes and species of fish. Saffron watched a big gray one labor its way across the center of the tank outpaced by a school of blue-striped fish. She saw the striped tail of an eel and bent down to get a better view. She couldn't see much more of the fish itself, but she could see the structure it was hiding in. The lawyer had taught her something. Examining the eel's cave, she could tell that it was man-made. In fact, the few items resting on the gravel at the bottom were all obviously manufactured. This, then, was probably a fish-only tank. Everything inside was spotless and in place. It was spectacular, and Saffron used up several minutes just watching plate-sized parrotfish and pairs of delicate angelfish approach the glass to check her out.

She shuffled through the house, trying to see anything significant. Her heart was still pounding. Her mouth felt dry, and her throat was raw. She coughed a couple of times. Being here again was more unnerving than she had expected. There were two bedrooms, a dingy kitchen, and a single bath, each filled with aquariums. Most of them were fish only, each a different species, in varying sizes and all the colors of the rainbow. In spite of herself, Saffron was enjoying it. Color delighted her, filled her soul. It was one reason she had stayed in the islands—the shades of green alone could keep her discovering new tones for a lifetime. Each tank was labeled on the front with its species written in marker in the upper left corner.

The tanks were immaculate, and the word could be used for the rest of the place, too. Nets, tubes, and bags were lined up by size on any available surface and containers of fish food sat on individual shelves, floors, and counters, labeled and arranged in groups. The species of fish was markered on each tank, in the upper right corner.

Saffron couldn't help feeling a little bit as if the house itself was a tank. Just as each artificial rock and coral had a place, so did everything in the house. Adding to the feeling of being in an aquarium, the windows ran with humidity, and the floor was gritty with sand.

The fish mostly ignored her, swimming in schools or singly through their immaculate tanks. But she studied them, crouching in front of floor level tanks, sitting on a kitchen chair, climbing a stepladder to peer into an aquarium next to the ceiling. In the second bedroom, she found over thirty tanks on specially-built shelving, each glowing with its own color of light. Saffron glanced at the fish, but studied the bulbs. Different ones had different degrees of opacity and mixtures of color. It made the fish under them seem even more varied. Saffron switched off a couple of the bulbs and looked in at the fish. Without the light, they appeared more or less drab. Their brilliant cobalt and mustard hues were barely distinguishable.

It was like people, Saffron thought, in the right light, they were dazzling. Without it, you never could see their real colors.

The whole house was a study in color. The paint on the walls had faded where the humidity had gathered, the curtains had frayed and worn, making them a variety of hues, and the floorboards shifted in color in the center of the room, where, Saffron assumed, shelves must have been moved to accommodate more tanks.

Saffron wondered briefly what would happen to these animals if Milo didn't come back. Were they hungry now? Bradley had said they seemed to be getting fed, so Milo must have made arrangements. But for the long term, who would look after them?

A sound made Saffron freeze. It had been quick, sharp, and muffled. Something falling? A door closing? Saffron's heart thudded. She stood very still, trying to figure out where it had come from and what it could have been.

The room was full of sounds—the filtration systems, the buzzing of the lights, the shush of her feet on the sandy floor. She shifted, suddenly very aware of the grit under her shoes—she couldn't move without making some noise.

But the sound was not repeated. The longer she listened, the more rhythmic the soundscape became. Everything in it belonged: the gurgling of the water, the soft shushing of the filtration equipment, even the ocean and the rain outside. The fish glided soundlessly in their tanks. It was strange to be surrounded by so much life and still feel so alone. Saffron never felt alone in her egg house—the chickens cackled to her, vied for her attention, made demands and alerted her to any discovery. They were excellent company. But the fish were wholly contained in their tanks, living their own lives, totally separate from each other and from anyone outside their glass walls. They were isolated.

Saffron recognized the similarities. Milo and Dorah were reclusive, too, out here in their lonely house. They had isolated themselves in their own tank, in a way, and glided through their lives without connections. Saffron felt, not for the first time, a little sorry for the couple.

When she walked again, she was particularly attuned to the sounds of the house, and of the empty, lonesome feel of it. The hallway seemed to have more grit on the floor, and at the end of it, near the door to Milo and Dorah's bedroom, she saw what it was: salt. A big bucket of "Speedy Sea Aquarium Salt" sat beside a scoop trailing a fine white powder. The bucket said, "The perfect mix of salts and minerals for any size aquarium." Saffron hadn't considered that the tropical fish would need particular conditions in their tanks. You would have to mix the right kind of salt into the water in just the right proportions to keep a healthy environment for them. Fish-keeping seemed, to her, like an exhausting hobby.

She checked her watch. Almost nine thirty. She really needed to get home. She would have gone straight down the hall to the front door if something in the master bedroom hadn't caught her eye.

It was a single, enormous fish in an equally large aquarium. Gliding through the water was the unmistakable multi-fanned shape of a lionfish.

But this was no ordinary lionfish. Saffron thought back to the first time she'd gone snorkeling with Nik. That fish had been about the size of her hand. This one was much, much bigger.

CHAPTER 12

S affron sat on the bed watching the slow, deliberate movements of the enormous lionfish. It was nearly two feet long. Each of its spines was easily the length of Saffron's forearm. Its cinnamon bands were two fingers wide, and the fanlike fins spread wider than two palms.

In the corner of the tank was scrawled, "Lion Fish. DO NOT SELL." The fish moved with purpose, unlike the smaller, flightier fish Saffron had seen, every ripple of its fins seemed purposeful. It held itself in the center of the tank, and it stared directly out at Saffron in a particularly unnerving way.

She suddenly wanted to leave. Standing, Saffron glanced at the massive oak desk the aquarium was sitting on. Here was something out of the ordinary.

Where everything else in the house was neat and organized, the desk was a catastrophe. There was a deeper organization, Saffron could tell, but the top layer was chaos. A box of fish food was scattered across strewn papers, a drawer was open, a cup was knocked over, an uncapped pen lay askew. Drops of what Saffron assumed was blood-flecked spittle had dried across the papers, probably from Dorah's last struggling breaths. Cyanide, Bradley had explained when Saffron first told him about the bottle she had found, was a terrible way to die.

Even the desk chair lay on its side. Saffron righted it and sat in it, closer to the glaring lionfish than she was comfortable with but also closer to the curious state of the desk.

What could have left it this way? The first thing that came to Saffron's mind was a struggle. If Milo and Dorah had fought, then this could be the evidence of that. Saffron looked for something heavy, something Milo might have struck her with. But what she saw was mostly papers. Maybe some of them would indicate where Milo was hiding. Did they own another house somewhere? Was there an itinerary for a boat or a train trip? None of those things seemed to jump out at her. A paper caught her eye, though.

Carefully, she picked up the paper from the top of the stack, brushing off fish food. Saffron began to read.

I, Leon Cole, being of sound mind and body, do hereby bequeath my mortal estate to my biological children upon the following conditions:

*-50% to my daughter Dorah if she have no children,
natural or adopted.*

*-50% to my daughter Rachel if she be married by 12:00
pm on the date of her 55th birthday*

*Should either violate the condition of receipt, the whole
of the estate will be disbursed to the remaining biological
child. Should the children be deceased, incapacitated or
ineligible, the whole of the estate will be disbursed to the
Fantail Foundation.*

It was the will. Signed by Dorah and Rachel's father, Leon,
and a notary that Saffron didn't recognize, it was clear, short,
and to the point. Due to its lack of obscure legal terms, she suspected that Leon had written it himself. This copy was accompanied by several forms detailing the sum of money as of a few days
ago—it was substantial—and how it would be disbursed. Those
forms had circles around some of the signature lines, indicating,
Saffron thought, where principle participants were to sign. The
names were familiar: Dorah, Rachel, and Cutler.

Saffron peered at the document, laid it aside, and looked
around. She already knew that much. What else was here?

It was then that she saw it. Scrawled in the corner of the desk
calendar, beneath the tip of the uncapped pen. It was scratched
onto the paper, the handwriting a world away from the careful,
clean signature Dorah had used on the documents. This was likely the last spasmodic word Dorah had written. Saffron stopped
breathing. It was her own name.

Saffron Skye. Why would Dorah have written it? Did she
still think, at that moment before her life ended, that Saffron was

locked in her garage? Was she trying to send a message to investigators to let her prisoner out?

Or—and this made Saffron feel queasy—was this a message
not about her, but *for* her? She closed her eyes. What had Dorah
said? What had she known about Saffron? She knew she was an
event planner. She knew that she was planning Rachel's wedding.
And she had also known that Saffron solved the odd mystery
now and again. What if Dorah had known foul play was on the
horizon? What if she had meant for Saffron to investigate and
find this?

She looked at her name again. The letters were made in a
jerky, tortuous script. If the medical examiner was right, and Milo had given her cyanide, she was feeling the effects of it by the
time she wrote this. The more Saffron thought of it, the more she
considered the plausibility that Dorah, in her last moments, had
been trying to communicate something to her.

The mess on the desk seemed more significant now. Another
paper caught her attention. Pulling it out from the others, she
saw that it was an application. An application to the Honorable
Piscine Order. She scanned it. It was dated just two months ago.
Saffron didn't even know that the Order was still functioning. To
Saffron's surprise, the applicant was Dorah Harrison.

Routine information like the woman's birth date, address,
and income were followed by a much more interesting section
focused on her eligibility for membership.

From the short paragraph at the beginning of that section,
Saffron gathered that in Order to be initiated into the Honorable Piscine Order, one had to meet specific criteria: one had to
be the child of a current or deceased member of the Order. A
parent could sponsor a single one of their children to join the

Order. Concurrent membership of siblings was prohibited, to avoid an imbalance in the power structure of the Lodge, according to the paper. Apparently, Dorah's father, Leon, had been a member. Saffron saw his name on the application.

But she also saw, at the bottom of the page, a glaring red stamp: Membership Denied. Under that were checkboxes with possible reasons: Failed Background Check, Applicant Does Not Meet Income Requirements, Current Member Objections (with a space for the objections raised by members of the Order), but only one was checked: Sibling Currently a Member.

Rachel was a member of the Piscine Order? Did they have the lodge back on the mainland where she had been living? Saffron began to wonder exactly what this organization did, anyway.

So Dorah had wanted to join and had found out that Rachel was already a member. One more barb in the sisters' already prickly relationship.

Saffron was sometimes glad that she had no siblings. They often seemed to bring stress. But, she had to acknowledge that having someone to share your life experience with could be nice. Nik and his twin sister Naia gave each other such support and strength that they made having siblings seem appealing.

Saffron searched some more. The rest of the papers seemed to be orders for Milo's fish: three Achilles Tangs, one Orangeband Surgeonfish, two Yellowstripe Ceris. It looked like Milo was bringing in a lot of money for these fish. But Saffron knew that animal husbandry was not lucrative, no matter how much your stock sold for. The cost of keeping so many fish, so many tanks, as well as shipping and feed, must be astronomical. Just as in chicken farming, and, she supposed all other types of agriculture, fish-keeping was only for people who loved animals, not money.

Saffron's watch buzzed her 10:00 bedtime alarm. Rising with the chickens meant she needed to get her sleep. And the quiet house was starting to feel very confining. Saffron took out her phone and snapped pictures of the desk, each paper, her name in Dorah's jagged handwriting, and even the lionfish in his tank, whose beady eyes still followed her.

She was just turning to leave when she saw one more detail. On the wooden arm of the chair, in a splintered joint between pieces of oak, red fluff had caught. Saffron leaned down close to it. It was, absolutely, the fuzz from Dorah's bathrobe. And with it, in the crevice, was a thin, black length of frayed cord.

Saffron scrambled in her pocket for the necklace. Pulling it out, she slid it from the bag and held it up to the chair. The piece of cord matched perfectly with the broken necklace cord.

Saffron sat back down, closing her eyes. She tried to imagine how the necklace could have tangled in that particular place. If Dorah had been wearing it—Saffron held it up to her own neck and tried to contort into a position that would catch the necklace there, but it was impossible. With the chair upended again as it had been when she'd found it, the positioning was even more impossible. She righted the chair and sat, laying the necklace on the table. Only if Dorah had snatched it, stood, and steadied herself on the chair would the necklace cord have hung in the right place to catch—with the cuff of her bathrobe—and leave the fragment in the joint.

She was carrying the necklace, then. Why? Why would she grab it, especially if she was staggering, gasping, as Saffron pictured that she was? If the cyanide had begun to affect her, then

why, in her last poisoned moments, was she clinging to a necklace her husband had probably stolen?

Saffron's head ached. There was no doubt in her mind now
that Dorah had been murdered, probably by mild-mannered Milo. Saffron tried to remember her conviction that the hen-pecked
rooster didn't want to hurt the hen, but that theory seemed
laughable now.

She took a couple of photos of the cord and the fibers in the
chair and texted them to Bradley. She thought about sending the
shots of the papers, but she wasn't yet sure what significance they
held, if any.

Almost immediately, a text came back. *Thanks for checking it
out, but GO HOME!*

Saffron watched the lionfish out of the corner of her eye as
she texted back: *Thought you wanted me to help?*

She could hear Bradley's raspy voice in his reply: *Help out in
the daytime. In public areas.*

Fair point, Saffron thought. Bradley probably didn't want to
have to worry about her just now, with Rachel to look out for
and madman Milo on the loose.

Ten-four. Heading home.

· · · ·

THE HENHOUSE WAS QUIET when Saffron checked on
her girls half an hour later. Most of them were roosting, their
work of foraging and laying eggs done for the day. A few of them
gave long, low calls of protest as Saffron's blacklight danced over
them. She still carried it when she went to check them at night,
though they kept the farm pretty free of scorpions.

Once she was sure there were none, she snapped on the light in the workspace, drawing even more objections from the hens.

"Sorry, girls. I've got to get these eggs taken care of." She turned the crank and brought the eggs swaying down the conveyor belt toward her.

She gathered and packaged the eggs, taking longer than usual since it had been a rainy day. The beautiful rainbow colors of the eggs were always hidden by streaks of mud and grime on days like this, but the washer did an excellent job of getting them market-ready. She'd need to drop off orders to her commercial customers tomorrow, so there was no sleeping until the eggs were ready.

The egg house was quiet, a soundscape not unlike Milo and Dorah's house. The egg washer whooshed and scrubbed rhythmically, the ocean and the rain filled in the rest of the space, and the chickens punctuated the night with occasional comments. But here it was quiet and calm, here Saffron felt safe, and here she wasn't afraid someone would jump out and get her.

So when the egg house door flew open, and Mrs. Jones stormed in trailing rainwater, Saffron was more than startled. She screamed and dropped a carton of eggs.

"Where have you been?" Mrs. Jones snapped. "I have been looking for you all day."

Saffron pressed her lips together, trying to be calm. She didn't look at the cracked eggs. She'd clean them up after her guest was appeased. "Did you text the number on the card in your kitchen?" Saffron knew the answer—she'd had her phone with her all day.

"I don't text." Mrs. Jones made a sniffing sound.

Saffron didn't say *well it's your own fault then*, even though she wanted to. What she said was, "How can I help."

"The ocean—" Mrs. Jones waved a hand, "it's too loud."

Saffron suppressed a smile. "The ocean's too loud?"

"Yes. Can't they turn it off at night or something? The waves—they just keep coming. In and out and in and out," Mrs. Jones held her hands to her ears. "I'll never get any sleep."

Saffron thought fast. Sleep deprivation was a real concern to many travelers, and though she found Mrs. Jones' demands somewhat humorous, she did want the woman to have an enjoyable vacation.

"I think I have just the thing," She gestured to Mrs. Jones, and the two of them went up to Saffron's bungalow, where she retrieved the Snoozaroo that Fumi had given her. It wasn't until Mrs. Jones turned and headed, grumbling, back to her cottage, that Saffron realized she'd never even tried the gadget out. She'd been so busy she'd barely slept for days. A wave of exhaustion hit her. She powered through it long enough to go back to the egg house and clean up, but she got tomorrow's eggs put away as quickly as she could and fell into bed already dozing.

• • • •

THE LETOA ANNIVERSARY party was a vast success by any measure. The day dawned clear and pleasant, the Piscine Lodge looked sensational, and the food arrived with plenty of time to set up. The Letoa's had several generations of family members there, including Mr. Letoa's ninety-six-year-old mother, Violet, who danced a stirring foxtrot with one of the grandsons. Saffron was relieved when the old lady sat down to catch her breath and eat an enormous piece of cake. Seeing the party was moving along fine, she went over to express her admiration to Violet.

The old woman waved off the praise. "I was doing that step on this dance floor before Claude was a sparkle in his daddy's eye. The day I can't do that, they might as well put me out to sea."

Saffron saw an opening. Nobody seemed to need her, or Violet, so she asked a couple of questions, trying to understand this place a little better.

"So, tell me about the Lodge. You've been coming here a long time?"

"Live right across the street," Violet said. "Used to come here all the time," Violet pinched an errant piece of pineapple cake and popped it in her mouth, licking the coconut frosting off her fingers. "Haven't been since Claude's daddy died nineteen years ago."

Saffron felt her heart go out to the woman. Since her mother had died, she knew something about loss. "Too hard to come without him?"

"Sure. And they haven't been getting together like the old days. Used to be, this was the swingin'est place on the island come Saturday night. Now, hardly ever see lights on in here at all. Just random afternoons sometimes, and never more than a couple cars at a time. That ain't a party, if you ask me."

That seemed strange to Saffron. "What was the Lodge for, originally?"

"For?" the word seemed foreign to Violet. "Socializing, I guess. Though the members said that they were all about philanthropy, trying to fund scholarships and buy boats for needy fishermen and such."

Philanthropy had not occurred to Saffron.

"They did a few things, but it never seemed like much for all the time and money they were putting into it. I know some of the other Lodges around the country did lots with their dues."

"So there are other Piscine Lodges?"

"Oh, sure, anywhere there are fish."

That seemed an odd answer to Saffron. "What do the fish have to do with it?"

Violet put down her fork and looked at Saffron with an expression of practiced exasperation. It was a look only the very old could pull off—people who had had a long lifetime's worth of restating the obvious. "Everything, honey. It's the Piscine Lodge. You have to have access to fish to be a member."

"Access to fish?"

"Right. A pond or a river or a lake or the ocean. You have to catch your namesake, and then you have to keep it alive."

"Your namesake?" This was all confusing and strange to Saffron, yet she couldn't get enough.

"Sure. When you get initiated, the Lodge takes you out fishing, and what you catch determines your nickname in the Order and your position in the structure. Like my Wilbur caught a triggerfish his first time out, so he was Triggerfish, a Noble Guard of the Order." She said it warmly, with remembrance in her eyes, and she stood, leaning heavily on the table. "He had to keep and take care of that triggerfish in an aquarium at our house." Her eyes had a faraway look, "never could keep that cat away from that tank. Wilbur was terrified it would eat that fish sometime, and he'd get kicked out of the Order." Saffron stood, too, and followed Violet around the room to the far wall. "But that's not what got him. He got kicked out for no good reason, just as the Lodge began to go downhill. Broke his heart."

She shook her head sadly. "I don't know what happened to it after that. Wilbur never would speak of it." Saffron didn't like the regret in the old woman's eyes. "I think it had something to do with the leadership around here. Something, funny, if you ask me. Of course, I wasn't supposed to know any of that, because I wasn't a member," Violet said, "but Wilber and I didn't believe in secrets of any kind." She turned suddenly, stopping just short of the wall, and grasped both of Saffron's hands in hers. Violet's grip was cold and bony. "That's good advice now, too, honey. Don't you ever keep anything from your man. Even if he don't like it, it's better he knows."

Saffron felt her breath catch. Did Violet know about Keahi? Of course not. Saffron had never met the woman until tonight. It was her own guilty conscience that was making her feel that Violet was talking specifically about the secret Saffron had been keeping.

"Okay," she stuttered.

Violet looked satisfied. She turned her cloudy eyes back to the wall and walked to a particular frame. "See, now? There's my Wilbur himself."

The picture was black and white, and in it was a man in what could only be described as a fish-inspired suit of armor. His helmet looked like the head of a fish, the breastplate was overlayed metal that looked like scales, and the sword at his side had a fish on the hilt. "Wow," Saffron said, because she couldn't think of anything else.

"Quite a looker, wasn't he?" Violet asked, poking Saffron in the ribs.

CHAPTER 13

S affron was still thinking about the Honorable Piscine Order the next day when she drove down to Honolulu with Nik. They were heading out for more snorkeling, and though she still needed to finish cleaning up the Piscine Lodge, she also very much needed a break. And Bradley had forbidden her to do any detective work until Milo was in custody, so that freed up a lot of her time.

She watched the ocean out the window. It skimmed along beside them, its vibrant cerulean hues making the chiffon seafoam on its crests pop out all the more. She was thinking of Keahi, of the color of his eyes and the richness of his laugh. She'd tried to call, but his phone had, for the last two days, gone straight to his message service, who explained that he'd been engaged in some urgent surgery. The woman who took his messages had no idea when he'd be free or how his operation had gone. Saffron didn't know if he was still dealing with it or if this current emergency was something new altogether.

Nik's voice pulled her back from Boston. "I never knew that old Lodge was so interesting."

Saffron had been telling him about the Honorable Piscine Order. She shrugged.

"And it's weird that Rachel's a member. I wonder what her job is." He squinted. "What did you say some of the others were? Besides the guard?"

Saffron ticked them off on her fingers, "There are Keepers, who are in charge of the 'artifacts' of the Lodge, whatever those are, there are Stewards, who are in charge of the kitchen and the food, there are Inductors that move newbies through the ranks, all kinds of positions, all the way up to the Most Grand Excellency of Honor."

Nik stifled a chuckle. "That's not a pretentious title at all."

"That's what I thought when Violet told me about it."

"And she said that was like the president? Or the boss of the whole Order?"

"Yes, at the international level."

"And we still aren't really sure what all the rest of them do?"

"Not really. Mr. Letoa came and gathered up his mother before she could tell me everything."

"Just when it was getting interesting."

"It was all pretty interesting."

"I like that part about having to catch and care for the fish you get your name from."

"That is an interesting twist," Saffron said. "It would be a lot harder in some of the other fraternal orders."

This made Nik chuckle some more. "Where would the Elks Club keep all their elk?"

"Or the Lions Club?"

"It's interesting, for sure," he said.

"Something's just eating me up with curiosity, though," Saffron said, shifting in her seat. "I am just super curious about Rachel's name and position in the Order. Did she catch her fish near her home on the mainland? Or here? Does she have a trout in a tank back in Wisconsin?"

Nik shook his head. "So the Order is all over the world, huh? And they catch the fish wherever they can? Any kind of fish?"

"That's what Violet said. Her cousin is a Piscine out in South Carolina, and he has a catfish."

"How long do they have to keep them?"

"The natural life of the fish. They can't let them be killed or get rid of them, or they lose their membership. But if the fish just dies, that's okay."

"They still get to be members?"

"Yeah, and they don't have to get another one. I guess they've proven their respect for the honorable fish beings and their dependability for their fellow members of the Lodge." She paused. "I guess taking care of something is a good way to show your character."

• • • •

THEY WENT TO A NEW beach today, one that Nik said would have some fish Saffron hadn't seen yet. The first part of their dive proved him right, when they came upon a blue and green fish he told her was an ulua.

Later, Saffron sat on the beach after a delicious picnic lunch and waited for Nik to bring back sodas from the manapua truck parked beside the beach. She loved the manapua men that drove around the island, stopping at beaches and parks and little towns. Their trucks were outfitted with candy counters and so-das, and of course, the best manapua in Hawaii.

The beach was busy today, but not overwhelmingly packed. People picnicked and peered into the tide pools on a long rocky outcropping. Kids built sand castles while their parents lounged on chairs nearby. Saffron watched two little boys scooping sand into a pile and decorating the pile with shells. They looked famil-iar. She tried to think if they were from Maika'i. Though it was far up near the North Shore and they were down near Honolulu now, it could be that they had come down for a day trip just like she and Nik. But she couldn't entirely place the boys.

"Kaleb Junior, stop it!" one of the boys pushed his brother.

"No! I'm putting it here!" His brother pushed him back. In a moment, they were fighting in earnest. Saffron looked around for their parents, but none of the grown-ups around seemed to take any notice. The boys were really getting worked up. She was afraid they might hurt each other, so she walked over.

"Hey, that's a nice sand castle," she commented, plopping down in the sand on the other side of it. The boys settled and beamed at her.

"We made it," said the smaller one. He had uniquely colored eyes—the pale brown of first light on the sand. Saffron's color memory filed it with only half-a-dozen other people she'd met whose eyes were that shade.

"It's awesome. You should show your parents!" she spoke with enthusiasm, hoping to get the boys to involve whichever adults belonged to them.

"We can't," said the bigger one, who had pale blond hair and no eyebrows that Saffron could determine. "Our dad can't get out of the car, and our mom's in there talking to him."

This was a surprise. "Oh. Is your dad hurt? Is that why he can't get out?"

"Nope. He can't get out because he'll get in trouble if he does, and we're not supposed to tell anyone he's here."

"He's been gone, but he had to go to work some days this week, so he came home, but he has to leave again tomorrow."

Saffron tried not to look surprised. "Oh. That's . . . Interesting."

"He's a good guy, but sometimes the cops think bad guys are good guys," said the little one.

The bigger one turned wide chestnut eyes to Saffron. She saw, in them, doubts about what his brother was saying. She remembered similar doubts about her own father. Looking into his eyes was like looking into a mirror.

Saffron heard Nik's voice behind her. "Well, you two don't fight anymore, okay?" she said. "Just play and have fun. It's a beautiful day."

"Okay," said the older one. Saffron walked up to where Nik was, feeling sorry for the brothers.

Their mother, a woman with a blank expression, came to get the two boys before Saffron was finished with her soda. They gave her a little wave as they went back up the beach to their car and their mysterious father.

Most of the families were packing up and heading home by the time Nik and Saffron went back out. He asked if she'd like him to take her home, but Saffron wanted to see a few more fish. Snorkeling had gotten in her blood now, and she couldn't get enough of it. She convinced him to go out for just a while longer.

Some of the reef fish had gone home, too, it seemed. There were fewer now than there had been this morning, and mostly ones she'd seen before. No lionfish, no octopus. Saffron still couldn't get over the feeling that the octopus were hiding right in front of her. It made her search every rock, question every lump on the sea floor. Near the end of the swim, she was looking so hard at the unremarkable rocks on the sea floor that she didn't notice the swirling waves near one part of the reef.

Saffron sensed something close to her and turned in the water just as an enormous wave hit her, pushing her directly into a basketball-sized spiny urchin.

Fire shot down Saffron's arm, and she swam as hard as she could away from the urchin, back toward the beach. She couldn't see Nik, couldn't call for him with her mask on, so she let the adrenaline pumping through her carry her toward the golden sand as her upper arm pulsed with pain.

The sand was soft and warm, and she was gasping as she hauled herself out onto it. Crumpling onto her side on the beach, Saffron tore her mask off and tried to breathe as she looked at her arm. Protruding from it were the eggplant-colored spines of the urchin, large and small, a dozen or more, as thin as wires and as long as pencils.

She could hear herself sobbing as the pain throbbed through her. She tried to get her mouth to form Nik's name, but it wouldn't work properly. All that came out was a little moan.

Suddenly, someone was beside her. Soft hands were stroking her hair back from her face. She saw a silver ponytail and looked up into the face of the diver who had caught the clownfish.

"Shhh," the woman said, "you're going to be okay."

Saffron felt someone supporting her back. She looked over her shoulder to see the woman's diving partner, his eyes pinched with concern, kneeling behind her.

The woman turned Saffron's face to her. "What's your name?" Saffron tried to think through the pain.

"Saffron," she managed.

"Okay. Saffron. I'm Allie. Are you visiting?"

It seemed an odd moment for a chat, but as Saffron felt new streaks of fire from her arm, she realized that the woman was distracting her as her partner began to remove the spines. Suddenly she was very glad to have something to look at. She shook her head slowly, her voice gone down a whirlpool of pain.

"You live here then?" the woman said.

Saffron managed to raise and lower her chin a couple of times. She glanced down. Several of the shining spines lay in the sand behind the man. He had a pair of forceps and was gently pulling them out one by one.

When she turned her face back, Nik was beside the woman, looking panicked and horrified. Saffron tried to say his name. The woman waved him off.

"Saffron here has met one of our *vana*," she said, stroking sweat from Saffron's face, "and the meeting did not go well."

"I'm so sorry," Nik said, "I looked around for you but..."

Silver ponytail stopped him. "She's going to be just fine. Just fine. Now, what's your name?"

"Nik," Saffron heard the tremor in his voice. Her vision was fading, so she closed her eyes.

"Nik," said Allie, "I'm going to need you to run up the beach there and go to my truck. It's the double cab one with the three square fish on the side. In the back seat is a duffle bag. You're going to want to get that back here to me as quick as you can."

Saffron heard Nik's footsteps as he ran away, leaving her alone with the two strangers and the searing pain in her arm.

"Saffron," the woman said. She sounded very far away. "Saffron, listen to me. Jeff's going to keep working on those spines, but you've got to stay with us. He's got a lot of them out. Just hang on a little longer."

Saffron tried to answer, tried to thank Jeff, but nothing came out. She lay moaning for a long moment, her eyes clamped shut. Every muscle in her body was tensed. She couldn't feel the warm sand anymore, or the sun, or the woman's touch. Just heat and ache and every breath—torture.

"Saffron, open your eyes for me."

Saffron forced her lids and was blinded by the sun.

"Okay. Your friend Nik is here, and he's going to be holding your hand for a minute. You watch me. Jeff's got all those spines out, and I'm going to put some of this on." She was holding a small spray bottle. "It's magic, Saffron. You just wait and see."

Nik traded places with Allie, taking Saffron's head on his lap and her hands in his. She could barely feel him. She looked down at her arm. Black dots and smudges lay under her skin like sapphire bruises, but the protruding spines were gone. The pain remained though, and the dots seeped blood.

Allie began spraying her arm. "This is amazing stuff. It was isolated from the digestive tract of the hawksbill sea turtle. They eat sea urchins, and we noticed they don't seem to mind these nasty spines. That's because they have a special compound that dissolves the spines. It's an acid. And once we figured it out, we started making it synthetically."

Saffron didn't care where it came from. A cool, sweet breeze was beginning to blow. Saffron could feel it. The woman sprayed some more. The screaming pain in her body was ebbing like the tide, easing with every beat of her hammering heart. Nik's face tightened into focus. Saffron tried to smile.

"There she is," he said to Allie and Jeff, then back to Saffron, "there you are. There you are. It'll be okay. Just breathe. Breathe."

Saffron did. She pulled in breaths as the fire receded to her right arm, then left her fingertips tingling as it centered back in each individual puncture in her upper arm.

And then it was gone. She choked on the relief it left in its absence. Her arm felt light and tight, but the pain was gone. She spoke, and her voice was back, too.

"It's gone. It doesn't hurt anymore." The woman moved back around and helped her sit up. Saffron saw a ring of onlookers. Nik ran a gentle hand across her knee.

"Saffron, I'm so sorry," he said. That tremble was still in his voice.

Saffron couldn't think of any words. Her head was light with relief—giddy with feeling the soft sand and the warm breeze. She wrapped her left arm around him and hugged him, burying her face in his shoulder. The onlookers burst into applause. Several of them were recording with their phones.

She sat up. "That stuff is amazing!"

Allie smiled, the crinkles near her eyes bunching. "Thanks. I'm sure glad we had it today. You're looking better. Your color is coming back."

"I'm a redhead," Saffron joked, "there wasn't any color to begin with."

"Aaaand your sense of humor is intact," Jeff said.

"That's made from turtles?" Saffron said.

Allie looked shocked, "no, no, it's synthesized to mimic a compound that turtles produce," she clarified. "No turtles were harmed in the making of this spray."

"It's amazing. Where did you get it?"

"We made it," Allie said proudly. "At the Reef People Coalition."

Saffron watched the crowd dispersing. "What's that?"

"We're a group of marine bio-chemists that study the interplay between marine and human biology, and how we can make life better for the reefs and for people."

"You're doing a good job," Saffron said, peering down at her arm. "You made my life better today."

Allie and Jeff stayed with them until dark, observing Saffron's recovery.

"So you're from Maika'i?" Allie asked. "We just set up a lab there."

"I think I saw you diving the other day," Saffron said. She remembered, with a little embarrassment, thinking they were up to no good. She described seeing them spray the weird alien eyes on their stalks, which the scientists identified as palythoas, and seeing them capture the clownfish. "What were you doing?" she asked.

"Ahhh. The 'auhuhu trials."

"I'm not familiar with that word," Saffron said. She looked at Nik, who shrugged his shoulders.

"'Auhuhu is a plant that Native Hawaiian fishermen used in hola—a type of fishing. They would pound this plant and put it in baskets or coconut husks and then put those in the water. The fish would be stunned by the poison in the plants, and then the fishermen could gather them up to eat."

Saffron shook her head, still not understanding.

The good thing about the 'auhuhu is that it dissipates quickly, and it doesn't hurt other organisms in the water. In small doses, it doesn't even do lasting harm to the fish."

"You were going to eat the clownfish?" Saffron clarified.

"No. See, in the aquarium hobby, there are thousands of fish collectors—not just here, all over the world, who are using much more dangerous substances to stun fish for capture and sale to the aquarium trade."

Jeff nodded and jumped in. Saffron could feel their enthusiasm. "When managed properly, fish collecting can be completely safe for reefs and fish populations, just like sport fishing or commercial fishing. It can even help control fish populations and balance the ecosystem if agencies give more permits for more prolific fish and fewer for less prolific fish. It can be a very good thing. But in many places, people are just trying to survive. They sell the fish they catch to aquarium dealers for their living, so they go diving to catch these fish, and they need to get as many as they can as quickly as they can. If there aren't good ways to do that, it results in terrible reef destruction and devastation."

"So we're working with the compounds from the 'auhuhu plant to make an easy, cheap, targeted compound that fishermen can use safely and that can make the fish more comfortable during collection, healthier afterward, and do no damage to the fragile reef ecosystem." Allie's excitement about the project shone in her eyes and in her animated gestures.

"There's a whole world of remedies and poisons in the ocean," Jeff said. "And a lot of the seafaring cultures have known about them for centuries. We're just catching up."

"I still can't believe how fast that worked," she said.

"It's the acid. It dissolves those spines like jello in hot water." Allie peered at Saffron's arm. "I put my number in your phone. You call me if you notice any bad reactions."

Saffron ran a finger over her wounds, touching the black smudges and dots gingerly. "Is that bruising?"

"Nope. That's the ink from the vana spines," Allie said.

Saffron tried to sound it out, "Va-na?" she asked.

"Yep. Sea urchin. Spelled in Hawaiian with a w: w-a-n-a, but pronounced with the Hawaiian v sound for the w. Like *Hal-i-e-va*."

"Will the ink wash off?" Saffron asked.

"Nope. You've got it for a few weeks until your body breaks it all down. Congratulations. We call that a Hawaiian tattoo."

CHAPTER 14

There were eggs everywhere—on the counters, stacked in cartons on the cart, in the washer and still more coming on the conveyor. The sunny days that had come on the heels of the rainy ones seemed to carry Saffron's hens to new heights of production. Saffron was glad for the abundance of egg cartons she had on hand and the abundance of time to get the eggs into them.

She was also glad to have guests in the three little cottages. She'd delivered a dozen eggs to each of them this morning, and though Mrs. Jones had not answered the door, the other two groups were delighted to get them.

She smiled, thinking of the little family in the Banana Cottage. The children found their way, every day, down to the egg house. Saffron had shown them where she kept the scratch grains—a mixture of corn, wheat, and barley that was basically candy for her chickens—and they loved to come in and toss scratch grains to the hens. The old couple in the Lagoon Cottage was equally enchanted with the experience of staying on a working egg farm, and they had chatted with Saffron over the carton she'd delivered, telling her all about their grandchildren, of whom they had twenty-six.

Saffron had been exhausted last night when she came home from the beach. Nik had helped her inside, made her some chicken long rice, an iconic Hawaiian soup with clear noodles that she loved, and she had fallen asleep on his shoulder in the living room. She hadn't been out to check the chickens, and he had dozed on the couch holding her all night. When the golden

163

light of the Hawaiian sunrise woke them both, he'd driven into town and brought back malasadas—her favorite Hawaiian donuts—for their breakfast. She'd sent him off to work with a quick thank-you kiss that had left her a little breathless.

Saffron's arm ached a little this morning, but it was nothing compared to the fiery torment she'd felt on the beach yesterday. The ink remained, making a messy blur punctuated by perfect circles. Sort of an abstract tattoo, Saffron thought.

Bossy scolded Saffron as she walked by. "Don't blame me," Saffron told the hen, "you're alone because you're so mean to everyone."

"I'm alone because I got on a plane to come to Hawaii and get away from everyone," a sharp voice made Saffron spin around. Mrs. Jones stood glaring at her.

"I—I wasn't talking to you—I mean, I didn't see you there. I was just talking to my chicken."

Mrs. Jones' incredulous scowl made Saffron stop talking.

"Well, no wonder my trip is a disaster. My hostess is in here talking to a chicken instead of attending to her guests."

"I'm sorry," Saffron managed. Bossy squawked in the pen next to her, sounding like Mrs. Jones' echo. "Was there something you needed?"

"Yes. I need you to do something about the sun."

Saffron blinked. "The sun?"

"Back home the sun just shines. Here it glares. It glares off the flowers, it glares off the leaves, it glares off the ocean. It's giving me a headache."

Guests were always asking for things—the old couple this morning had asked for some extra towels. The family had asked to borrow some boogie boarding equipment to play at the beach.

But nobody had ever asked Saffron to alter the star at the center of the solar system before.

"Um," Saffron tried to think, "is it bothering you in the cottage? I can see if we can cover the windows more completely?"

"No, you silly girl, of course, it's not bothering me in the cottage. It's when I'm out. At the beach."

"The sun is too bright at the beach." Saffron tried to say it without smiling. "I can help with that—I have a great beach umbrella. I'd be happy to bring it to you."

"No, no, no," Mrs. Jones shook her head forcefully. "Not *shade*. I don't want to be in the shade, I want to be in the sun, but the sun is too glaring."

Saffron held her hands up in helplessness. What was she supposed to do about the way the sun shone?

"You're useless," Mrs. Jones spun around, stomping out through the still-open doors of the egg house into the apparently-too-bright sunshine.

Saffron stifled a giggle and followed her.

"You know what? I thought of something," she said, trying to make her voice more compassionate. "It will just take me a minute."

Mrs. Jones made a noncommittal sound as Saffron rushed into her house and began to look through the drawers in the spare bedroom.

In less than a minute, she was catching up to Mrs. Jones. Saffron held out her hand. "I think these might help."

Mrs. Jones studied the sunglasses in Saffron's palm with a skeptical expression before snatching them and putting them on.

There was a long, breathless moment while she peered around the farm.

Finally, Mrs. Jones gave a tight nod. "These will do."

If Saffron thought she'd get a thank-you, she was wrong. Mrs. Jones went into her cottage without another word, and Saffron went back to finish her work in the egg house.

To her, Mrs. Jones seemed like a cautionary tale: don't get into the habit of criticism, or you may not get out. She'd criticized the sun, the surf, and the sand since she'd come, finding fault with everything that made this place special. Saffron did not want to be that way.

"I even like you," she said to Bossy, tossing her a handful of scratch grains just to be nice. "Whether you like me or not."

Bossy squawked a reprimand, then went after the grains. Saffron watched as she picked out only the cracked corn, scratching the wheat and barley out of her way and sending them flying, with a measure of sand, toward Saffron.

The sand hit Saffron's shoes and the boardwalk center aisle of the egg house with a shushing sound. Saffron stepped back, feeling the grit of it under her feet. Suddenly, she was not in the egg house anymore. She was two other places: out on her lanai the night Milo had shown up, and in Milo's house. The lanai. The hallway. Both covered in sand that had seemed, somehow, too fine.

Because it had been too fine. The sand he'd left on the lanai wasn't sand. It was aquarium salt. Milo had been at his house before he came creeping onto her lanai, the color of his shirt Saffron closed her eyes and remembered his two-toned shirt. She'd seen the color difference that night, but she hadn't realized that the shirt wasn't faded. It was dusty. Milo had been covered in that fine, powdery salt. Which meant he'd been at his house.

Saffron called Bradley. "I think Milo's hiding out in his house," she said. "And I think I know where."

• • • •

SAFFRON WAS GLAD SHE wasn't alone as she stood in Milo's living room half an hour later. Bradley had his gun drawn, and he'd only allowed her to come if she promised to stay behind him. Nik had come, too, and he stood behind her, his hand protectively around hers.

"So, you think he's been coming back here?" Bradley asked. His voice was tight.

"No," Saffron said, moving forward with him through the living room and down the hall, "I think he's been staying here."

Bradley was quick to object, "Can't be. We've had people all through this place."

Saffron moved into the spare bedroom. She ran her eyes over the gritty floor, picturing Milo's shoulders, dusted with powdery salt.

Saffron pointed. In the center of the aisle between the rows of tanks, the caramel-colored floorboards shifted to cinnamon. Nik raised his eyebrows in a question, and Bradley shrugged before Saffron realized that they couldn't see it. Whether it was the strange lights from the many colored bulbs above the tanks or whether it was the fact that they didn't have the same sensitivity to color that she did, Saffron didn't know, but when she pointed again, more emphatically, all she got was the shake of their heads.

So she stepped forward herself, kneeling on the gritty floor. Bradley moved in with the gun, and Nik squinted down at the floor, obviously trying to see what she was seeing.

Saffron ran her fingers along the floorboards, wedging them into a crack near the edge of the color shift. "You've had people all over the house," she said, "but not under it." She lifted, and there was Milo Harrison.

Blinking up at them, the suspect held his dusty hands high. "Don't shoot," he said, though there was a weariness in his voice that suggested he wouldn't mind if Bradley did.

"What in the world?" Bradley's explosive voice was back. "Get up out of there. Saffron, back away."

She did, and watched Milo use a worn ladder to ascend out of the crawl space.

"You've been in there this whole time?" Bradley asked, stepping forward.

"More or less," Milo coughed almost in time with the clicks of the handcuffs. Saffron walked back over and crouched down, peering into the space under the house. It was as damp and unpleasant as she would have thought. There was a chair, and a cot, as well as an old nightstand table with a book, a headlamp, and a box of crackers on it. A spartan existence, Saffron thought, until she realized that Milo probably only went down there for a short amount of time if someone was in the house. When the house was empty, he would likely climb out of the hole and live normally—well, as normally as he ever did—in the home he'd shared with his wife.

As Bradley read Milo his rights, Nik led Saffron out onto the porch. "That was weird," he said, "how'd you figure it out?"

"Well, when Milo came to see me, there was salt on his shoulders and in his hair. I kept trying to figure that out because it didn't make sense. But this afternoon, I realized that he could be *below* the floor, and that salt was sifting down onto him through the floorboards. And when I was here before, I heard a sound in that bedroom. It must have been him under there."

The thought gave her a shiver. Though there were still many unanswered questions, Saffron felt some comfort in seeing Milo's bathtub ring of colorless hair framed by the window of the police cruiser as Bradley hauled him away.

• • • •

SAFFRON POURED ANOTHER cup of coconut cocoa for Rachel as they sat in the garden of the Sweet Pineapple Bed and Breakfast. It was her own recipe, and she'd brought it over to break the news to Rachel about Milo's arrest.

Blake had returned. He sat on the wicker love seat with Rachel, his arm around her shoulders, his ever-present sunglasses obscuring his expressions, but his voice conveying frustration and anger.

"I hope they hang him this time," he said vehemently. Rachel's eyelids dropped briefly over her teary eyes.

"Well, seeing as there is no death penalty in Hawaii, that's unlikely," Saffron said.

Blake fixed his sunglassy gaze on her. "I'm picking up that you don't think I should be so harsh."

"I didn't say that," she said, although he was absolutely correct. "I just think there's been too much death."

"Or not enough," he grumbled. Saffron tried to remember that he had been through a grueling week—the wedding, the discovery of the body, questioning from Bradley, then a trip to the mainland, several days of work, and a trip back here. She tried to have sympathy for him.

"Well, whatever happens to that monster, at least now Rachel's safe," he said grudgingly.

"Right," Saffron said. "That's what matters."

Rachel took a sip of cocoa with a shaking hand. "It's hard for him to understand," her tone was apologetic, "why Dorah's death upsets me, and why it's sad to me that Milo is back in prison."

"It is hard for me to understand," Blake shook his head. The hand that was resting on Rachel's shoulder was clenched into a fist. "I'd think she'd be glad, especially with that close call for her this week."

Saffron looked pointedly at Rachel. "Tell us," she said, "Why you're upset instead of glad."

Rachel's eyes held gratitude, as if she'd been wanting someone to ask. "Because even though our mom left before I can even remember, and even though our dad was crazy, and even though the money made a mess of what sparse friendship we'd held onto through our adolescence, Dorah was still my sister."

The simplicity and sweetness of the phrase erased Saffron's next words from her mind. She didn't know what to say to that.

Rachel went on, "You don't get an unlimited number of siblings in this life. Once your parents are gone—and mine were gone early—they're the only ones who truly know who you were. Even when I was angry at her or hurt by her, I still wanted the best for Dorah. Maybe I didn't want her to get all the money, but I didn't want her to die."

Saffron knew when she heard it that she would need to call Bradley. Rachel wasn't on her suspect list anymore, in spite of the money and the motive it represented.

But as she looked at the reflective surface of Blake's sunglasses, she wasn't so sure about him. Quickly, she downed the last of the cocoa in her cup and reached for the teapot.

"Oh, we seem to have emptied this," she said, hefting it. "Blake, there's more in a pan on the stove in the kitchen there in the B&B. Would you mind refilling this?" She held the teapot toward him expectantly and breathed a sigh of relief when he stood and took the pot. She waited until the door of the house closed behind him before she leaned forward and put a hand on Rachel's knee.

"I have to ask you a tough question now," she said, "and I have to ask it quickly."

Rachel's eyebrows raised in surprise. Saffron knew her voice was full of intensity as she formed the question with as much clarity as she could manage, "Does Blake get the money if you die?"

Rachel's expression clouded over. "What?"

"The inheritance. Does Blake get it if you die?"

"Why would you ask that?" The usually open Rachel drew back, her face a mask of confusion.

"Because he's the perfect suspect," Saffron said, "we've all been so busy looking for Milo that I didn't even think of it, but if Blake killed Dorah, and then he—" she stooped herself from saying, *and then he kills you* and softened it to, "and something happens to you, then he's suddenly a very rich man."

Rachel's expression went from horrified to angry. "First of all, that is not the kind of person he is. I wouldn't have married a murderer!"

"But you said it yourself—that many zeroes can be very persuasive," Saffron began, "and he would have had access to cut your brake lines."

"And second of all," Rachel leaped to her feet in agitation, "I'm not that stupid. As you know, I don't even have the money yet so it would have done him no good to cut my brake lines. And even if I did have it, Blake will never receive a cent of it. In case of my death, it would all go to Dylan!"

She spun around, stalking off toward the same door through which her new husband had disappeared.

Saffron let the sunshine sink into her skin. She was sorry she'd upset Rachel, but the truth was that they had to consider it. Saffron didn't like Blake's flippancy toward Milo's fate, although it was understandable. She didn't like other things about him, either, like the fact that he'd been "so perfect" for Rachel, and that he never took off those stupid sunglasses, and that he'd been so quick to jump on the marriage bandwagon.

But maybe that last part was just bitterness. Saffron acknowledged that she may be a tiny bit jealous of how easily Rachel and Blake's relationship seemed to have worked out. She wondered again why Keahi hadn't called her back.

Just then, she heard the buzzing of a phone. She checked her pocket, but it wasn't hers. Saffron looked at the little wicker table where the used tea service sat, missing its pot. Nothing there. A third buzz led her to the loveseat. There, behind the cushion, was a black smartphone.

Saffron snatched it, knowing before she saw the screen that it was Blake's.

A call was coming in. The number was emblazoned across the screen, but there was no contact information, and to answer it Saffron would have to unlock the phone.

Instead, she snatched her own phone and snapped a photo, saving the number a heartbeat before the call went to voicemail and the number disappeared from the screen.

The lock screen was uninteresting: a charcoal background with the time and date in red numbers in the center. There was no more information that Saffron could find.

She laid the phone on the tea tray and gathered up the cups, then took them back to the kitchen in the Sweet Pineapple.

Inside, she found the teapot full on the table and the kitchen empty.

Saffron sat down the tray with the cell phone and headed for the door, calling a "thank you" to Bunny Monroe for letting her use the kitchen. She didn't stop to find Rachel and Blake, and she didn't stop to chat with Bunny. She had a lead to follow.

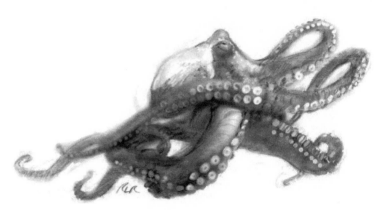

CHAPTER 15

The number rang twice before a cheerful female voice answered, "Jay Burton Agency, this is Linda. How may I direct your call?"

Saffron realized that she hadn't thought out her strategy very well. She needed to find out why they were calling Blake, but she wasn't sure how to ask that.

"Um, yes, I'm returning a call for Blake Morgan," she said, "he is . . . Indisposed at the moment and cannot respond himself." *Indisposed?* She wished she had thought of something better. That seemed like a word people would only use when they were lying.

"Okay," the pleasant office assistant didn't seem bothered by the word, "I don't recognize the name, but I can look and see who his account is with and transfer you to that agent," she said, "They would probably know why they were calling him."

"That sounds great," Saffron tried to hide the relief in her voice. In dealing with so many companies as an event planner, she'd found that the best problem solver in any organization was the secretary.

In a moment, Linda was back, "Aw, I'm sorry, I couldn't find any accounts with that name."

Saffron felt her chest deflate. "Oh. Okay."

"Usually our agents are good at following up, though, so if someone called him once, I'll bet they'll call back if they don't hear from him."

"Yes," Saffron said. "Thank you. Just a couple more quick questions, Linda, if you don't mind. My boss likes things organized."

Linda laughed. It was a musical sound that made Saffron wish she felt as light as Linda, "Don't they all?"

They commiserated about bosses for a few more minutes until Saffron said, "So, remind me what kind of agency you are again?"

"We're an advertising agency," Linda said, "the best in Honolulu!"

The words sunk into Saffron's stomach like an avocado pit. "Wait, Linda?" She said. "Could you check one more thing for me? Could you check that there's not an *employee* by the name of Blake Morgan?" She let a couple of seconds pass as she listened to the clacking of Linda's keys. "He might be an old employee. Like maybe from a few years ago?"

Linda kept searching, punctuating her exploration of the company directory with phrases like, "Nope, not there," and "that's as far back as that goes." Finally, she said, "I'm sure sorry, but there's no record of a Blake Morgan here."

Saffron managed a thank-you before she hung up.

But that wasn't going to be all. After the egg line in the morning, Saffron was going to Honolulu.

• • • •

SAFFRON HAD JUST PULLED into a parking spot in front of the Jay Burton Agency when her phone rang. It was Keahi's ring—a gentle ukulele number that had played at the Laki Luau the night of their first real date. She answered it with butterflies in her stomach.

But Keahi's voice was neither light nor playful. "Saffron, are you alright?"

"Wh—What—" she managed, putting away her questions about how the surgery had gone.

"I saw you. I saw you on the news."

"The news?" Saffron had not been interviewed since the last big Maika'i case she'd worked on. That hardly seemed current or urgent.

"You got stung by an urchin?" He asked.

Saffron's head spun. The news? She hadn't seen any reporters or news vans at the beach that day. But then it dawned on her. She had seen cameras. All those people with their phones.

"The news?" she repeated.

"Yeah, I watch the news from back home online. They were running a story about this new biomedical company in Maika'i, and they showed some woman spraying you on the beach," his voice broke, "Oh, Ipo, you looked like you were in so much pain."

The pieces were beginning to fit together now, and she wanted to reassure him, "I was. It was awful. But whatever she sprayed on me was like a miracle."

"I saw that, too," he said, the tension in his voice easing slightly, "it seemed to take the pain out on contact."

Saffron told him about it, giving Allie's explanation about why and how it worked.

"I'm glad they were there," he said, "but you did go to the emergency room, too, right?"

"Yes. I did. They said it would be fine."

Keahi was still worked up, "send me a picture of it. I want to see how it's healing. Are you sure you don't have any infection?"

The concern in his voice made Saffron miss him so much she couldn't breathe. "Okay," she said, "just a minute."

Switching her phone to the camera mode, she pulled up her sleeve and snapped a photo, which she sent to him before getting back on the line to say it was on its way.

She heard his phone chime through the call, and he was quiet for a minute. "Okay," he finally said. "It's looking pretty good. But you need to keep an eye on it. Your skin is so fair and so sensitive, it could go bad quickly if an infection starts to set in."

"I'll watch it," she said. "Keahi, how did your surgery go?" She was afraid to ask, worried that he had lost another young patient and having to relate the news to her would cause him more pain. And he was quiet for a long moment. But when he spoke again, his tone was warm.

"It went perfectly," He said. "Really well. My patient has already gone home. I saw him this morning, and he's going to live an active, healthy life from here on out."

She was bursting with pride and relief. "I told you it was going to be okay. Where have you been? I've been wondering about it for days."

"I know. They told me you called. It's a little embarrassing."

"What is?"

"Why I haven't been available. I guess, see, one of the other docs at the hospital teaches at Harvard Medical School, and he watched part of the operation. He was teaching some of his advanced students about those very same techniques this week, so he asked me to come up and give a couple guest lectures."

"What?" Saffron felt herself grinning, "you say that like it's trivial, 'Oh, I was just teaching at Harvard,' K! Really? Harvard?"

"Well, it's not that exciting," he said, but she could hear in his voice that he was pleased she was excited, "it's just up the road from the hospital."

"It's HARVARD MEDICAL SCHOOL!" she said, and her sentence ended in a laugh as light as Linda's had been.

"I will say, it was fun. I never thought I'd be there."

"They were lucky to have you," Saffron said, "you are a skilled surgeon. Those students better appreciate learning from such a gifted teacher."

Her praise must have been too much, because Keahi stopped her with a little humility, "Well, it wasn't all me. There was a whole team, you know, of doctors and nurses," as soon as he said the word, Saffron saw Evelyn's face in her mind. She couldn't stop herself from bringing it up.

"How did Evelyn do? Was she the supernurse you thought she'd be?" She tried to keep it light, but there was a current of bitterness even she could hear in her voice.

Keahi was quiet for a heartbeat, then, as always, honest. "Yes. She was a superstar. I couldn't have done it without her."

The thing about honesty was that it was hard to be mad at someone when they were being sincere. And it sparked sincerity in Saffron, too. When she spoke again, the bitterness was gone.

"K, you know, I'm really glad she was there for you. I'm glad you had her help when you needed it."

This time, the silence on the line was longer. Keahi's voice was weary when he answered her, "Thanks, Ipo. It looks like we both had good nurses when we needed them."

It was not what she had expected him to say. Saffron searched their conversation to give his statement context. Was he talking about Allie?

But then, in one horrible moment, she knew. Her mind flashed back to the urchin sting, back to the cell phones pointed at her, back to the blinding pain, back to lying in Nik's arms on the beach. Keahi had seen. He knew.

She let the silence lay along the miles between them.

• • • •

BY THE TIME SHE MADE it into the lobby of the agency, Saffron's enthusiasm for the case was gone. Her enthusiasm for everything was gone.

Keahi had been as understanding as she could expect under the circumstances, but when she'd come clean and told him about the time she'd spent with Nik, about the kiss, about her loneliness, he'd said what she had been afraid to hear since she'd kissed him goodbye at the airport months ago: "It's not fair to keep this going when we're five time zones apart."

And so, just like that, in a ten-minute conversation, they'd decided to take a break. Neither of them knew what that meant, exactly, but when Saffron heard the tears in his voice as they hung up, she knew it wasn't good.

She'd cried off all her makeup in the car before coming into the lobby, and her eyes felt prickly as she walked past a row of photos and awards to Linda's desk.

The woman was just as Saffron had pictured her: neat, Asian, and brilliantly cheerful. She noticed immediately that Saffron had been crying.

"Hold on right there," Linda said, "I'm going to get you a bottle of cold water." When Saffron tried to protest that she wasn't a client, Linda held up a hand. "Hup," she said, "Just sit over there, and I'll be right back."

"Over there" was a 'U' of wide leather furniture punctuated by stark white side tables. She sat and flipped through a folder from one of the tables. It was a portfolio of the firm's best work.

There were ads for everything from shoelaces to vitamins, from roof shingles to organization apps. Saffron let herself get lost in them, wishing she was in the market for a new pair of sneakers rather than a new heart.

When Linda returned with the water bottle, she didn't go back behind her desk as Saffron expected her to. Instead, she sat on the couch next to Saffron.

"Now," she said, and somehow even her compassionate voice still held that note of cheerfulness, "what in the world is wrong?"

Saffron didn't picture herself as someone who spilled her feelings easily, but she didn't stop herself from giving Linda a summary of her heartbreak. Saying it out loud didn't make it hurt any less, she discovered.

Linda was equal parts consolation and dismay. She struck just the right balance of grieving with Saffron and being angry about the whole situation. By the end of their conversation, when Linda asked how she could help, Saffron didn't bother with pretenses.

She told Linda she was the person who had called the day before, and she was here to see if she could find any connection, no matter how small, between this office and Blake Morgan.

Linda, now Saffron's dear friend, pulled her back behind the desk and together they poured over the CRM—the customer relationship management system, looking for anyone like Blake. Then they looked at old employment records, independent consulting contracts, and every document they could find in any file they could discover.

The clock read 4:48 when Saffron heard voices coming down the hall behind the glass doors to her right.

"Your boss?" she asked Linda.

Linda nodded, her eyes wide, and Saffron realized her new friend could be in serious trouble for having Saffron back here. Knowing she couldn't make it around the big desk and over to the waiting area before they came in, Saffron scrambled directly over the desk instead. She made it to the couch and snatched the portfolio just in time to make a reasonable impression of composed waiting.

The two men nodded to Linda and walked out.

It was only then, as Saffron's heartbeat returned to normal, that she realized what she was looking at. On the page in front of her, behind a glossy page protector, was an ad with a blue background and a single rose in the center. Only it wasn't an ordinary rose. It was a rose made of berry-red dinner plates.

The *plates* were the *petals*.

Saffron remembered then. The morning after her kidnapping. The drive to Uwē Beach. Blake's best campaign. He had used anagrams, he'd said. This was his most significant account. She gripped the portfolio and walked over to the desk.

"Linda," she said, "I know that in a minute your bosses are going to be streaming through here, and I truly, truly don't want you to get in any trouble. But I need to ask you one more question: who designed this ad?"

Linda looked at it, squinted, then typed on her keyboard and stared at her computer screen. She let out a long sigh. "I'm sorry again, Saffron. No Blake Morgan here. The Petals and Plates campaign was headed up by Kaleb Gorman, one of our junior associates here."

Saffron couldn't let this go. It was too coincidental. "Wait, he works here *now*? Currently?"

"Right. But he's not in today," Linda looked at her screen, "or you could ask him what he knows about this person."

Something was tickling at the back of Saffron's mind. "Linda, can you tell me what Mr. Gorman looks like?"

Linda waved a hand toward the wall of photos. "You can see for yourself. The junior associates are the third row down."

Saffron crossed the room, her head feeling light and floaty from the emotional ups and downs of the day. And there he was. Third row down, sixth picture over: Blake Morgan, Rachel's new husband, with a plaque under his picture that said, "Kaleb Gorman."

It was Saffron's turn to say, "What in the world?"

Linda was at her elbow, and she told her about this striking turn of events.

"Something's fishy here," Saffron told her. "Look, I need one more favor."

And, as Linda went to her computer to find an address and phone number for Mr. Gorman, advertising genius, Saffron studied the man she knew as Blake Morgan.

It was his eyes that struck her first. Maybe because she'd never seen them in person before, or maybe because his photo was hung right at eye level, but mostly because they were the exact color of the sand at sunrise. When the seven other people she'd ever seen with that eye color flashed through her mind, she stopped on the little boy she'd met two days ago on the beach. His eyes were this shade. This. Exact. Shade.

• • • •

SAFFRON WAS NOT FAMILIAR with the rules of a stakeout. Mostly, she'd seen movies where people sat in high-tech vans, ate donuts, and watched their targets on banks of tiny screens.

This was different. She was sitting at a bus stop directly across the street from the address Linda had given her. She could see, in the front yard, the two boys from the beach playing tag, and a woman—a weary-looking woman—sitting on the lanai steps talking on the phone.

Saffron could hear that the woman was holding off a creditor, and doing an admirable job, Saffron thought. When she hung up, she called to the boys to come for supper.

"What about Daddy?" the older boy—the one with his father's eyes—called, looking hopefully down the street.

"I'm sorry, hun," his mother said, "he won't be home tonight."

At their protests, she held up her hands, "Listen, he's got a really big account at work that he has to finish up."

"But he's *always* gone," the littler boy howled.

"Just for the last few weeks," their mother said. "And a couple more, then, he says, he might not have to go back at all!"

The boys cheered as they bounced past their mother. "Can we call him before bed?"

"Sure. He may not be able to talk to you, because he's so busy. But he'll love to hear your message." The woman stood on the lanai, gazing down the street for several minutes until she, too, turned and went into the house.

Saffron rode a bus to the next stop, then circled back around to her car on foot. She sat in the driver's seat and used her phone to go to the dating site Rachel had told her about.

It wasn't hard to find the "Flags of Fame" wall, where she searched for Rachel and found the page devoted to their courtship. From there, she clicked into Blake's profile.

Sitting in her car as the sun went down, Saffron half-hoped she was wrong. Maybe they were just look-alikes, or maybe she was overstating their resemblance. After all, half of Blake's face was always hidden by those sunglasses, so she could be filling in information that wasn't really there.

But a quick scroll through his photos told her they were one and the same. In fact, one of his photos was taken in front of the house where she'd just seen his children playing.

As she let the truth sink in, Saffron glanced at the name at the top of the page, and everything became clear.

Blake Morgan

Kaleb Gorman

The king of anagrams. That's what Blake had called himself. And apparently, they weren't just for selling products. When selling a new version of himself to Rachel, he'd used his old strategy.

Blake was an anagram of *Kaleb* and *Morgan* was an anagram of *Gorman*.

Now that she saw the same letters in the names, Saffron couldn't *stop* seeing the scheme he'd used. Just shake up the life you have now and rearrange it into something different.

She saw the pictures of the horse ranch, of the bank, and a quick search showed her he'd gotten them from the internet. She needed to tell Rachel, but Rachel wouldn't answer her calls or her texts. Saffron swiped through a few more photos. She stopped at one of them and stared for a long moment. Was that what she thought it was? She cracked the window and let in some of the sweet island air, then zoomed in on the photo. She held her breath and squinted at her screen. In the photo, Blake—or Kaleb—was at what looked like a beach barbeque. He held a can in one hand and a hot dog in the other. He was smiling in an aloha shirt and shorts. And around his neck, peeking through above the top button of his shirt, was a lava rock carving in the shape of a fish.

CHAPTER 16

T hough she looked all over town for Rachel and Blake, she had no luck locating them. Finally, she stopped in at the police station and filled Bradley in on what she'd discovered about the groom.

"Ah. I wondered why he'd left again," Bradley said, reaching for the phone on his desk.

It was a short conversation with Honolulu PD, but they said they'd go around and see if he was at his residence or at the ad agency. Bradley said he'd been having trouble finding Rachel, too, and Saffron had no luck the rest of that night or the next rainy morning tracking her down.

Rachel still wasn't answering her calls or her texts, and Saffron was nearly wild with worry. If Blake was not who he said he was, if he was deceiving Rachel to get the money, what happened if he found out she wasn't going to give it to him?

She had one hope to catch Rachel—the traumatized bride was holding a memorial service for her sister at Iki Bay. The Hawaiian word in the bay's name meant little, and it was a tiny, peaceful place alongside the road. Saffron didn't know if she would actually approach Rachel at that solemn time, but she could at least see if she was there and verify that Rachel was still okay.

Her phone rang—the explosive chicken dance—while she was dropping off her last egg delivery at the Paradise Market.

The Honolulu police had no luck finding the slippery anagrammer either, but his family was pretty surprised to see them. For now, Bradley said, they'd just have to wait until he turned up.

Tale and Baruti had sensed from her shining eyes and trembling lip that she was in no mood for being teased about her love life, so they'd offered more warmth than cheer this morning, and they promised to keep an eye out for the groom, too.

It was overcast and drizzly. Saffron huddled into a light jacket as she went back to her car. She missed Keahi, missed his strength and clear thinking. She wanted to talk to him, wanted him to comfort her in this confusion and pain as he had comforted her in so many others. But that wasn't his role in her life anymore, and the pain was hers alone to carry. She wondered if it was raining in Boston, too.

When the egg deliveries were done, Saffron drove to the Piscine Lodge. She had been so wrapped up in her investigation and in her trip down to the ad agency, that she hadn't taken time yesterday to finish cleaning up from the party. Now, tidying up in the quiet, dusty old place, she tried to hold her tears at bay and not think of Keahi.

She was always surprised at guests' ingenuity. Rather than face the inconvenience of finding a trash can for their napkin or bread crust, they often found unusual places to stick them. Today, she found programs with the Letoa's smiling faces stuck in plants and rolled into the wooden scrollwork of the chairs. She found half-eaten cake in two fake plants and a glass of punch perched atop one of the thick picture frames on the lodge member's wall. Saffron saw with relief that that was the only frame on the long wall that was empty. At least the punch couldn't have destroyed a historic photo.

She had to reach high and remove the glass carefully, as it was one she'd borrowed from Fumi, and she also didn't want it to spill on the photos that lined the wall.

She took a moment to peer at the pictures again, looking at the serious faces of the Honorable Piscine Order as she walked along. Many of the photos were black and white, and a glaring smudge on each of them caught her eye.

Stepping closer, Saffron saw what she had not seen before: every one of them had a carved fish necklace like the one she'd been carrying.

In the newer photos, the colored ones, Saffron could see the fish better. It didn't take long to recognize that they were carved in the shape of their namesake fish—each one a different species, but the same stylized look that she'd seen before.

So the necklace likely belonged to a member of the Lodge. And maybe if she could figure out who it was, she could figure out why Dorah had been carrying it when she died.

Saffron suddenly felt the emptiness of the lodge around her. She would likely never have a better reason to snoop around here than she had right now. She decided to take advantage of that.

The big main floor led to a wide staircase that took Saffron to the basement. In it were several smaller meeting rooms, a lounge area with chairs and a television that looked as if it had been there for decades, and, finally, an office.

The office, like the rest of the lodge, was open. Saffron went in and sifted carefully through some stacks of papers on the desk. They were dusty and brittle as if they'd lain undisturbed a long time.

There was a plaque that said "Secretary," and a couple of filing cabinets.

As Saffron leafed through various folders in the cabinets, she found several types of documents. There were membership records, including snapshots of the initiation fish for each member. Saffron spent a while looking at all the unusual types of fish. She tried to see if the members had any resemblance to their namesakes, and in some cases, the answer was yes.

There were accounting files, showing the members' dues and donations over the years, and any disbursements of those funds. The balance was substantial, but there were relatively few withdrawals. Some of the payments were to local schools or businesses. After looking through several files, Saffron noticed a striking trend. All the records seemed to stop about five years ago. There were no more applications, no more disbursements of funds, no more dues. There were also no more meeting minutes and no more flyers for ballroom dance night or potluck Friday. That matched with what Violet had told her: that the only people left visiting the lodge were three or four old men that scheduled the building and occasionally played cards there—it seemed this chapter was mostly defunct.

Except that Saffron sensed it wasn't. There were other signs: fresh ink on the rubber stamps in the drawer, a shiny new lock on one of the filing cabinets, and, of course, the application she'd seen at Dorah's house. Someone was operating the Maika'i Chapter of the Honorable Piscine Order without the knowledge of its founding members, and Saffron wondered why.

She had to talk to Eke and find out who had commissioned the fish necklace. Maybe it could lead her to more information.

For now, she had to stop investigating and finish cleaning up this lodge. She turned away from the photos, wondering what secrets lay in her own snapshots.

• • • •

WHEN SAFFRON WALKED into Barkadoodle, she was more than a little surprised by Echo's enthusiastic greeting. The big bird flapped immediately over to Saffron's shoulder and said "Pretty Girl" three times just to be sure Saffron heard.

In the middle of that, Saffron was trying to have a conversation with Eke and Bernie.

"I was just wondering," she said, "Eke, you said that the necklace I showed you was commissioned. Would you mind telling me who wanted it made?"

"Sure," he said, "I don't think it's a secret. The Picene Lodge commissioned it."

"Really?" Echo flapped away, and Saffron moved closer to the counter.

"Yeah. They message me sometimes and have me do fish for them."

This was just what Saffron needed to know. "Could you tell me who you worked with, particularly?"

He shook his head. "Nope. It was just an email from their generic account. No name. They just transferred the money and never gave me a contact. They said they'd pick up in person on that particular day, but then it got stolen. In fact, I feel really guilty that they didn't get it after they paid me, but I couldn't find out who to transfer it back to."

"So he spent it," Bernie laughed. "That made him feel better."

"I've been working on a replacement," Eke said, waving a hand toward the counter, in case the cops won't give me that one back. I won't charge the buyer for it since they didn't get the first one."

Suddenly, Echo was back, landing with a thud on Saffron's shoulder. Saffron was about to protest when Echo dropped something into her hand. "For you! For you!" Echo said lightly.

When Saffron opened her hand, she gasped. In it was another fish necklace, half-formed from a lump of lava rock. She held it up.

Eke swore. "Echo! Stop doing that!" he snatched it back from Saffron. "This is the one I'm working on. But stickytalons here can't keep from swiping it."

"Oh?" Saffron led them to keep speaking.

"Yeah. She steals my stuff all the time," he said, "If I have to get my hands into the tanks and take off my watch, she steals it. If I lay down my sunglasses or my cellphone, Echo's off with it. I'm telling you, she makes for a hostile working environment."

"Call the union," Bernie challenged.

But Saffron was less worried about what Echo stole than what she did with what she took. "So, how about this idea? Instead of Milo stealing the necklace, what if Echo stole it and gave it to him, just like she gave me this one?"

"Hmmm," Bernie said, "Sounds plausible."

"And maybe he thought it was a legitimate gift and took it home," Saffron finished.

"Yeah," Eke said, "that makes more sense anyway, because why would Milo steal something from here? He could just get it with all the credit he's got from bringing us awesome specimens."

Saffron was only half-listening. She was watching the big parrot, who had flapped off and fetched a small treasure chest aquarium decoration, which she'd also given to Saffron. Saffron watched, reconstructing Milo's visit to the pet store in her mind—he'd come in, brought his boxes full of bags full of fish, stopped at the desk to record what he'd brought in, then Echo had brought him the necklace. He'd thought it was for him and had taken it home to Dorah.

Only Dorah had known what it was. As a hopeful Piscine member, she was familiar with the rites and rituals. She would have recognized the significance of such a necklace. So she had kept it. But why? And why would she have stopped to grab it when she was likely fleeing for her life?

• • • •

DRIVING HOME, SAFFRON passed Iki Bay. Though Dorah's body was still at the medical examiner's office, today they would lay her memory to a rest she had never found in life.

A little group stood at the water's edge. Saffron was partly relieved not to see Blake, and partly disappointed that he was still missing. It would be hard to arrest him and question him if he didn't show up. Saffron recognized a local Kahu—or minister—standing at the head of the group, draped in leis and bright fabric. Rachel was there, and Dylan. That was all. Though a few tourists meandered on the beach, only three people were there to celebrate Dorah's life.

Saffron watched for a moment. The mourners were pulling flowers off their leis and scattering them in the waves at their feet. It was a calming sight. The bright petals—the colors of tangerine, strawberries, and peaches—rose and fell on the cobalt waves, some of the tiny spots of color sweeping out beyond the breakers and toward the open ocean.

From the corner of her eye, Saffron saw a still figure at the upper edge of the beach. Watching the solemn proceedings intently, camera raised, was Mrs. Jones.

Saffron's annoyance with the woman flared again. Had she no decency? Who took pictures of a funeral service? Though the Hawaiian way of saying goodbye was unique and beautiful, it wasn't just another tourist attraction. Did she not understand that these were real people, real *grieving* people, who were saying goodbye to someone for the last time? Saffron hoped with all her heart that Rachel didn't notice the cranky old woman.

Saffron backed out, leaving the mourners to do their difficult work. She sent Bradley a text telling him Blake was still missing.

When Saffron drove into her parking spot behind her house, she saw a familiar station wagon. Nik was in a chair on the lanai. His golden skin was warm in the light of the setting sun.

When she met him on the porch, he immediately reached for her arm. Lifting her sleeve, he ran light fingertips over her Hawaiian tattoo, watching her face intently.

"How is it today?"

Saffron smiled. "It's actually great. I have a little ache, but not too much."

"Do you feel like going out tonight?"

Saffron winced, "I'm not sure I'll be up for snorkeling for a little while," she started.

Nik interrupted her. "No, no, not snorkeling. A party. A beach blast. Eke's having a hukilau," he let his fingers trail down her arm to take her hand in his. "Good food," he said teasingly, "and good company."

Saffron didn't feel like a party, but she didn't feel like being alone, either. Birds were crying in the monkeypod tree above them, and the ocean waves made a lonesome sound tonight.

Nik seemed to sense her conflict. She saw the slight color shift in his face that signaled his concern: a pale bluish cast around his mouth, and reddish cheeks and forehead. She loved that he was anxious about her feelings.

"Is everything okay?" he asked, giving her hand a little squeeze.

Saffron didn't know how to answer that. Everything was not okay. Keahi wasn't officially hers anymore, if he ever had been, and Rachel was in danger from someone who, if not a murderer, was at least a lying creep. But neither of those things could be changed right now, and a kind, handsome surfer was offering to take Saffron to a party. That wasn't bad. The hens had produced a bumper crop of eggs, which had brought in extra cash along with what Rachel had paid her to plan the wedding.

When she answered Nik, she was honest. "Everything's not okay, but some things are."

A blue tinge mixed with the red in his cheeks and forehead, giving his tan skin a slightly plummy undertone and telling Saffron that he was still concerned, but also a little confused. She made herself smile. She wasn't ready to tell him about Keahi, and she was weary of worrying about the strange situation that had haunted her since she'd gotten in Milo's car. "You know what? I'd love a hukilau. Let me get changed and we'll go."

At this, the blue faded and Nik flushed the currant color of happiness. Seeing it made Saffron smile for real.

• • • •

THE BRIGHT SOUND OF a ukulele wound through the underbrush and reached Saffron and Nik long before they reached the little stretch of beach where the party was. Saffron could hear voices: singing, laughing. Torches tossed flickering light through the dense foliage and along the twisting trail.

She'd worn her lightest dress—a linen sundress the color of fresh-cut pineapple—to ward off the oppressive heat and humidity the week's rains had left behind. It felt good to be out, good to be walking hand-in-hand with Nik, leaving her worries behind her. The torches on the beach cast flickering shadows the color of warm caramel across the sand.

She let herself be drawn by the singing, by the sight of the snatches of indigo ocean that lay beneath the moonless sky. She let the smell of kalua pork—the sweet signature dish of the islands—lead her.

And when they reached the half-circle of palm logs and stones where the music came from, she felt new.

Eke was there, raking coals from the fire into a small pit on the side. Saffron wondered what that would be for—the pork, she could smell, was already cooked.

Saffron sat down next to Nik on the end of the log closest to the sea. The air tasted like laughter, and she couldn't stop herself from singing along with the current song, even though it was in Hawaiian and she knew she was just guessing at most of the words. She felt the beat of the pahu drums in the air, through the log, in the soles of her feet on the sand. It was the kind of music that moved you, made you want to move. Around the circle, people were leaning together, talking, telling stories.

Nik draped an arm around Saffron's shoulders and handed her a can of soda. Cracking it open, she glanced up just as he leaned down for a kiss.

Before Saffron had come to the islands, she hadn't known how many kinds of kisses there were. Reggie, her only serious relationship, was a Washington DC kisser—procedural and a little pretentious. All of Reggie's kisses were pretty much the same.

This one was playful and light, a peck that tasted like the orange soda Nik was drinking. It made her heart flutter, and her hand find his.

He was still looking down at her when the fist flew between them and caught Nik on the jaw with a harsh *whap*. Nik tumbled backward off the log and landed in the sand.

Saffron spun and looked up into the face of Vernon Kaliki, one of Keahi's oldest friends.

Nik was on his feet before Saffron could scramble to hers. Suddenly, the half-ring of cheerful onlookers looked more like spectators at a prizefight.

"You trying to move in on Keahi's wahini?" Vernon was smaller than Nik, but built, and he was not holding back.

Nik wiped blood from his mouth, bobbing lightly on his feet as he advanced toward Vernon. "I don't see Doctor Kekoa around here anywhere."

"That doesn't matter. You know they've been dating."

"Hey!" Saffron pushed in between them, "Stop it!"

Vernon looked at her with the accusation she'd expected to see in Mano's eyes that first day. She remembered how Mano had chosen, instead, understanding and gentleness. When Vernon blurted out, "What you gonna tell Keahi?" Saffron suddenly felt tears springing to her eyes.

She was conscious of all the eyes on her. She reached for Vernon's arm, pulling her face close to his, keeping her voice as steady as she could manage. "Thanks for being a good friend to him. We broke up." Her voice cracked in the middle of it. He looked at her incredulously for a minute, then over to Nik, who stood visibly vibrating with the anticipation of throwing a punch.

"Oh," Vernon said, and Saffron saw pale green embarrassment creeping across his nose and under his eyes. He turned to Nik, holding his hands wide in an apology. The two walked off together toward the waves, leaving Saffron standing in the middle of the circle alone.

CHAPTER 17

Nik was much quieter after he came back, but he put an arm around Saffron's shoulders and sang along a little with the song that had started up.

They'd only been sitting for a few minutes, though, when a call came from the water's edge, and nearly the whole group was on its feet. The music stopped abruptly, and the guests all moved down toward the ocean. Nik held Saffron's hand as they made their way to the edge with the crowd.

Before she knew it, Saffron was wading into the water. The surf was warm and playful, and someone handed her a wet, slimy handful of what felt like a net. Together the whole party pulled the net up onto the beach. Leaves were woven into its rough ropes, and in between them were the wriggling, shining bodies of fish.

These were not reef fish, rather broad meaty eating fish, and Saffron spent the next hour watching Eke, Vernon, and the others prepare and cook them over the coals on the beach. When they were finished, everyone had a plate heaped with mac salad, kalua pork, and the fresh fish.

Nik had shaken off the unfortunate altercation from earlier, and his cheer had returned. He was telling Saffron about the upcoming Surf championships being hosted near the surf shop where he worked when Saffron heard a snatch of conversation from behind her that pulled her attention away from Nik as effectively as Vernon had earlier.

"It was a shadow diver," someone was saying, "someone who the akua had taken for their sacrifice before, whose spirit is trapped at the waterfall forever."

The term "shadow diver" would have been enough, but the mention of the akua—the major spirits that inhabited the island—secured her focus. Ever since she'd come to Hawaii, she'd seen enough unexplained phenomena to suspect other forces at work than those she could see. She'd had some experience with ancestral spirits, the 'aumakua, and she'd felt, like many others, the raw power of the island. She had read several books on spirits and demigods and had discussed them with Mano for hours sometimes while he carved or she gathered eggs.

She tried not to feel the pang of anxiety and sadness at the thought of telling Mano about her and Keahi's conversation. She pushed his smiling face from her mind and listened harder.

She wasn't the only one. Most of the circle had quieted down to hear the story, and when it was finished, a guy Saffron had seen surfing with Nik told a story of the menehune, tiny people who roamed the island at night building incredible structures and causing various kinds of mischief.

Time slipped by, and the fire began to die down. Someone started telling another story, this one about a ghostly battleground on the North Shore, where an ancient battle had taken place. A girl with firelight in her eyes told the tale. She claimed that the people who lost their lives still wandered, looking for the peace their people never found.

Saffron shivered in spite of herself, and Nik pulled her closer, smiling. Saffron told herself there was nothing to be afraid of. She supposed these were no more than the ghost stories kids on the mainland told around their campfires, of bigfoot and lost teens, of unexplained disappearances and haunted hotels. But somehow they seemed more plausible out here, with the salty breeze ruffling the hem of her light dress and the dark wall of bushes shielding the secluded beach from civilization.

The dark night didn't help either. The only light was what came from the fire and the torches. It was an eerie light that left shadows dancing at the edge of Saffron's vision. The sound of the waves, usually calming, seemed only to cover more sinister sounds that might be rumbling out in the bushes.

Eke waved off the story. "That's nothing. What can a ghost do? Scare you? Walk around trying to catch your attention? What you should be afraid of is the curses—the things the gods have left behind to punish humans for our trespasses."

The circle quieted. "There's the drowning waterfall, you know, like you were saying, where the akua waits for sacrifices," he waved to the first storyteller. "There's the crying tree, where people come looking for a person they can swear is crying, but once they enter the circle of the tree's branches, they are never seen again."

It's just a story. Saffron told herself. But Eke's voice modulated down another key, and suddenly it didn't seem like he was telling just a story.

"None of those are anything, though, compared to the poison pools." He drew out the last two words, then paused. Nobody asked him to go on. It was as if they were hoping he wouldn't. Saffron wondered briefly if that was out of fear about the story or out of fear of kapu—the taboo surrounding things that were forbidden to discuss. She had learned about it from Keahi's family.

But Eke went on anyway. "There was, long ago, a shark god who married a beautiful human woman. She gave birth to a child with a gaping shark's mouth on his back—but the shark's mouth was toothless. She kept him wrapped in a cloak to hide it. The shark god told her to never, never feed the child any meat, but as he grew he one day got hold of some—" here Eke took a big bite of kalua pork and chewed it dramatically. "Immediately, the shark's mouth on his back grew horrible teeth, and from that moment on, his appetite was insatiable."

"Like Vernon's!" Someone called from the other side of the circle. Because Vernon was, at that moment, taking a huge bite out of a grilled fish he was holding by its head and its tail, everyone chuckled. But it was a nervous kind of laugh, a tense and uncomfortable sound that didn't make the shark story any less unnerving. In fact, the forced laughter made it more so.

"Many villagers disappeared before they realized that the shark god's son was a monstrous killer. They caught him, tore him to pieces, and burned what was left, then scattered the ashes in a tidal pool so that he could never, ever return."

Eke was into the story now. Saffron could see the red tones of excitement in his cheeks and nose. The breeze ruffled his hair. He moved in that smooth and graceful way around the circle. "But that's not the worst part. Little did they know that the shark god's destruction would live on. In the pool grew strange creatures, and from them seeped a potent poison. If the villagers dipped their blades in the water, then contact with them caused horrible, torturous death." The word hung heavy in the circle. "The pool spread it's poison to the other islands, finding pools on them that lay in plain sight and infecting them with the curse. The poison waited in them until someone stumbled upon their cursed waters and spread the shark god's destruction again. Thus, he continues to consume the human race one at a time, to feed his voracious appetite until this very day."

A heavy silence hung around the circle. Saffron's wounded shoulder hurt from pressing it into Nik's chest so hard, and she eased away a little as someone said, "I've never heard of a poison pool," But there was a slight tremor in the voice that told Saffron that the story had been convincing enough.

"Think what you want. It's true whether you believe it or not," Eke said. "Believe me, I know. My uncle stumbled onto one of those pools, and he died a day later."

"No way. There's no pools like that on this island."

"There sure is," Eke was losing his crowd, and Saffron could tell that he didn't like it. "I know where."

"No you don't, brah," this voice was different. It was not light, scared, or teasing. It was quiet and solemn. Saffron sensed in it the wisdom of someone who knew, too, but didn't want it said aloud. She couldn't see the speaker, but his words definitely erased the last of the curiosity.

People were losing interest. They were standing and stretching, embracing, picking up their soda cans and tossing their paper plates into the fire. The party was breaking up.

"I do know," Eke said, "my uncle, brah, he was messed up from that pool, man. He was coughing and shaking, and he couldn't even see straight. Nearly walked into the ocean. And then he couldn't breathe. Don't tell me it's not true, I've totally seen what that poison can do."

Nik was turning away from the fire, gathering things up, reaching for Saffron's hand. She was still half-listening to Eke. "I'm telling you, it's off the Breadfruit Road, way out there by the old bunker. My uncle died." Saffron saw the moment that Eke gave up trying to convince people. A girl about his age had come over to tell him how scary his story was and he shifted his focus.

But Saffron kept hearing his words in her mind. Over and over. Poison pool. Coughing. Shaking.

"Nik," she said, catching his hands, "Is tomorrow your day off?"

"Yeah."

"And do you know where the Breadfruit Road is?"

"Sure," he said, "Why?"

She looked him in the eye. "Because tomorrow I need you to take me to the poison pool."

• • • •

THE NEXT DAY SAFFRON learned that the Breadfruit Road was really more of a Breadfruit Path. They left Nik's station wagon a half-mile in and walked the rest of the way to the beach. When they broke out onto the narrow strip of sand, they found themselves on a little rise that sloped gently down to a vast stretch of flat black lava rock. On its far side, the ocean lapped at the stone, breaking in lacy sprays up and over the rock with each incoming wave. In the stone were indentions, hollows, and dips that glowed like lapis lazuli in the morning sunlight. They were full of water, some of them five or six feet deep, some bare inches.

Deep blues and teals and aquas played in their depths, and golden reflections danced on their surfaces. Tide pools.

Saffron's heart beat a little faster. "Do you think one of those is the poison pool?" She asked.

"From what you said you heard Eke say, I'd say so," Nik said. This is the right place. Look."

He pointed to the far side of the beach, where the rocky mountain climbed out of the water. If Saffron hadn't been looking for it, she never would have seen the bunker, but knowing it was there helped her to pick out the unnaturally straight lines, the gap in the foliage, the massive cement structure underneath the vines and fallen trees. This was the place.

Together, they climbed down the little stretch of sand.

"Which one do you think it is?" Saffron asked, hesitating as they stepped onto the lava rock. What if the story was true? She must at least think it was possible, or she wouldn't be out here. And if it was possible, then one of these pools could hold certain death.

She peered into the first pool. As long as a school bus and twice as wide, it was the color of peacock feathers. In its crystalline depths lay starfish of every color: lime green ones whose legs were tipped in cherry red, bubble gum pink ones, grapefruit orange ones, and blueberry ones with vibrant amethyst nubs on their legs. It was disorienting, looking at a field of stars below her instead of above. Like the world had become inverted and the new night sky was technicolored.

There were crabs in the pool, and coral. There were stubby alien eyes like she'd seen the scientists fogging with the 'ahuhu compound. What had Jeff said? "There's a whole world of remedies and poisons in the ocean. And a lot of the seafaring cultures

have known about them for centuries. We're just catching up."
She would bet that he and Allie would believe the story of the
poison pool. She peered at the alien eyes. What had they called
them? Palythoas, a soft coral that grew in a colony. These were
stunning: a whole bouquet of neon bullseyes in brilliant watermelon, sunflower, and chartreuse shades. Their multihued disks,
surrounded by waving tentacles, made small mounds across the
bottom of the pool.

Other pools held different palys. Some were dove-colored
with violet centers, some whole pools looked like psychedelic
dance floors, with fluorescent tangerines and lemons.

"These are incredible," Nik murmured, peering into another
pool. "I've never seen so many of these things or so much varia-
tion between them."

"They're spectacular," Saffron said. "When I see things like
this, it makes me understand why people keep aquariums in their
houses. I just want to sit and look at these colors." She took
out her phone, and, balancing on the rocks, held it a few inches
above the perfectly clear water. She shot a couple of pictures, trying not to fall in or drop her phone.

Saffron was careful not to touch the water in any of the
pools, Eke's story still rang in her ears. But honestly, none of
the pools seemed terribly dangerous. Little fish darted around in
them, crabs took their lazy, sideways routes along the bottoms of
the pools, and the strange palythoa polyps swayed softly and rippled their eyelash-like tentacles. It was all very peaceful and hardly seemed deadly to Saffron.

Caught up in the exploration, she wandered from pool to
pool. She glanced up, noticing that she was nearing the edge
of the tidal pools, where the big bunker loomed above on the

mountainside. The last pool at the edge of the lava rock was less impressive than the others. It was smaller, about the size of two cars side by side, and the lava rock in it shifted from the more familiar charcoal gray color of the rest of the pools to a drab reddish brown that Saffron had seen in dead leaves and old blood. The palythoas in that pool hardly held her attention, either. Instead of vibrant shades of varied colors she'd seen in the black pools, these were a dingy sage green and pale brown, with a fine spray of tentacles around them that appeared to have a slightly bluish tint. The tentacles made it seem like there was a slight haze over each cluster. They sat in grumpy little clusters on the red lava rock of the pool. Waving between them was a slimy looking moss. Saffron leaned closer to see if it was seaweed or something else. There were fewer creatures in this pool, but the light brown palythoas were abundant. It was there, when she was peering at the boring palys, that she heard her name on the breeze.

She looked over at Nik, who was a few pools away. He wasn't saying anything. She stood and looked beyond him, out onto the ocean past the edge of the lava rock, and saw a canoe slicing through the water toward her. In it were Mano and Akoni.

Saffron's cheeks grew hot. Did Mano know that she and Keahi had broken up? Was he coming to address it with her? She felt a knot in her stomach as she wondered whether she and Mano could still be friends if she weren't dating Keahi. Mano was her first friend here in the islands, and she didn't want to give him up, but she knew how much he loved his grandson.

His voice became clearer as he and Akoni came closer, and Saffron's heart dropped when she heard the desperation in her friend's voice. She scrambled across the lava rock toward him, one thought in her mind: what if something had happened to Keahi.

As the canoe came up and Mano jumped out, Saffron was caught up in a tight hug.

"Are you okay?" he asked, stepping back and looking at her. "What are you doing here?"

Saffron's mind was spinning. She didn't answer him, but asked her own question, "Is Keahi okay? You look terrified."

He made a chiding sound. "I'm terrified for *you*. Do you even know where you are?"

Akoni was out of the canoe now, and he'd called Nik over. As Nik approached, Akoni began to speak to him in Hawaiian. Saffron didn't understand all the words, but she knew enough of them and knew the tone. Akoni was giving Nik a harsh reprimand.

"We—we came out to find a pool they were talking about last night," she said. "A poison pool." The horror on her friend's face made her talk faster, "But these aren't poison, they're stunning. No, no," she laid a hand on Mano's arm, "really. They're all clear and mostly really beautiful. There's just this one red pool that's not too interesting, but the rest are—"

Mano touched his fingertips to his forehead. It seemed, to Saffron, a gesture of anxiety. "That is the poison pool," he said, "Did you touch the water?"

"What? No, no, of course not. But it really wasn't that interesting," she said.

"Saffron. People have died from just being in this area. They've died horrible deaths from swimming in that pool."

She tried to explain, "Are you sure that's it? I didn't see anything."

Mano closed his eyes and shook his head, "You don't know." He said, "there are things you can't see with your eyes."

Saffron wanted to keep arguing, to assure him that there was nothing dangerous here, but she suddenly and powerfully remembered the octopus she'd seen at the reef her first day snorkeling. It was there all along, but so perfectly camouflaged that she couldn't see it. A clammy feeling crept across the back of her neck as she realized that the little fish and crustaceans the octopus prayed on couldn't see it either. They'd been skittering along the reef without any sense of the danger they were in.

Mano's eyes were on hers. She closed her mouth and nodded to show that she understood.

"We need to go now," he said, taking her elbow and turning toward the canoe.

"What about Nik's car?" Saffron said.

"I'll come back out here with the Kahu and get it later." Mano walked across the lava rock to the canoe, and Saffron followed him.

"The Kahu?" Saffron wondered what the spiritual guide would have to do with it until she saw Nik and Akoni next to the canoe.

Akoni was standing near the water, facing Nik. He was holding half a coconut shell and raising his voice in what Saffron recognized as pule—a prayer.

As she watched Akoni dip fresh water from the sea, as she listened to him pray, she realized the severity of what they'd done. This was a cleansing ceremony. Mano leaned close and gave Saffron a summary translation, for which she was grateful.

"This is to remove kapu—taboo," Mano explained. "He is asking the gods for pardon for you and Nik, explaining that you are young and foolish," here Mano looked at her pointedly, and Saffron felt the weight of his words, "and that you need forgiveness and cleansing and protection from the spirits you may have disrespected."

Akoni sprinkled the water across Nik as he continued the pule. Saffron heard the name of a god she recognized and the words *limu make*, which Mano translated for her as "seaweed of death." Saffron felt trembly.

When Akoni was done, he gestured Nik into the canoe and then performed the same ritual for Saffron, Mano, and himself. They were all cleansed before they were allowed in the boat.

Saffron felt blessed, and she felt the very real weight of what they'd done. If Mano believed so strongly in the danger of this place, then so did she. She offered a little pule of her own as they rowed away. The tidal pools grew smaller and smaller behind them.

They sat in silence as Nik helped Akoni row into the ocean. Saffron and Mano sat in the middle of the canoe, facing each other, with Akoni behind Mano and Nik behind Saffron, also facing the center and each other. Saffron could see that they were moving parallel with the shoreline, probably heading to Akoni's house on the beach.

When the two old men began to converse again, in low tones, Saffron took that as a cue that it was alright to speak.

"I'm sorry," she said, "I didn't consider the seriousness of going there. I guess I wanted to know what it looked like."

The old men listened, and Mano responded. "We all make mistakes, moʻopuna. Just remember and don't make the same one a second time."

"I won't," she said.

"Why did you go there?" Akoni asked, shaking his head as if such a thing were inexplicable.

"I was just curious if something in the water could truly be as poisonous as they said."

Mano gestured at her arm. "It looks like you've already had an encounter with the poisons of the sea," he said. "But if you are still curious, let me answer your question. Yes. Poisons beyond your imagination lay in the pools of the *limu make*."

CHAPTER 18

B radley was at Saffron's door the next morning.

"Problem," he said, holding out another evidence bag. She took it. Inside was the bottle of cyanide.

She met Bradley's gaze with a question in her eyes.

"It's not cyanide," Bradley said.

"What?"

"It's not cyanide. In fact, the lab has no idea what it is. It doesn't match anything they have on record."

With shaking hands, Saffron rolled the bottle out of the bag and into her palm. The label clearly read Sodium Cyanide. Except. She held it up and looked closer. There were some smudged letters above that, and below it—her heart stopped—three square fish stacked diagonally.

"Any idea what it could be?"

Limu make—seaweed of death—flashed through Saffron's mind, but she didn't say it. Could her friends at the Reef People Coalition be making poison? They had saved her. And if they were making it, what was it for? And how did Milo get it?

"I don't have an answer," Saffron said, "but I have a lot of questions, and I know who to ask."

• • • •

THE REEF PEOPLE COALITION'S Maikai building was a big cement building formerly used as a warehouse by a local fish company. Saffron was unsure whether the lingering smell was from its previous use or its current one because as a reception-ist led Saffron and Bradley through the big, echoing rooms, Saf-

211

fron saw plenty of tanks containing live fish of all varieties. She assumed that they were part of Allie and Jeff's research.

Indeed, when the receptionist deposited them in Allie's lab, the biochemist was crouched down talking to a large pink fish in a tank on the floor.

Allie immediately stopped what she was doing, jotted an observation on a clipboard, and then turned her attention to Saffron.

"Let's get a look at that urchin sting," Allie said, and Saffron showed her the smudged area. It wasn't aching anymore, and if not for the tattoo and the memory of the searing pain, she might have forgotten about it by now. "It's looking good," Allie said.

"That stuff is magic," Saffron acknowledged.

"You know," Allie said, "we got contract offers from several major retailers in the last couple of days. Apparently, someone sent in a video of us all on the beach to the news stations, and they played the footage all over. We're ramping up production. It's going to fund our other projects for a long time." Her eyes were shining.

Saffron was glad that some good had come out of the news coverage that had destroyed her relationship with Keahi, but she didn't say anything about it.

Bradley cleared his throat and jerked his head slightly. He wanted her to ask about the bottle. He was a busy man, and he didn't waste much time chatting. Saffron held up the bottle, "I have a question, Allie. About this."

Allie's face was neutral. Saffron saw no change in the underlying colors, no cooling of her features to indicate fear or reddening of her cheeks to show that she was happy to see the bottle. If

Saffron had to name the expression Allie wore, she would call it indifference. The researcher took the bottle.

"Sure," she said, "shoot."

Saffron chose her words carefully. She didn't want to jump in with the fact that it had been found at a murder scene. "What is it? Is it sodium cyanide?"

Allie squinted at the bottle. "Hmm. Our ink isn't as waterproof as we thought." She pivoted and snatched her clipboard from the counter. Without excusing herself, she jotted some things down before answering the question.

"See," she pointed to the smudged line of text, "it's smudged out here." Allie crossed the room and opened a high cupboard. As she did so, Saffron exchanged a wide-eyed glance with Bradley—more than a hundred identical bottles were stacked on shelves inside the cupboard. Allie extracted one and brought it over to Saffron. "Here you go. See, above that, where it is smudged out, it should say *'auhuhu compound, substitute for.'*"

"Substitute for," Saffron tried to make sense of that. Then she saw. "Oh. *Substitute for sodium cyanide.*"

"Right. Remember? I told you about the compound we've been working on? The derivation of the chemicals in the 'auhuhu plant?"

"Used to stun fish during collection," Saffron remembered.

"Right. We gave some samples out to local fish collectors for field trials," Allie said. "This is one of those bottles. I can see we need to rethink our ink." She chuckled at her rhyme.

Bradley cut in. "How is it used?"

"Well, the goal was to make it as close to the process some of the fishermen in the Philippines, and other places are already using. So we made it in tablet form. Now, the fishermen take cyanide tablets, crush them into plastic water bottles, shake them up until they dissolve, and then take them out onto the reefs. It's cheap, easy, and relatively effortless. The fishermen don't need special equipment or a lot of time. When you're trying to survive, both time and money matter. They can do it in just a minute and then dive down to puff it on the reef and collect the stunned fish."

A deep voice came from behind them. "Some of the more shady fish dealers actually supply the cyanide tablets to the fishermen without charge. It's despicable." It was Jeff. "Cyanide is murder on our fragile reef systems," Jeff added. He glanced at the bottles as he came around to stand by Allie. "Three square feet of coral is destroyed for every fish collected with cyanide," he said. "Kill the coral, kill the reef. The whole ecosystem falls apart."

Saffron couldn't get enough air. In her mind, she was back in the bay, watching that incredible underwater city. She imagined it empty and barren, desolate without the creatures that made it beautiful.

Allie picked up the dialogue, "And in Sri Lanka, the Philippines, and Indonesia, they're spraying the reefs with it every day. A huge percentage of tropical fish imported into the US are caught using cyanide. Nearly all of them, in fact."

"Why don't they stop it? Make it illegal?"

"It is illegal. But cyanide is nearly impossible to detect," Jeff said. Saffron caught Bradley's eye. That's what they'd said about Dorah. That after a few days, the cyanide couldn't be found. "So how do you enforce the law? We think it's more effective to replace the cyanide with something reef-safe."

Saffron was as impressed with this compound as she had been with the one they'd sprayed on her arm.

"So, is this compound poisonous to humans?" Bradley gestured at the bottle Allie was still holding.

"Not at all," she said proudly. "It only works on fish, and it's not poison. Rather, a mild anesthetic that wears off within minutes."

"It doesn't hurt reefs, invertebrates, humans, birds, or Cnidaria," Jeff added.

"What was that last one, now?" Bradley asked.

"Cnidaria," Jeff clarified, "a type of symmetrical aquatic animals with mouths surrounded by tentacles—think jellyfish, coral, anemones."

Saffron thought of the alien eyes—the palythoas. She was sure they were cnidarians. Before she could say so, though, Bradley asked another question. "So you're saying that the stuff in that bottle could not be used to poison a human being?"

"That's right," Allie said, it's completely harmless."

Bradley sighed. "Alright then, I guess we're done here."

• • • •

THE OCEANSIDE CAFE was having a lunch special, and it was spectacular. Garlic shrimp scampi, swimming in butter, over sweet pineapple rice. Three slices of buttery avocado graced the plate, and beside it, for dessert, grilled banana bread. Saffron dug in, savoring a rare quiet lunch at the popular eatery.

She had been disappointed to learn that the tablets she'd found were not cyanide. That made so much sense. Bradley was going back to the idea that Dorah's death had been an average marital brawl gone wrong, but Saffron had a feeling that it was more. She kept seeing the desk, kept seeing her own name written there: a message, a plea.

Saffron left the cafe and walked down the street. She found herself in jail. Bradley was out on patrol, and the only other staff at the office was the dispatcher/secretary who did the paperwork and answered the phones. She knew Saffron pretty well by now, so when she asked to go back and talk to Milo in the jail, Betsy waved her through.

The jail was old-fashioned, with four cells and a walkway down the middle. It reminded Saffron of her egg house. She sat on a narrow bench that ran the length of the walkway. Milo, in his cell, peered out at her from the edge of his cot.

He seemed calm and pleased to see her. Saffron reminded herself that he was a kidnapper and probably a murderer. Still, she could see in him the defeated posture of the henpecked rooster, and she couldn't help but feel a little sorry for him.

Saffron skipped the chitchat.

"Something's been bothering me, Milo," Saffron said. "A couple of things."

"Okay," he said. He didn't look at her directly. Instead, his gaze swam around in the general direction of her face.

"First of all, did you kill your brother-in-law? Did you kill Rob?"

Milo sighed. "I told the judge I did."

"That's not the same thing. I have a hunch that you didn't, but I can't figure out why anybody would choose to spend more than a decade in prison for something they didn't do."

Milo pressed his lips together.

"She's gone, Milo. You can say whatever you want to say."

He dropped his head back and fixed his eyes on the ceiling. "Not back then, I couldn't."

Saffron stayed still and quiet, letting him ease into his reverie.

"Back then, I didn't say anything."

"Were you protecting Dorah? Did she kill him?"

At this, he looked fiercely at her, "Not Dorah. Leon. Leon killed him."

Saffron kept her voice quiet, though she was reeling. "Tell me what happened, Milo."

Milo closed his eyes. Saffron saw a particular tinge to his face—a soft violet that was, she'd noticed in many people, the color of remembering. He was going back a long time. His voice was small when he spoke.

"Rachel and Rob came for a visit. I liked them. They were so happy, so *nice* to each other."

Saffron remembered that at this time, Milo would have been living with both Dorah and Leon. Both so controlling, manipulative, cruel. His must have been a difficult existence.

"They brought Dylan. He was fascinated with the fish. I loved showing him all the different kinds." Milo opened his eyes and looked at Saffron. "It was the first time I'd really wanted kids. And I told that to Dorah and everybody at lunchtime." He shook his head. "That mean old man wrote the will that afternoon."

Saffron felt his disappointment.

"He told them that afternoon, read out what he'd written, and the strangest thing happened. Instead of them being mad at him, they turned on each other. Dorah told Rachel that he was right, she could never take care of herself—she needed a husband because she was incompetent, and Rachel told her she should never have any kids because she would totally wreck them with her cruelty. They were screaming at each other, and Leon didn't do anything. You know what? I looked over at where he was sitting in the corner by that big lionfish in the tank, and he was . . ." Milo trailed off, then said, very softly, as if the word tasted terrible to him, "smiling."

Saffron could tell the night held unresolved trauma for Milo, and she didn't want to make him go on, but there were still so many questions.

"How did Rob get involved?"

"He couldn't stand the fighting. He tried to break it up. The girls stormed off separately, and luckily Dylan was taking a nap. Just Rob and me and the old man left in the front room." Milo had warmed to the story now, and it poured out of him like he'd been wanting to tell it for a long time.

"Rob challenged Leon about the will—he was always braver than me. He told the old man that it was just cruel to do that, that it would pit the girls against each other's happiness for the rest of their lives."

"What did Leon say to that?"

"He said *he knew* that's what it would do. Then, he started rambling about Lionfish."

Saffron remembered the big fish with the spines she'd seen at Milo and Dorah's house.

"Like you have at your house?"

"That's the one. It's a mean sucker. He was saying how they were going to eventually take over the ocean because they had evolved stronger and stronger and developed all these advantages over other fish, and he said he wanted his daughters to be predators, not prey. That if they were toughened up, nobody could get the best of them. And they could practice by facing off with each other. He said the will would ensure that the stronger of them got the money, whichever one was most determined. And if both of them were, they'd benefit equally. He was obsessed with that stupid lionfish."

Saffron remembered it: sullen, predatory, staring out from its tank. She remembered the vicious spines, the vacant eyes.

"That's what really got Rob in trouble," Milo said, his tone hollow.

"The lionfish?"

"Right. The old man went on so long about it, and totally ignored Rob trying to talk about the damage Leon was doing to his daughters, that Rob just snapped. That was back when I was trying to get into coral propagation, and I had this set of long tools—spatulas, shears, and tweezers, for working in the tanks. He snatched up the feeding stick—the handle was like two feet long, and the end was pointed like a spear. Rob said that not even the Lionfish was invincible, and he lunged for the tank, knocked the top off, and speared that lionfish with the feeding stick."

Saffron was riveted, imagining the scene from all those years ago.

"He left the stick in it and stepped back and looked at me. I knew how he felt. It was like that thing was a symbol of Leon, and it was like striking back at him."

Milo's hands were shaking. There was sweat on his forehead. "But Leon, madder than I ever saw him—and I saw him furious more than once—had this total silence. Instead of panicking, he turned cold, and I saw this cruel look on his face. Rob stood there watching, waiting for the old man to say something. But Leon didn't. He just stood up and walked to the tank. He grabbed the end of the stick with the lionfish was still speared on the end."

Milo was talking fast now, wrapped up in the memory. His voice was trembling along with his hands.

"And he pulled that fish out of the water. I thought he was going to try to save it. But he pulled it out, took two steps toward my brother-in-law, and swung it directly into Rob's chest."

Saffron gasped. Her arm burned where the urchin had stung her, whether from some physical response or from the memory of the pain, she wasn't sure.

"Are they poisonous?"

Milo shook his head, "venomous. They won't kill you, but if you get stung, you will wish they had."

"What did Rob do?"

At this, Milo's face flushed with the green and red tones of disgust. "He screamed," he said, "the worst sound I've ever heard. And he fell to the ground. Leon turned back to the tank and shook the fish off the stick back into the water. Can you believe that thing still wasn't dead? And he turned back toward Rob, who was passed out on the floor from the pain."

"What did you do?" Saffron said.

Milo looked away.

"At that moment, I looked up to see little Dylan coming down the hall rubbing his eyes. He'd just woken up, probably from the scream, and I didn't want him to see his dad like that. So I ran and intercepted him in the hall and took him to another room to show him some other fish."

Milo ran his hand across his forehead. "So you see, it really was kind of my fault. I could have stayed. But I knew that Rob wouldn't die from the sting, that it would just be agony for a while. I thought I could find Rachel and Dorah and send them to help. I never expected Leon to do what he did."

Saffron's words were barely a whisper. She was standing now, leaning against the bars to hear every word. "What did he do?"

Milo looked around. She saw him take in the bars and the high window, the bleak cell, the cot. She wondered how long he had wanted to say this out loud, all those years in prison.

"He threw him off the point into the waves at Uwē Beach."

Saffron breathed. There was a relief in the horror story coming to an end. "They said he was beaten to death."

"He was. By those waves. They hit the shorebreak with awful force. He wouldn't have been able to swim, in pain like that." Milo shook his head violently as if trying to knock the memory out of it. "I shouldn't have left the room."

Saffron knew regret. "But Milo, you didn't kill him. You took Leon's punishment. Why would you do that for him?"

Milo stood, too, and there was agitation in his voice, "I didn't do it for him. Not for him. For Dorah. Because he convinced her he'd die in prison and said that if that happened, he'd leave all the money to the Fantail Foundation, some auxiliary of the Piscine Lodge. They hatched a whole plan for me to take the rap. They said I'd only get a couple of years."

She believed Milo. And if he wouldn't kill someone that horrible, she didn't think he'd kill his wife. The henpecked rooster came back to her mind. He still wanted to be near Bossy, even though she attacked him every time he approached. Saffron made a mental note to rehome him with the Friends of Hens, to give him a shot at a healthier relationship.

"Milo, I'm trying to figure out who killed Dorah. The police think it was you, but I don't. I think something else happened."

"Of course I didn't," he said wearily. "This time, I'm telling the truth no matter what."

"Okay. If you didn't kill her, what do you think happened to her?"

"I think she wandered out too far on the rocks, fell in the water, and the breakers—" he closed his eyes, unable to go on.

"Just like Rob. But she'd lived there all her life. Wouldn't she know how far she could go?"

"Usually. But she was sick that night, though. She was coughing and dizzy, and maybe she had the flu coming on. I don't know.

From his weary, anxious tone Saffron could tell that these were questions he had answered before.

Milo laid down on the bed and turned his face away. "If that's all, I'm tired. I'd like to rest."

But Saffron had one more question. "Milo, something else has been bothering me. Why did you deliver an ornate butterflyfish to Barkadoodle? They said they couldn't sell one."

He rolled back over and stood up. Saffron backed rapidly away from the bars.

"I explained that in the note I left!" It was the most animated she'd ever seen him. "They had a guaranteed buyer for that fish. He was going to pick it up!"

This was new information to Saffron. "A buyer? You had been in contact with someone who wanted an ornate butterflyfish? Who was the buyer?"

"I don't know. Just called himself Butterflyfish. He contacted me through my online store and asked if I could get my hands on an ornate. He was going to pay top dollar, plus some great frags in trade."

"Frogs?"

"No, frags. Rock fragments. Reefers trade them around. He had some really nice ones, and he had left them in a bucket on the lanai while Dorah and I were out diving that day. So I nabbed the ornate that morning after you were at our house and dropped it off with Barkadoodle's order. I told them all that on the note. They were supposed to sell him the ornate and collect the money when he came in. He said he was picking something else up there anyway."

"You left a note?"

"In Barkadoodle. I arranged the trade with him, and I was going to tell Bernie about it, but he wasn't there when I came by. So I left a note. But I don't know if he got it. That stupid bird probably stole it. She's obnoxious."

"She does have a little problem."

"Only good thing she ever did was give me that necklace," he grumbled.

"So Echo did give you the necklace? Eke was wondering where it had gone."

Milo ducked his head. "I probably shouldn't have taken it, even though she gave it to me. But it looked so much like the one that Dorah wanted. Except it wasn't carved to look like a lionfish."

Saffron tried to push the big fish with the spines out of her mind. "Lionfish?"

"Yeah. Like her dad's. After Leon died, she got as obsessed about that fish as he had been."

"Wait, the fish lived? After he used it against Rob?"

"I told you. It's a mean sucker."

The perfect piscine representation of Leon Cole, Saffron thought.

"You know, even after it got speared, it hung on. It even thrived. You saw it. It's still going strong. He kept it alive a long time, and it even outlived him. Dorah's been keeping it, seeing if the Lodge would let her in. She was convinced that she was going to be the next Lionfish of the Honorable Piscine Order, but they wouldn't even let her join."

"What's the lionfish's job in the Lodge?"

Milo scoffed. "That seems obvious," he said. When Saffron raised her eyebrows and her shoulders at him, he grudgingly explained. "The Lodge royalty. The leader. Lionfish. And they also are in charge of discipline—kicking people out of the Lodge and stuff." Milo leaned forward. "Her dad kicked a bunch of the members out. It was a big scandal. Wouldn't give them their dues back. People around here were pretty upset. They said he just wanted them out so he could get his hands on all the money."

"Tell me more about the Piscine Lodge."

"I don't know that much. Just that Dorah wanted in, but they denied her. She had the lionfish and everything. But I guess her sister got accepted first. She was pretty angry about it. You know, they said that all that money was still out there in the lodge somewhere, and I think she was after it, too."

Saffron's head was spinning. "Wait, you said the necklace Echo gave you wasn't a lionfish?" She pulled out her phone, and there was an uneasy silence while she navigated to the picture of the pendant. Why hadn't she seen it before? It was, clearly, a butterflyfish. She asked Milo, and he confirmed.

"I saw pictures in the lodge. It looked like the necklaces were all carved to look like different fish?"

"Sure. The necklace looked like the fish that the member had caught, the fish that determined that person's job in the Lodge."

"That's what I thought when I was looking at those pictures. So what's the job of a butterflyfish in the Lodge?"

Milo shrugged his shoulders. "I've never heard of anyone being a butterflyfish. But that would make sense because nobody could keep one alive, and that's part of the deal."

Saffron considered this. "Do you think whoever asked you to catch that fish wanted to pass it off as something they caught?"

"Maybe. It's hard to catch fish if you're not practiced at it."

"I can't figure out how Leon caught his lionfish," Saffron said. "It seems like that would be so hard, with their defense mechanisms. And like you said, they're mean."

Milo's voice was subdued when he said, "not even they are as mean as Leon Cole was. He could capture anything." He heaved a deep sigh, "and keep almost anything captive."

Saffron's ears perked up, "*Almost* anything?" she asked.

"Not his wife, of course. She had enough spunk to leave. I just wish she had taken the girls with her. They would have had a very different life."

Saffron nodded.

"Of course, she was a member of the Lodge auxiliary. The Fantail Foundation. At least, that's what Dorah said. She said her mother set that whole thing up. But it didn't take off. Apparently, the members didn't think much of it, and none of the other wives of the Lodge members ever joined it. Must have been kind of lonely for her."

Saffron could hear Milo's own loneliness in his words. But she couldn't stop thinking of the butterflyfish. Who had asked

Milo to catch a butterflyfish? And who had asked Eke to carve one? Saffron was putting pieces together as fast as she could. Could they be the same person? Someone trying to choose a particular position in the Lodge hierarchy? It seemed likely. She needed to figure out who this mysterious online buyer was.

• • • •

SAFFRON WAS MULLING it over the next morning at the egg farm.

She had put in a call to Birdie, her friend from the chicken rescue group, and Birdie had arrived to collect the lovesick rooster.

Saffron was sad to see the bare patch where Bossy had snatched the red feathers away from the rooster's neck.

"She's a mean one," she told Birdie.

"She's just too obsessed with being on the top of the pecking order," Birdie responded. "She needs to be rehabilitated and reintroduced into a new flock."

"Rehabilitated?"

"Right. Trained not to pluck feathers and encouraged to make new friends who are above her in the flock hierarchy." Birdie said.

"How do you do that?"

"The first step is chicken spectacles." Birdie said.

"I'm sorry?" Saffron had an image of tiny, wire-rimmed glasses. "How would they stay on? Chickens have no ears."

"They do have ears, but their ears don't stick out. And they don't need ears for chicken spectacles. They just clip onto the beak. It keeps them from being able to see right in front of their beak. They can still do everything a chicken loves to do except pick feathers. They have to be able to focus on the feather to pull it. We decorate the spectacles to look adorable. Sometimes we put on googly eyes."

Silly, but it still sounded like a good idea to Saffron. They had loaded the rooster into a dog crate and set it in Birdie's car outside. "I think she might do better in another flock," Birdie said kindly. "Do you want me to take her and send her to the ranch on the mainland?"

Saffron had seen pictures of the Friends of Hens sanctuary. It was beautiful.

"Will she be able to pick on that poor rooster?"

"Oh, no. They'll be in different flocks."

Saffron leaned down. She hadn't had to say goodbye to any of her hens yet. The prospect made her feel a little melancholy. She pulled some grain from her apron pocket and reached toward Bossy. Bossy ignored the treat and promptly pecked her hand, hard.

"Take her," Saffron said.

• • • •

BIRDIE WAS GONE BY ten, when Saffron sat in her cozy living room watching the rain. Eleven o'clock was checkout time for the cottages, and the day had finally come for Mrs. Jones to go back to wherever she'd come from. Saffron had seen the woman through the window of the coral cottage, packing, as Birdie drove away, so Saffron expected her any moment.

While she waited, Saffron was savoring a rare moment of reflection in the swirling current of chaos this week had been.

She'd never known the many moods of the ocean when she lived back on the mainland. Here, she felt it change from playful to mournful to vengeful by the day, sometimes by the hour. She thought of the gargantuan breakers at Uwē Beach, and a little shiver ran up her spine.

What a horrible thing his death had been. But something still seemed off about Dorah's death. Maybe she was ill, but what could have made her so sick that she wandered off like that? And what had she been trying to tell Saffron?

The ocean had seen so much sadness whenever it visited Uwē Beach. Maybe that's what made the water so tormented there.

Outside, at Saffron's beach, the sea was pensive. Gray and foamy under the stormy sky, it chased itself up the sand and swallowed the raindrops as they fell.

She couldn't get Milo's story out of her head. Leon Cole had tormented everyone close to him: his daughters, his lost wife. Saffron wondered about the girls' mother. Had she just left, like Saffron's own father had, never to make contact again? Had the girls known how to reach her? Was she still alive?

Saffron thought back to the last few days, to the significant events in the sisters' lives. Saffron had planned and executed so many events now, she knew they came in many varieties. Certainly, weddings could be stressful, and funerals were sad, but the best of both were also joyous celebrations of life. The best were surrounded by loved ones and music and good food.

Rachel's wedding, Dorah's funeral, both events were solitary and both were ultimately sad. The girls had endured these moments alone, with only the ocean and the tourists to share them with.

Tourists.

Saffron sat up. The beach. The onlookers. Her mind began to spin. Her heart pounded in her ears.

One uninvited guest had been at both events, and Saffron was having a terrible realization.

She had to go to the Coral Cottage. In her bare feet, she ran to the back door and pulled it open.

But she didn't have to go any further. Mrs. Jones was waiting on the back lanai, suitcase in hand.

Saffron opened her mouth. What could she possibly say? She saw it now, the resemblance between the two women—the downturned mouth, the pinched eyes, the hot red overtones in the skin of her hands.

"You're Dorah Harrison's mother." She blurted it out.

Mrs. Jones flinched as if the name hurt her. Saffron supposed it did. But then the woman nodded, and her angry eyes had tears in them.

"And Rachel's?" Saffron asked.

"That's right. Although I haven't spoken to her for many years." Mrs. Jones was quiet and solemn as if her usual crankiness had melted away with the rain.

Saffron didn't know what to say. How could she have not seen this before? She had only seen Dorah alive for such a very short time, and under such difficult circumstances, that she could forgive herself for not noticing the physical resemblance. The cantankerousness, though, should have been a giveaway.

"This has been an incredibly memorable stay," Mrs. Jones said. Saffron looked for a hint of sarcasm in her voice but found none.

Saffron couldn't bring herself to criticize Mrs. Jones. Not now that she knew what the woman had been through. "I hope your trip home is safe," Saffron ventured.

"It doesn't matter," the guest said, setting down her suitcase. "I'm ready to go anytime. Once you've outlived your children, you realize that your own death isn't the worst thing that can happen."

"Oh," Saffron felt suddenly very sorry for Mrs. Jones. "I'm sorry. I know how it is to lose someone."

"Yes," Mrs. Jones said, "I came here for a wedding, but I ended up at a funeral."

Saffron made her voice as gentle as she could. "I'm sorry."

"Thank you."

"Mrs. Jones, I know this subject must be terrible for you, but I'm trying to figure out what happened to your daughter. There are some things that just don't make sense."

Mrs. Jones looked at her skeptically for a moment, then leaned closer. "I agree. Like her being in the water."

"Oh?"

"Yes. I taught her to stay away from that point when she was a little girl. She never would have gone out there if she was thinking straight. And she was an excellent swimmer."

"How do you know that?"

Mrs. Jones looked down. "I've been to see her. Several times since her father died. We would go diving together, and eat at the Oceanside Café."

Saffron's eyes widened. She remembered Bernadette talking about Dorah coming in in a wet suit and eating lunch with an old woman.

"I think that's wonderful, that she had you in her life. I don't think she made many friends."

"Thanks to her father. He was heartless."

Saffron had heard nothing that would convince her otherwise.

"But you haven't talked to Rachel? How did you know about the wedding?"

Mrs. Jones hung her head. "My grandson tipped me off. He thought I should be here. He was right. I've been in contact with him for a few years. But I could never face his mother. She was so destroyed when I left." In a moment of desperation, Mrs. Jones reached out and grasped Saffron's hand. "I couldn't get away from him otherwise. I was afraid of what he'd do. He had me convinced that they didn't love me and didn't need me anyway. But he was wrong, and I was wrong to go. I never should have left them."

But Mrs. Jones wasn't finished talking. "I didn't leave because of them. I left because of their father. Because of his affairs."

It was an old story, and a sad one. "I'm sorry, Mrs. Jones."

"Oh, you know. He wanted much fancier women. I was a goldfish in a sea of damselfish. He went for the flashy ones, and I was too ordinary."

"I wanted to come back for my girls, but he wouldn't hear of it," she sighed. "Things were different then. Women had fewer choices." Mrs. Jones retrieved a check from her pocket and handed it to Saffron before picking up her suitcase. "But I did do some things right." The woman said. "And maybe someday Rachel will know what those things were. And then maybe I can face her again."

"I hope you can," Saffron said, suddenly, painfully aware of what she would give for one more conversation with her own mother, or even with her father.

"I guess this will be my last trip to the island," Mrs. Jones said. "There's nothing here for me anymore."

Saffron nodded sympathetically, too emotional to say anything.

When Mrs. Jones spoke again, Saffron heard the guest she'd come to know. "At least I won't have to deal with all this sand and sunshine anymore." Mrs. Jones straightened her raincoat and stepped off the lanai to her rental car.

CHAPTER 19

Saffron couldn't stop thinking about the octopus. Dorah's mother had been staying at her place all along, and she'd never known until today. The groom was a liar, Milo hadn't killed his brother-in-law at all. Saffron wondered briefly if anyone around her was really who they appeared to be.

And now Rachel's mother was on her way to the airport, and Rachel didn't even know she'd been there. Saffron tried to call her, but Rachel still wouldn't answer.

Dylan.

She called the number he'd called from when he arrived at the airport. He answered on the first ring.

"Dylan," Saffron said, "I know you invited your grandma. She wants to see your mother, but she's afraid to because she left. Do you think you can break that news to her?"

"Sure," Dylan said, mild surprise in his voice, "as soon as she gets back."

"Where is she?"

"She went to the lawyer's with Blake."

The air went out of the room. "Blake is back?"

"Yeah. He came back this morning. Said he was going to help her settle this inheritance thing. I let him, because I don't know how to help with it."

Saffron kept seeing Blake's lying face, shapeshifting into Kaleb the advertiser like the octopus had done. "Listen, Dylan, I think Blake cut your mom's brakes. He's not who he says he is." It took her a moment to fill Dylan in. "I don't know what he's up to, but I don't trust him. Can you get to them? Stick with your mom? I will go look for them, too."

Dylan agreed. The tightness in his voice revealed how much he cared for his mom and how scared he was.

"I'll meet you there as quickly as I can," Saffron promised.

She drove as fast as she dared, hoping that if they were at Cutler's office, at least they'd be in public and Blake couldn't do anything terrible.

But when she arrived at the law office, Phyllis said she hadn't seen the bride and groom, and Cutler wasn't there. She thought he might be at his house, getting ready for court this afternoon.

Saffron needed to fill him in. She needed him to make sure the money didn't get disbursed before Blake was arrested. She'd have to go catch him at his house.

She bluffed, "Oh, right. He lives in that big blue house on Mahalo Crescent, doesn't he?"

Phyllis, always chatty, corrected her, "No, no, he's over on Pueo Drive. The ugly house." Saffron was glad that Phyllis was more concerned about accuracy than she was about privacy.

If Saffron were worried she wouldn't be able to guess which of the Pueo Drive houses was Cutler's, her anxiety disappeared as soon as she saw it.

It was, Saffron couldn't deny, an aquarium. Boxy. Made entirely of floor-to-ceiling windows with thin strips of steel as bracing, she could see why Phyllis had described it as she had.

Saffron knocked and rang the bell, but there was no answer. Maybe he'd already gone to the courthouse. Just to be sure she didn't miss him, Saffron went around to the back.

She didn't mean to look in the windows as she went, but to be fair, it was *all* windows. And inside, the open layout was filled with freestanding reef tanks, some of them the size of Saffron's whole living room.

She didn't mean to lean so hard on the back door while she was trying to get a better look at the tank in the solarium, and she certainly didn't mean to fall directly into Howard Cutler's kitchen. But when she realized the overarching theme of the decor, she didn't rush back out.

There was a magnificent carved table bridging the space between the kitchen and the dining room. It was shaped like a fish. Three weeks ago, Saffron wouldn't have known that it was a butterflyfish, but she knew now.

And she knew that the glass tiled backsplash featured butterflyfish, and that the heavy brass bookends were butterflyfish, and that in the twelve-foot-high reef tank that divided the kitchen from the living room, butterflyfish glided through the water.

Saffron saw it now—Cutler was the butterflyfish.

It made sense that a man with his passion for the hobby would be a member of the Piscine Lodge, and it made sense that a man with a passion for butterflyfish would want one to be his namesake.

But Cutler had said, himself, that he was not a swimmer—that he knew too much about the ocean to want to go into it. So he must have wanted to buy the ornate butterflyfish from Milo to avoid catching it himself.

Saffron peered into the reef tanks. There were more species of fish in them than she had ever imagined. She even saw some of the butterflyfish that Cutler had in his office tank: the saddleback butterflyfish.

But as hard as she looked, as closely as she peered, she couldn't find, in any of the tanks, the slate body and tangerine stripes of the ornate butterflyfish. Maybe that was why Cutler wanted it: simply because he didn't have one.

The fact that he didn't have one was confirmed when Saffron got to the end of the large living room and saw what appeared to be a solid gold tank. The sides were still glass, of course, but the frame holding them together was gold. Engraved into the gold above the center of the front wall of the tank were the words "Ornate Butterflyfish." But there were no fish inside. A beautiful, colorful reef stretched across the middle of the tank, populated by more species of coral than Saffron had seen even in the ocean. What had Cutler said? That most people wouldn't put the work into finding the particular coral that butterflyfish would eat. He had apparently committed to growing whatever kind an Ornate Butterflyfish would like.

Saffron called out Cutler's name, forcing her voice into a friendly tone. But the house was silent. And it was fascinating. She climbed a spiral staircase whose banisters were shaped like coral. At the top of it, a short hallway with several rooms caught Saffron's attention.

Saffron knew she shouldn't be here, but a nagging realization drew her onward down the hall. A man like this did everything deliberately. If he wanted an ornate butterflyfish, he had a reason. And she was willing to bet that the reason was not simply a desire to have all the species.

To the members of the Piscine Lodge, these fish were symbolic. They said something about you—who you were and what place you deserved to hold. If Cutler wanted to be the Lodge's ornate butterflyfish, it was because that meant something. Saffron just wasn't sure what.

The second door was open into Cutler's private office, over-looking the ocean—a million dollar view.

On his desk, a photo. Saffron recognized it as the one missing from the Piscine Lodge's wall before she even drew it near enough to study. It was Cutler's biggest client: a younger Leon Cole, dressed in a robe and hat that were unmistakably patterned after the long spines and fans of the Lionfish. Saffron saw the symbolism, and it turned her stomach.

Leon Cole looked at home in that outfit because he had been like a lionfish: he had stung everyone who got close to him, infusing them with his own venom.

Saffron raised the photo and looked at Leon's face—looked at it closely, trying to see if she could see a trace of the cruelty, of the torment, he'd heaped on the people around him.

Her gasping breath echoed in the little room when she saw something else: on Leon's face, three freckles were aligned.

Cutler had taken off his glasses when she was in his office, and Saffron remembered the exact shade of the three freckles that had lain in the same place: on one side of his nose, under the rim of his glasses. Leon had the same three freckles. It was an undeniable match.

Saffron forgot about caution. She wrenched open the file drawer under the desk and snatched the folders inside. They were full of unpaid bills, letters from creditors, and plummeting stock projections. From the looks of it, Cutler was living far above his means. Even this house was at risk for repossession, according to the documents.

One folder was a mystery. In it were papers marked "invoice." But that was the only English word on many of them. There were numbers, and what looked like amounts, but the rest of the words were in different languages. Cutler must be selling something to people in other countries. Perhaps fish specimens?

Every paper was in place, though. Every one creased precisely. Every folder new and carefully labeled. Except one. Hidden inside a crisp folder full of warranty cards, was another folder, worn and tattered by constant review. It was labeled *Leon Cole Will*.

This was the folder she'd seen in his office that day. The one he had refused to let her look in.

Inside, more photographs, a copy of the will, and exactly what Saffron had been looking for. Something that stopped Saffron's blood and proved the suspicion that the freckles had sparked—a paternity test.

She knew what she would read as soon as she touched the paper.

Child: Howard Cutler

Alleged Father: Leon Cole

There followed then a list of words and abbreviations that Saffron only marginally understood: amelogenin; alleles; CSF1PO; Penta A. There were columns of numbers, and at the bottom, in bold lettering, "The alleged father cannot be excluded as the biological father of the child. Probability of paternity: 99.99999%."

Here it was in hard numbers. Cutler was Leon Coles' son. The woman Leon had an affair with must have gotten pregnant. The test was not that old—it was dated just a few years ago, at the end of Leon's life. Cutler must have convinced him or coerced him into providing a genetic sample for the test. Saffron wondered if he'd shared the results with his biological father.

Saffron looked up, breathing deliberately. Her heart was hammering. Her eyes settled on a cut-glass butterflyfish on a shelf. It was the size of a football, its patterning etched into the glass in smoky stripes.

And suddenly she knew why Rachel had seemed so confused at the mention of the Piscine Lodge. It wasn't an act. She had no idea what it was. Cutler was the sibling that had beat Dorah to membership. But why? What did he possibly have to gain from staking claim to his father's sponsorship in a tired, mostly-defunct social club?

Just as the coral reefs hid thousands of tiny fish, it seemed that behind every answer lay more questions. Saffron didn't even know where to go with this information. Bradley would only be interested if it seemed Cutler had an obvious motive—something to gain from Dorah's death. If the Lodge had denied her application, then he had already achieved his goal of claiming his father's spot before she died.

Saffron thought of the will. It didn't seem to make a good motive, because it was so clear that one or both of his daughters would get the money as long as the stipulations were met. It seemed Cutler had little to gain from killing his half-sister. He knew that the money would simply go to Rachel if Dorah were dead. And if both were, Saffron remembered, the money went to the lodge auxiliary that Mrs. Jones had set up years ago.

Saffron snapped photos of all the papers, but she was reticent to send them to Bradley on account of the fact that she was, technically, breaking and entering. She paced around the room, then out into the hall.

Glancing toward the end of the hall, Saffron saw an unusual sight. At the end, where a regular door should be, stood a door sealed with a thick rubber gasket. It reminded Saffron of the kind of doors she'd seen on the USS Bowfin, a submarine in Pearl Harbor, when she and Keahi had spent a day down there before he left.

She approached the submarine door and found, hanging next to it, a complex breathing mask.

Saffron had been in enough sticky situations to know she should put that on before she opened the unusual door, so she did. Opening the door, she walked into a small room, bare except for buckets spread around the floor and three tanks in the center. Within them, swaying softly, were the palys from the poison pool.

· · · ·

SAFFRON DIDN'T KNOW why she was whispering. She had no indication that Cutler would be back anytime soon. Allie was having trouble enough hearing her on the phone with the mask over her mouth.

"Say that again? What did you find?"

"Palythoa. They're light brown with bluish tips on their tentacles. They seem dingy. Can you tell me what you know about them? Mano said they were poisonous, and I saw them in a pool out on Breadfruit Road."

"If they're what I think they are, then he's right. There are lots of kinds of palys, though. Some are dangerous, but some aren't. Where are you, Saffron?"

"I'd rather not say. I'm not exactly . . . Supposed to be here."

"Well, listen, it's unlikely that any palys are going to hurt you for just looking into their tanks, but if you can get out, do it now.

Let me tell you, if they're *Palythoa toxica*, you do not want to be in there any longer than you need to be."

"I need to know more about them."

Allie sounded exasperated. "What do you want to know? That palytoxin, which they produce, is the second deadliest poison *on Earth*? That one gram of it will kill a hundred-" here she cut out, and Saffron moved toward the window.

"It will kill a hundred what?"

"Not a hundred, Saffron. One gram of it will kill *a hundred million* mice."

Saffron tried to fathom that.

"How do the palys administer the poison? Do they bite?"

Allie laughed. "Bite? No, they don't have to. If they're disturbed or agitated, they can release the poison in a slime," the word rang a bell in Saffron's memory, "and even aerosolize their poison. It's deadly, Saffron."

"What would disturb them?" Saffron asked, edging toward the door.

"Anything. A shadow passing over or a fish jostling them. Lots of people break up the rocks they live on and sell or trade them to other people with reef tanks. That really upsets them."

"Frags," Saffron said.

"Right."

Saffron looked at the rocks they were on. They were perfect lava rocks—the color of rust. Red lava rock from the poison pool. These were, without a doubt, the deadly *limu make*.

Saffron looked around the room, describing not only the tanks and palys but also the setup and equipment. Allie grew more alarmed with each detail. "Saffron. Where are you? Whoever is doing this is not just an ignorant hobbyist. This person is *cultivating* palytoxin."

This explained the foreign invoices. She told Allie about them, and the scientist let out a low whistle. "This is bad, Saffron," she said.

There were buckets along the wall of the room. They were labeled "live" and "inert." In them, the red lava rock chunks looked the same to Saffron, and they looked exactly like the chunks in the bucket that Dorah was scrubbing the night she died.

"Don't touch them," Allie was saying. "If they release their poison, and you breathe it, it will do permanent damage to your lungs. If your skin comes in contact with it, it will *kill* you. If it gets into your bloodstream through a cut, it will kill you even quicker."

Saffron found herself breathing shallowly, trying not to draw any more air through the mask than necessary. Her hands were curled up and pulled back into her sleeves.

Though she still didn't know Cutler's motive, Saffron knew that this was how Dorah had died. Cutler had arranged to trade a tainted frag with Milo. He'd dropped it off at the home of his half-sister. And he'd dealt with her before. He'd known her obsession with cleaning, had seen her hands. He'd known she would scrub the grungy-looking rocks and prompt the palys to release the world's second deadliest poison.

And Dorah had figured it out, too. Saffron slipped her fingers out, retrieved her phone, and looked at the pictures of the desk in Dorah's bedroom. Her own name, the necklace, and the legal documents. The circles around the signature lines had not been meant to show Cutler where to sign—Dorah had put them there the night she died. They were intended to point Saffron to Cutler.

She imagined Dorah's forceful voice as if it were speaking the three clues:

Saffron Skye, the Butterflyfish is Howard Cutler.

Dorah must have figured out that she'd been poisoned. She must have pieced the puzzle together just as the worst of the toxin hit her. She had known Saffron played detective, and she may have even thought Saffron was still locked in the garage. She had assembled the clues as best she could on the desk.

Saffron thought of the necklace. She imagined Dorah putting it on the desk, scrawling her name, circling Cutler's. And, as she pulled away, Saffron saw how the necklace had tangled in the sleeve of Dorah's bathrobe, how she'd steadied herself against the chair, catching its cord in the arm. She wouldn't have even noticed the necklace clinging to the fuzzy bathrobe. She'd known, and she'd wanted someone else to know, that the Butterflyfish had killed her.

And if he was selling this stuff, there was no telling how many other people were his victims. He had to be stopped.

Saffron snapped photos of the room as quickly as she could and backed toward the door. Allie was still hammering away in her ear, citing statistics, giving warnings.

"Are you listening to me, Saffron?"

"No," Saffron said. "I'm getting out of here. Thanks, Allie."

She slipped out and hung the mask back on the hook by the submarine door. Saffron stood in the quiet hallway for a moment, trying to judge her breathing. Was she okay? Could she sense any burning or irritation in her lungs? She looked at her hands over and over, remembering the cracks on Dorah's hands, and shivering when she realized that when the woman had scrubbed the frags, the world's second most deadly poison had entered her body through those cracks.

Dorah had staggered out into the night in the final throes of the palytoxin poisoning, after leaving all the clues she could. She may have been looking for Milo when she'd fallen off into the water, and like with her brother-in-law years ago, the breakers had finished the job.

• • • •

SAFFRON CALLED BRADLEY on the way to the courthouse. She was surprised to find him at the station. Though he was confused, he promised to meet her there.

When she arrived, Bradley strode confidently toward the single courtroom. She was glad he knew his way around the building.

Cutler was at the front of the courtroom, and the traveling circuit judge was speaking.

"As the stipulations of the will have not been met, I'll approve the motion to disburse the estate of Leon Cole to his remaining biological child, Howard Cutler." He raised his gavel. Saffron sprang to her feet.

"No! Wait! Your Honor!"

The old man looked up at her from under eyebrows that looked like palm fronds. "Excuse me?"

Saffron didn't know what to say. She blurted, "You can't give him the money. He killed Dorah Harrison!"

Cutler's face, for several long seconds, pulsed with a pale blue undertone. It was, in Saffron's experience, the facial color of fear. But he was a lawyer, and he had complete control of himself in the courtroom. There was no other indication that he was panicking.

His voice was steady as he said, "Objection, Your Honor. This is not a trial. This is merely a formality."

"I'm interested in what the young lady has to say," the judge said.

"Your honor, I believe that Howard Cutler sent a deadly biological agent into the home of his half-sister, Dorah Harrison." Saffron wasn't looking at the judge. Instead, she watched Cutler just for the pure satisfaction of seeing his shock that she knew this. "Dorah Harrison was poisoned and subsequently died."

"That's ridiculous," Cutler scoffed.

"Is it?" Saffron said, "because the medical examiner has just, on my suggestion, started a thorough search for signs of palytoxin poisoning. Are you willing to bet your freedom that she doesn't find it?"

Cutler shook his head. "Preposterous."

"You have a lot of words for that concept. But tell me this. If you didn't kill Dorah Harrison, why are you here trying to settle the will while you've sent the beneficiary off on a wild goose chase?"

"What are you talking about?"

"I just got off the phone with Dylan, who says you sent Rachel running around town with some phony paperwork looking for a notary public while you slipped over here to the courthouse early. Why wouldn't you want her here, unless you're making a play for her money?"

Saffron saw the hard look creep into Cutler's eyes. He looked so much like Leon Cole in that moment that Saffron's muscles tensed in fear. He knew she knew, and he changed his approach.

"Your representation of the situation is inaccurate," he said. "I'm not stealing anything. I am here to get the money. *My* money. I am a legal beneficiary, and the will is binding. Read that will out, would you, clerk?" He called to the clerk, who looked like he would rather be doing anything else. But it was his job, and he obliged:

I, Leon Cole, being of sound mind and body, do hereby bequeath my mortal estate to my biological children upon the following conditions:

-50% to my daughter Dorah if she have no children, natural or adopted.

-50% to my daughter Rachel if she be married by 12:00 pm on the date of her 55th birthday

Should either violate the condition of receipt, the whole of the estate will be disbursed to the remaining biological child. Should the children be deceased, incapacitated or ineligible, the whole of the estate will be disbursed to the Fantail Foundation.

She heard it now: *disbursed to the remaining biological child.* Leon had taken it for granted that his daughters were his only biological children. He had failed to specify "daughters" in the second paragraph of the will.

"I am Leon Cole's biological child. The court will find documents attesting to that in the packet I provided." The judge leafed through a stack of papers and made an affirmative noise as he perused one. Probably a copy of the paternity test Saffron had seen earlier.

Cutler was the only one who knew that he could qualify as a biological child. Like any decent lawyer, he had seen that loophole and exploited it.

In the back of the courtroom, Saffron heard a ruckus. She turned to see Rachel standing there, listening. By her side were Dylan and Blake.

"Not so fast," Rachel said, "I don't care if he is a biological child. I have met the stipulations of that will, so it doesn't matter what he says. I was married by my 55th birthday. I earned that money."

"Did you now?" Cutler said. Saffron saw a look pass between him and Blake, and it became clear to her.

"It was you!" she cried. "I kept trying to figure out how Blake worked into all of this!"

Cutler didn't stop to listen. He kept talking. "Rachel, I'm afraid I have to inform you that you were not legally married as of your 55th birthday."

"Are you kidding me? You were there at the ceremony." Rachel said. She turned to Blake, "Tell him, honey."

Blake looked down. Saffron thought she saw a glimmer of humanity in him at that moment, and she was glad for Rachel's sake. This was embarrassing enough without her groom gloating over his betrayal.

When the silence stretched on, the air in the courtroom became as fragile as glass. Saffron shattered it by speaking. "I'll tell you. Your husband's name isn't Blake Morgan. It's Kaleb Gorman." Rachel took a careful step away from Blake. He still didn't look at her. "He doesn't own a ranch, and he's not a banker in Missouri. He's an advertising executive down in Honolulu who decided to go fishing for a little excitement on a dating app, even though he was already married. But Cutler was on the lookout for just such a stooge."

Rachel looked at the lawyer in surprise, then looked back at Blake. "What? He's *married*?"

"Unfortunately, that's right. And I can tell you, as a legal advisor, that you're not legally wed, Ms. Kimball. The state of Hawaii does not recognize polygamous unions." He took out a handkerchief and wiped the corners of his mouth. "You are not married now, and you were not married as of your birthday."

Saffron felt sorry for Rachel.

"Why? Why would you do this?" Rachel was talking to Blake, and Saffron could see her trust in people crumbling away.

She tried to help. "He's doing it because he's in some financial trouble, and so is Cutler. They're both members of a club called the Honorable Piscine Order, so Cutler used that brotherhood to get Kaleb here to go along with his scheme."

"Honorable . . . what?" Dylan asked.

"Piscine Order. Also called the Piscine Lodge. They used to be a service organization that gave money for scholarships and fishing boats until your Grandpa Leon ran out most of the members and hid the money they'd donated and raised for worthy causes."

Saffron turned back to Cutler. She saw, with some satisfaction, that his temples were slick with sweat. He was gripping the back of a chair so tightly that his hands were eggshell white.

"And I think that your grandpa told him about that money, didn't he, Mr. Cutler? And you immediately repaid your client's confidence by going directly to the lodge and extracting every cent."

Cutler cleared his throat, but Saffron didn't let him talk. Cutler looked like he may be sick, and it didn't take Saffron's extraordinary color vision to see that Blake was scarlet with embarrassment.

Cutler pressed his mouth closed. It was a look she hadn't seen on him before.

"And you used it to build up your little frag farm. Gotta be expensive, tanks like that."

Cutler unstuck his lips to demand, "You were at my house? Your Honor, please, I—"

The old man just held up a finger. "Shhh-shh," he hissed, "I want to hear this."

Saffron went on. "And the money ran out, but you had orders you needed to ship, and your customers, I'm guessing, are not patient people. So you needed to get your hands on this inheritance."

Saffron stepped closer to Cutler and lowered her voice. "But your half-sisters were in the way, weren't they? And how do you get rid of them, but keep the inheritance from going to the Fantail Foundation?"

She turned and pointed to Blake. "This is where you come in. You had money troubles of your own, hmmm? So, Cutler promised you a cut of the inheritance to reel Rachel in and play husband until the deadline had passed for you to be legally married."

Rachel sat heavily on a bench at the back. Saffron couldn't tell if she was talking to herself or not. "But we were perfect for each other. The program matched us," her voice revealed the hurt in her heart.

Saffron hesitated, giving Blake a chance to answer. He kept staring at the floor.

"Cutler gathered info and had Kaleb here become the perfect man for you, Rachel."

The bride was looking up, searching Blake's face. She didn't say anything, just sat staring at him as if she'd never seen him before.

"Why—" she started, "why would you do that?"

"I haven't got another big account since the plates and petals campaign. We're running out of money. My family—" Blake started. He saw the words hurt her, and he stopped. "I'm sorry. I didn't mean for you to get hurt. He said it would be over by noon the day after the wedding. I didn't mean to drag it out."

"And what about the brake lines?" Saffron said. "Did you mean for her to get hurt when you cut those?"

Blake's jaw tightened, "I don't know anything about cars. I thought that was the fuel line. Rachel said she might go down to Honolulu one day while I was away. I was terrified she'd see me down there and figure out that I wasn't who I said I was. I just wanted to make the car not start so she couldn't drive down there. I wouldn't have wanted her to get hurt."

The judge sat watching the chaos in his courtroom. Saffron turned to him. "So, what do you say, judge?"

"I don't know what to say," he growled, his palm fronds waving, "This is a mess. All I can say for sure is that the dead sister doesn't get the money, and the polygamist sister doesn't get the money. I think we can assume that if what you say about Cutler here is true, he's going to fall under that 'ineligible or incapacitated' clause, especially if he's in prison. So, I guess the money goes to the Fantail Foundation, whatever that is."

Saffron didn't argue, and she tried very hard not to smile as the judge brought the gavel down on that decision. Rachel looked devastated. Saffron was glad that Dylan was there to reach out and put an arm around his mother.

"And I guess you'd better look into this poison farm, Bradley," the judge huffed. "Cutler may have more charges to face in addition to killing his sister."

Cutler found his voice and began to argue. Saffron caught the words *circumstantial* and *inadmissible*, even as Bradley hand-cuffed him and arrested him for the murder of Dorah Harrison.

CHAPTER 20

It was midmorning the next day when Saffron gathered up her keys, phone, and purse. She'd been on the phone all morning, talking to the Most Grand Excellency of Honor of the Honorable Piscine Order.

He had been far less pretentious than she had expected from his title. He was keen to hear of the situation with the Lodge in Maika'i, and he'd pledged to make a trip to the island himself to straighten things out. He would, he said, replace the stolen money from the international administration's coffers and be sure they were used for the purposes their members had intended. He would also reinstate the members that Lionfish Leon Cole had ousted, though some would be posthumous membership restorations. Saffron thought that Violet would be very glad to hear that her Wilbur would once again be known as an Honorable Member.

"Sir," she asked, then amended to address the president in the way she'd read she should on the internet, "Your Excellency, can I ask you a couple of questions about the Order?"

"Some things I can't answer, but I'm happy to share with you what I know that isn't protected by the Code of the Order."

Saffron talked to him about the Fantail Foundation, confirming what she'd put together.

When they were done with that topic, she said, "There's something I still can't figure out. The man who was operating the Lodge secretly, who had taken the money, who was denying memberships, his name was Cutler. And on the paperwork my friend Officer Bradley retrieved from the file cabinet Cutler had locked in the Lodge's office, we saw that he had appointed himself Ornate Butterflyfish of the Order."

There was a little gasp on the other end of the phone.

"Cutler was obsessed with Butterflyfish, and he was working very hard to obtain an Ornate. Why would that be?"

Saffron stopped talking to hear the Most Grand Excellency speaking in urgent, hushed tones with several other people on his end of the line. When he spoke, his voice was grave. "This is a most serious situation," he said. "Are you aware if he has such a fish in his possession? Has he kept one alive?"

"No. He has other butterflyfish, but not the Ornate. He has a special, enormous reef tank set up for it in his house, all ready for the fish, but the tank only has various species of coral and live rock. The Ornate didn't get delivered. It was set free back into the ocean."

"That's a bit of luck then. We owe you a debt of gratitude, young lady."

"Can you explain why he would want to be the Ornate But-terflyfish of the Honorable Piscine Order?" Saffron asked.

There was a little tremble in the Most Grand Excellency's voice when he said, "Because that fish is known for its focus on a single objective. In the order, we haven't had a Butterflyfish for a long time. That position in the in the original charter of the Order is the International Financial Officer, with control over all the Order's collective funds. Because we haven't had a Butterfly-fish, we have been managing the accounts with a committee, and that has revealed weaknesses in the financial model, but those weaknesses have not been addressed yet. Should anyone at this time be named Butterflyfish, the stipulations of the Order would allow them full and exclusive access to all funds. They could dec-imate the Order within hours, should we appoint someone who was not trustworthy, as we would have done if you hadn't pro-vided us with this information."

Saffron blinked. It was an unusual quandary, but the Honor-able Piscine Order seemed a pretty unusual group. And now she knew why Cutler had wanted to be the Butterflyfish. He hadn't just been trying to become the president of all the Lodges. He had been aiming to bring about the Honorable Piscine Order apocalypse. Somehow, that didn't surprise her at all.

• • • •

SAFFRON DROVE THE GREEN stretch of highway south of Maika'i, headed for the airport in Honolulu. She had to catch Rachel and Dylan before their plane took off.

Bradley called her on the way there.

"Hey," he said, "good detective work there."

"Thanks," she said, "So, you got the search warrant?"

"The judge couldn't sign it fast enough," Bradley said, "there was smoke coming off his pen."

"That's good. There's enough evidence there to put him away for a long time."

"And I heard back from the medical examiner," Bradley said, "You were right. Palytoxin. Worse than she's ever seen."

Saffron thought of the room with the submarine door, and she felt her heart pounding. "But Bradley, you did what I asked, right? You warned the investigators? Told them what they were dealing with? Did you have them call Allie?"

He chuckled, "Oh, yeah. Allie is in on it, and we've got a whole, specially trained FBI Hazardous Evidence Response Team in Maika'i this morning."

Saffron breathed a sigh of relief.

"You did good, Gumshoe," Bradley said. "Now go play Santa Claus." Saffron liked the sound of that.

• • • •

AN HOUR LATER, AT THE airport, Saffron sat on a planter and looked again at the paper with all the zeroes on it. It was the bank statement for the Fantail Foundation, obtained by Bradley and their new friend, the judge, just in time for this meeting.

At the top of the paper was a beautifully embossed fantail goldfish. Seeing it made Saffron smile.

She'd looked the organization up yesterday before she walked into the courtroom, and though she had needed the Most Grand Excellency's confirmation, her hunch about it had been right.

She was sliding it back into its envelope when Rachel called out. Her voice held confusion. "Saffron?"

The woman approached, her son and her carry-on bag in tow. "What are you doing here? Is everything okay?"

Saffron nodded. "Everything is fine."

"I'm glad we'll get to say goodbye," Rachel said kindly. "Even though it didn't go exactly like I'd imagined, I'm glad I came. I learned some things."

Saffron nodded. They'd all learned more than they'd expected to.

Rachel went on, "Saffron, do you think, when Howard Cutler is sentenced, that you could send me an address where he'll be serving his time? And Milo, too?"

It was Saffron's turn to be surprised. "Um," she started, "Of course." She assumed that Rachel would want to send a scathing letter telling them the ways in which they had wrecked her life. But Rachel surprised her again.

"Thank you, so much. I want to keep in touch with them."

"May I ask why?"

"Well, I want to thank Milo. He's given Dylan his entire fish breeding operation." When Saffron turned her gaze to Dylan, he was smiling.

"Yeah. He said he remembers that I loved them as much as he did, and when he gets out, he just wants to travel. The fish keep him too confined, he said." Dylan looked different. His hair was combed back out of his eyes. He looked like he had a purpose. "I'm going to start working to see if I can get enough money to get the fish and the equipment out to Wisconsin."

"And I want to write to Howard, too," Rachel said. Saffron couldn't stop her eyebrows from arching. Rachel hurried to explain. "I know it's hard to understand, but you know, I've been looking back on this feud with Dorah, and it all seems so futile. I wish we hadn't wasted all the time we had fighting over the money. You only get one family, and I don't know what kind of life Howard Cutler even lived. I want to understand him better, to reach out and see if we can heal some of the damage our father did . . . to all of us." She smiled a gentle smile, and Saffron felt admiration for her, and relief that she was not saddled with Blake anymore. She was glad the marriage hadn't been real. Rachel finished, "Because good or bad, he's still family."

Saffron saw the opening, and she took it. "So, did Dylan get a chance to tell you about the guest who was staying in my cottage?"

Rachel's eyes widened, then closed briefly. "Yes. Yes, he told me."

"So you know your mother is on the mainland? And she'd like to see you?"

Rachel gripped the handle of her carry-on. "Yes. I know. But I'm not sure I want to see her."

Saffron understood that, and she said so.

"Do you?" Rachel seemed doubtful. "Do you understand how it is to lose a parent?"

I understand that better than you realize, Saffron thought, but she said, "I imagine it's really difficult."

"I don't know if I want to see her," Rachel said, but the phrase she'd said, *still family*, hung in the air. "She never did anything for us," Rachel finished. Saffron recognized the fight within her. Wordlessly, she held out the envelope.

"What is this?" Rachel asked, taking it.

"One thing your mother did for you. A little sleight of hand she arranged all those years ago before she left." Saffron was grinning, waiting for Rachel to open it. She couldn't stop the flow of words.

"I talked to the Honorable Piscine Order this morning. There was no auxiliary organization within the Order. Your mother knew something was coming, that your father would be as duplicitous with you as he had been with her. So she set up the Fantail Foundation and made him and Cutler think it was a legitimate part of the Order. I did some research. If you look on the founding documents for the foundation, filed with the State of Hawaii, you'll find that there are only two beneficiaries of the Foundation: you and Dorah. Your mother put what little money she had in it when she left, hoping it would come to you someday. Before your father's death, she heard about the will from Dorah, and she hated that he'd done that. So she contacted Cutler and convinced him to convince Leon to write that in. Cutler was only too happy to oblige, as he thought he was going to get his hands on any money that went to the lodge anyway. It was like a back up for him."

Rachel was speechless. "What do I have to do?"

"Nothing. There are no stipulations. She made sure that, if the money came to the Foundation, her daughters would get it."

Rachel pulled out the statement and unfolded it. Saffron saw the reflection of the goldfish in her eyes as she grasped how much money was now hers.

"Your mother was giving you the money, no strings attached. She was ensuring that you would get it either way, whether you complied with his unreasonable demands or not."

"She did give us something," Rachel had tears in her eyes as she said, "thank you. And, if you have it, I'd like her contact information, too."

• • • •

THE WATER WAS WARM.

Saffron stayed well away from the jutting edge of the reef as she flew over the remarkable city under the sea.

The rains had cleared and the new morning sun warmed her back as she skimmed along, watching the underwater soap opera she'd come to love. And now, because of her bizarre adventure, she could identify many of the fish.

A humuhumunukunukuapua'a kept pace with her as she swam, and she squinted at an outcropping that just didn't look right. Reaching down, she brushed the humu away from the outcropping just as a tentacle materialized and reached for it. She was getting better at spotting creatures who weren't what they seemed to be.

Saffron watched a school of yellow tangs merge with a half-dozen red and green parrot fish in a dazzling display of color.

There was still so much to be discovered here, and she was starting to feel more at home in the water. It was a good thing, too, because Nik insisted that he was going to teach her to surf. She lifted her head out of the water.

There he was, getting a picnic ready on the sand. Nik tossed her a wave from across the bay. She didn't know where things were going with him, and she still missed Keahi terribly, but a new day was dawning, the colors were bright, and the sand was golden. Whatever was on the horizon, she was swimming out to meet it.

• • • •

HOME TO ROOST

ALOHA CHICKEN MYSTERIES: BOOK 5

Chapter 1

One slip and Saffron could ruin the whole thing—or lose a finger. She was carving a tiki—helping carve a tiki—and she'd already dug one of its intricate teeth out too deep. She was determined not to mess up again.

But the chicken roosting on her feet among the curls of bitter-smelling palm chips was not making her job any easier. Neither was the bank of cameras focused on her.

This was the Kahuna Kalai Championship, the premier competition for the world's master tiki carvers. Every four years, ten masters were invited to participate, and the competition was held in one of their hometowns. This year Mano had been invited, and the Kuhuna Kalai had come to Maika'i.

Saffron's business, Brightblossom Events, had been contracted to organize the whole thing. She had arranged to hold the event along Shell Beach—the broad golden stretch of sand on Maika'i's north edge. She had rented the durable canvas pop-up tents each carver had to work under, had arranged for all the visiting Kahunas' tools to be shipped, had planned the luncheons, the decor, the reception and auction that would take place at the end of the competition. The only things she hadn't arranged were the participants' travel and the publicity.

The publicity was being managed by a young and dynamic brother-and-sister team from Ems Communications who were staying in two of the rental cottages on Saffron's egg farm. Their names—Morgan and Megan—seemed to always come out wrong when Saffron tried to address them. And she'd been talking to them a lot. They'd been over to her bungalow every day this week, working out details of this ad or that radio spot. She wondered if they ever slept.

One of the publicity events was a tiki carving demonstration, where a master taught an amateur some of the basics of carving and the television stations filmed their attempts. Saffron could see why it was good publicity. The Kahuna Kalai—the master carvers—made their craft look so easy, slicing chips of wood away as easily as if they were carving butter. But put the chisels and mallets into an amateur's hands, and what should be a fearsome tiki became, with a lot of sweat and strain, a gap-toothed nightmare.

But Saffron's friend Mano, who had asked her to do the demonstration with him, was a tiki expert. He had carved everything from the enormous tiki totem poles outside the Oceanside Cafe in town to the tiny, intricate tiki buttons on his shirt.

Saffron glanced at them now, the fierce faces against the colorful fabric of his aloha shirt. His work was so detailed, so precise, that even at that tiny scale the tikis radiated with enormous personalities.

But he wasn't just a carving expert. He was also Saffron's friend, and he gently stepped in when she was having the most trouble and shaved off a curl of the soft palm wood here or scraped a too-sharp edge there.

Still, Saffron could feel her arms aching with the effort of holding the chisel and pounding it with the mallet. Small blows, Mano had said, and Saffron thought how the sound of carving matched the tap-tap-tapping of her chicken pecking at the shavings near her feet.

Typically, all her chickens would be at home in their lovely Egg House. But Cupcake, the remarkable creature sharing the demonstration space with her, had gone broody.

Hens went broody when they felt that universal urge to become mothers. They began collecting eggs—their own and anyone else's—and settled down on a nest to hatch those eggs.

Saffron's egg farm, called Hau'oli ka Moa—the Happy Chicken—usually didn't get too many broodies, thanks to nest boxes specially constructed so that the eggs would roll out of the nest boxes onto a little conveyor belt, which Saffron hand-cranked at least once a day and gathered the dozens of eggs to sell.

But Cupcake had been quite determined. She had made herself a nest on the floor of the indoor run, tucked into a corner. She'd even convinced a few of her pen-mates to lay their eggs there and had settled herself in.

Saffron wouldn't have minded, but the eggs weren't ever going to hatch. Her only rooster, Curry, lived on the porch most of the time and only occasionally visited the first pen when she felt he might be in danger. None of the other eggs were fertilized. Cupcake, no matter her determination, could never get a chick out of an unfertilized egg.

A broody hen, Saffron had learned, can be very stubborn. At first, she thought Cupcake would just give up eventually. But she didn't. In fact, she got so focused on hatching those eggs that she stopped leaving the nest to eat or drink. Saffron read that a broody can actually starve to death if no action is taken, so she set about trying to distract Cupcake from her goal.

But Cupcake, despite her name, was no pushover. She was tenacious. She ran back to the nest whenever Saffron moved her off of it. She built a new one if Saffron put her in a new pen. She wouldn't eat or drink unless Saffron were there beside her. The only thing that kept Cupcake from nesting was to bring her along on adventures to new places with new sights. Today's adventure was the carving demonstration.

Saffron slotted the tip of a fine, curved chisel into the groove she'd been making and tapped it gently with the mallet. A small curl of ocher wood peeled off and Mano blew it away from over her shoulder.

Saffron could see her latest row of cuts. The wood along that line was a shade lighter: an egg-nog shade of beige next to the more oaty color from her earlier marks. It made placing her chisel for the next slice much easier.

"You're doing great," Mano murmured. He was more reserved, more contemplative, than usual. Saffron figured it was partly because of the cameras, but she knew it was also because of things he was facing.

She tapped the mallet against the chisel, feeling the reverberation of the movement in her wrist, elbow, and shoulder. Small taps, moving the tip of the chisel in the tiny space between each blow. The wood smelled bright and bitter. The breeze from the ocean next to them tasted sweet in comparison. She saw Cupcake taste a newly fallen chip and flick it away from her, shaking her head. She didn't like the taste of them.

Saffron detected the slightest variations in the wood. Palmwood was like a bundle of fibers, and she could see where one ended and the next began. Saffron had what her friend Nik called "supersight" but what was really just an extreme sensitivity to color. She could see shades where others saw one flat tone, could see colors nobody else could see at all.

It had started out as a curse but here in the islands, working with her chickens and living among the bright island foliage, Saffron had found it useful more than once.

Mano laid a hand over hers, and she realized that she had let her mind wander and gone a little crazy on the eyebrow she was working on. The tiki now looked slightly incredulous, with one eyebrow higher than the other. Carving, Saffron had discovered, was strangely meditative.

Mano waved off the mistake. "We'll adjust it with this," he held up a blowtorch.

Saffron, conscious of the cameras, widened her eyes at him and shook her head slightly in an attempt to send him a signal that she wasn't good with open flames. Mano's eyes simply twinkled a degree brighter as he popped the trigger and a blue flame shot out like a scorching tongue.

There was an appreciative murmur from the reporters. Saffron was seeing a new side of Mano: the showman. He ran the flame around the cavernous eye of the tiki, turning any space he touched a toasty gingerbread color. It added definition and clarity.

"Some carvers," he said to the cameras, "use paint to make the details pop. Some use flame. Some don't do anything but carve. The thing is, the wood will age this way, anyway. Especially on an outdoor tiki, the rain will settle in the cuts and color the wood as it ages. But sometimes, you want something more dramatic, or more controlled, so you can use a blowtorch."

Saffron had thought he might downplay the arched eyebrow, but he didn't. Instead, he accentuated it, and ran the blowtorch around the inner edge of the other eye, making it appear even smaller than they'd carved it. Saffron was going to ask why, but he started explaining before she could.

He was talking half to her and half to the cameras, "See, one thing that makes carving so rewarding is that you think you ruined your tiki by making a mistake, but if you keep working, you figure out that the mistake is part of the . . ." He paused, and Saffron realized he was searching for the right word, "the specialness of the piece—the uniqueness. That mistake, and what you do with it, will make a different kind of beauty in the carving." He glanced up at the cameras. "It's like in life."

The torch hissed as Mano took Saffron's hand and maneuvered the tool into it. She gripped it, imagining what would happen if she dropped it into the pile of dry shavings she was holding. The shavings would ignite. The tent would go up in flames, and they'd probably have a fried chicken, too. No pressure, though.

Mano, using a chisel, pointed toward the mouth of the tiki. Saffron lowered the flame to the wood and moved it as she had seen him do, around the gaping teeth. Instead of gingerbread, the wood scorched coffee black. Mano guided her hand further back and moved it more quickly, gently toasting the wood rather than burning it in a concentrated spot.

The effect was lovely. Except for the black streak she'd begun with, the teeth popped amid a grid of warm brown lines. Saffron ran the torch along the rim of the nose.

"CHEATER!" the word rang through the calm quiet of the tent like a hammer blow. Saffron jumped, her torch hand jerking and making a wide espresso slash across the cheek of the tiki. Some of the cameras swiveled. She looked to her right and saw

Luka Tai, the youngest of the seven competitors. He was standing with his hand raised, glaring at Mano accusingly.

Saffron felt Mano take the torch. He had not yet looked toward the younger man. She glanced back to see Mano's eyes still on the tiki. He studied the slash across its cheek, then, calmly and deliberately, replicated it on the tiki's other cheek. Then he slowly turned the torch off and set it down before finally raising his eyes.

Luka went on. "You messed with my pendant!" He strode in, wood chips splashing ahead of his steps as if he were wading into the surf.

Saffron could see that he was holding the first of the competitors' challenge pieces. A tiki pendant meant to be worn as a necklace. Over the course of the competition, the participants would carve five pieces:

-A pendant
-A mug
-A mask
-A tabletop tiki
-A large tiki statue

The idea, Mano had explained to her, was that if an artist wanted to begin with a design, then try it out on the little pendant, they could use the same design for bigger pieces and save themselves some work.

Saffron was acutely aware of the cameras, of the reporters' buzzing voices as they filled their viewers in on this shift in events.

Mano seemed oblivious to all of it. He was focused on Luka, and the furrows in his forehead told Saffron that Mano was worried about the young carver.

"What's wrong?" he asked.

Luka held out the tiki pendant, and Mano took it from him, studying it.

"You cheated!" Luka cried, wringing his now-empty hands, "You changed it."

Mano shifted his gaze and peered at the young man, "Changed it?"

"I carved that yesterday, and the mouth was smiling," Luka's hands were like leaves in the wind: skittering around with abandon.

Mano was nodding. Saffron leaned around his shoulder and peered at the pendant.

The mouth had changed. It was no longer smiling—instead, a long, curved tongue extended from between grimacing lips.

"You didn't carve the warrior mouth?" Mano ran a hand over his silver beard.

This seemed to enrage Luka, "No, I didn't! I carved an open mouth. It's turned out amazing. And you couldn't stand how well I was doing, because you haven't even started yet!"

Saffron's stomach twisted. It was true. Mano hadn't begun carving his competition pieces yet. When the other competitors had all been waiting with chisels in hand for the starting horn yesterday, Mano had been drinking a cup of tea in his tent. Saffron's anxiety for him had grown all day yesterday as she watched him turn his blocks of wood over and look at them, set them upside down, watch the waves, then absentmindedly polish his chisels. It was as if he were in his little roadside stand instead of in the most prestigious carving competition in the world. The other competitors had made piles of shavings, heaps of them. He had never made one cut all day yesterday. And the only carving he'd done today was the few corrections he'd made on the demo piece.

Ten days and he'd already wasted one and a quarter of them.

But Mano wasn't bothered by Luka's accusation. Saffron was stunned and slightly annoyed to see that he was genuinely concerned about Luka's problem. She would have liked to snap at the younger carver and tell him there was no way Mano would alter his pendant, make him apologize, and make the cameras delete the footage of the accusation. She didn't like the idea of people thinking Mano was a cheater. He was the most upstanding person she'd ever met. But Mano was more concerned about Luka than he was about his reputation.

"Lotta hana, brah," he said. Saffron recognized hana—the word for work. He was worried about all the effort Luka had put into the piece. "Frustrating to have it shift on you." He said it as if this was a normal occurrence.

One of the reporters, a brunette from channel KKEY—Voice of the Florida Keys—noticed this, too. She crowded in, shoving a softball-sized microphone in front of Mano.

"I'm Bren Keely, KKEY 2 News. Did you say the tiki shifted?" she asked, "Like, changed?"

Mano glanced up with a mildly surprised look on his face, as if he'd forgotten she was there entirely. "Sometimes, the tikis do that," he said, "if the wood is too wet or the weather changes a lot, they warp, and they can sometimes look a little different than when you first carved them . . ." He trailed off as he realized she wasn't listening anymore. She'd taken back the mic after he'd said "sometimes the tikis do that" and was leaning close to her camera lens. Her voice was low with urgency as she spoke.

"You've heard it here first. Tikis are mysteriously changing here in Hawaii. KKEY brings you exclusive coverage of the Shifting Tikis of the Kahuna Kalai Championship. Stay tuned for developments." She gave a cut-off signal to her cameraman and tossed her long hair back over her shoulder. All around her, the other reporters were speaking to their cameras, taking up the refrain: The Shifting Tikis of the Kahuna Kalai.

Cupcake pecked at Saffron's shoelace, and she bent to pick up the chicken. There were a lot of people here, and a lot of feet. She didn't want Cupcake to get hurt. Cupcake was pecking at a wood chip, and she held it in her beak a moment before shaking her head and flipping it away from her, where it landed in the hair of the brunette reporter.

The woman put a hand to her hair, pulled it out, and turned. She fixed her gaze on Saffron, and her expression was one of pure hatred.

Saffron's eyes stretched wide. It seemed an unnecessarily harsh response for a little wood chip. She turned away from the scalding glare as Luka's voice caught her attention.

"You're the only one who would have had access to my tent. You probably went in the flap between our tents and messed with it!"

Luka's carving area was right next to Mano's. They were quick setup canopies with canvas side panels separating the carvers. It was possible that someone could slip through and interfere with the workspace, but the area was cleared each night.

The tents were guarded, and nobody was let in or out but those who were directly involved with the event.

She spoke up, "All the competitors are let in at the same time, Luka. Mano wouldn't have been here before you."

"Except that I overslept. My alarm didn't go off," Luka said defensively. "I just got here, and my tiki was all wrecked."

Saffron held out a hand, and Mano put the pendant into it. It was beautifully done, with the chunky cuts and rough edges that were hallmarks of Luka's work.

"See?" He cried, "it's obviously Ku—look at those eyes—that headdress. And see? The tongue is out."

One of the reporters hovering at his elbow spoke up, "Pardon me, I'm Chip Gaither from KBEN—the Bean!—Channel 11 Boston. Would you expound on what the trouble is here?"

Luka turned to him, looking into the camera as confidently as if he'd been doing it all his life. "Yesterday I carved a tiki pendant for the competition, but it's different today." He pointed at Mano, "He must have sneaked in and changed it."

"In what ways is it different?"

"In every way! It was a Lono, and now it's a Ku."

"Ummm," the reporter stammered. He obviously hadn't read up on tikis before he came to cover this event. Even Saffron knew that Luka was talking about the four major akua—gods—that were often the subjects of tiki carvings.

"See?" Luka asked, snatching the pendant back from Mano. "Its mouth is different. My carving from yesterday didn't have the warrior tongue."

This one definitely had a curved tongue, intricately carved and prominently protruding through its bared teeth.

"What is the warrior tongue?" Bren Keely asked, leaning past the other reporter to edge her way in beside Luka. Saffron could imagine that the shot her cameraman was capturing made it look as if she and Luka were the only ones in the tent.

"Its when the tongue of the tiki is sticking out," Luka said. "A sign of bravery and courage."

"And what is a Ku?"

"The god of war," Luka said. "But I didn't carve Ku. I carved Lono—the god of good fortune and peace—to ask for his power during the competition."

"God of war?" Bren was fascinated by this concept. "So he's an evil figure then?"

"No, no," Mano broke in gently. "It's different than in other traditions. These akua," Saffron recognized the word used for the major gods Mano had taught her about, "are complex—they are not just one thing. They are each in charge of many aspects of life. Ku is over war, but that is because he is a protector—a warrior with energy and focus. He can help you with your own battles." Almost as an afterthought, Mano said, "everybody has battles."

"And how does the tiki help you?" Bren asked. Saffron realized that she was leading him, looking for sound bites for her story.

"It gives you strength," Mano said. He was looking around at the crowd intently, but his voice held no fervor. Instead, he seemed almost preoccupied.

Bren stuck her microphone in Mano's face again, and the camera pivoted to focus on him and Saffron. She smiled over the chicken in her arms.

"How is that? How would a carving give someone strength?"

Mano ran a hand through his silver beard and gave an answer Saffron had heard him give to many malihinis—tourists—at his little roadside stand, "Tikis are special. They're more than just knickknacks," she loved how he pronounced all the k's distinctly in that word-ka-nika-ka-knackas—making it sound almost like a Hawaiian word, "they are representations of powerful akua—gods—that can lend you a hand in your life."

The reporter snatched that up, "You're saying they have a power of their own?"

"I'm saying they borrow power sometimes, and they lend it to us, sometimes." He was serene.

Saffron saw how the reporter leaned in, how she fixed that cold gaze on Mano's face, every gesture and every expression meant to intimidate him, to increase his discomfort in front of the camera.

But Bren Keely didn't know Mano. He was comfortable anywhere. It was something Saffron admired about him.

"How do you respond to these claims, Mr. Kekoa?" Bren asked, her voice accusatory, "Did you tamper with this man's carving in an attempt to get ahead in this competition?"

"Nope," Mano said, that puzzled look still in his eyes. He offered no more information.

"But the tiki is different?" Bren led, "It has changed?"

"That's what he says," Mano nodded, showing that he believed the story.

"You said yourself that Tikis have power," she said, "of a supernatural variety." She didn't give Mano time to respond. "So, could this shifting tiki be due to some kind of otherworldly influence? Is that possible?"

Mano glanced at her. "Anything's possible," he said, "but it's not too likely."

But Saffron had seen Bren's face the moment he said 'anything's possible.' The reporter would cut the clip there—and leave Mano claiming that the shifting pendant was caused by tiki magic.

• • • •

CONTINUE READING HOME TO ROOST: ALOHA CHICKEN MYSTERIES BOOK 5

• • • •

Thank you for reading!

DEAR READER,

Thank you for visiting Maika'i and the Hau'oli ka Moa Egg Farm! I hope you enjoyed Hen Pecked, and I hope you'll read more of Saffron's adventures in Book 5: Home to Roost. If you did enjoy the book, please consider writing a review on Amazon and Goodreads. I love hearing from my readers, and your reviews help other readers find my novels! I truly appreciate every review and every reader who spends time with Saffron, the hens, and me!

—Josi Avari

Made in the USA
Monee, IL
20 December 2022

23258262R00159